"You'll crea   town,"

Liz told Matt bre~~athlessly~~, hurrying a few steps ahead of him. Her son, Jeremy, for one, would be thrilled to meet his uncle Matt.

"Jeremy," Liz called to her son. "Look who's—"

But Liz never got a chance to finish her announcement.

Her son turned around, and his eyes grew as wide as saucers. To her amazement, Liz could see his hands begin to shake. A look of hunger filled his face, a look so intense that Liz almost cried out.

There was a definite quaver in Jeremy's boyish voice when he spoke, and his eyes were shining.

"Dad?" he whispered.

Liz's heart stopped. "Oh, Lord," she murmured.

"Damn," Matt muttered under his breath.

And from the look on Matt's face, his trip back to Stony Mountain wasn't going as planned…

Dear Reader:

Welcome to Silhouette **Special Edition**…welcome to romance. This month's six wonderful books are guaranteed to become some of your all-time favourites!

Our THAT SPECIAL WOMAN! title for August is *The Sultan's Wives* by Tracy Sinclair. An ambitious photojournalist gets herself in a predicament—the middle of a harem—when she goes in search of a hot story in an exotic land. And she finds that only the fascinating and handsome sultan can get her out of it.

This month Andrea Edwards's new series, THIS TIME, FOREVER, returns with another compelling story of predestined love in *A Rose and a Wedding Vow*. And don't miss *Baby My Baby* by Victoria Pade, as she tells the next tale of the Heller clan siblings from her series A RANCHING FAMILY.

Jake's Mountain by Christine Flynn, a spin-off to her last Special Edition title, *When Morning Comes*, rounds out the month, along with Jennifer Mikels's *Sara's Father* and *The Mother of His Child* by Ann Howard White, a new author to Special Edition.

I hope you enjoy these books, and all the stories to come!

Sincerely,

The Editor

A Rose and a
Wedding Vow

ANDREA EDWARDS

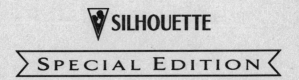

SILHOUETTE

SPECIAL EDITION

*First published in Great Britain in 1995
by Silhouette Books, Eton House, 18-24 Paradise Road,
Richmond, Surrey TW9 1SR*

© EAN Associates 1995

*Silhouette, Silhouette Special Edition and Colophon are
Trade Marks of Harlequin Enterprises II B.V.*

ISBN 0 373 09944 4

23-9508

Made and printed in Great Britain

In loving memory of Zach, Belle and Abby. We will never forget the love you brought into our lives.

ANDREA EDWARDS

Anne and Ed Kolaczyk have been writing together for more than fifteen years. Their four kids are pretty much grown, but their cats and dogs are still around to occasionally wander through their stories.

Anne and Ed have always believed that our present is the result of our past, be it hair colour, temperament or emotions. Living in northern Indiana, where the past has not been entirely obliterated by "progress," they have the time and space to listen to the voices from yesterday. It is in these voices that their characters learn to listen, and in doing so, find truth and happiness.

Other Silhouette Books by Andrea Edwards

FAMILY TREE

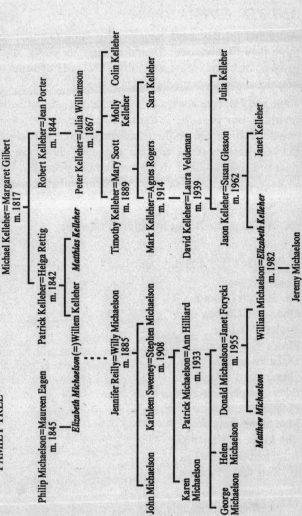

Prologue

The rain had been falling for so long it seemed like forever, flooding the fields and the roads, and keeping Betsy prisoner on the farm. Rain, rain and more rain. It was as if the heavens could not stop crying. Betsy's heart ached from the days of isolation, from the fear someone was calling out to her and she could not hear them.

Finally she could wait no longer. She waded out through the ankle-deep mud and muck to saddle the mare in the barn.

Her father followed her. "These rides out to the mountain each week are foolishness," he said. "Willem isn't coming back. He died at Gettysburg. The same as Amos Kirkland and Geoff Fitzpatrick."

She threw the saddle over the mare's back and tightened the cinch. "There's been no word from the army."

Her father's tight-lipped sigh spoke his disapproval. "Even Matthias believes his brother to be dead."

"He has no proof."

"Four years of silence is proof."

Betsy led the horse to the door of the barn, then wrapped her father's oilskins around her before stepping out into the yard. Her feet sank into the mud, each step a chore as the wetness of the mire tried to hold her back.

She knew Matthias would scold her. He would tell her not to be silly, but something was pushing her, making her go. This drenching rain would not stop her; neither would her father's anger or her mother's displeasure.

"You will be waiting forever, and the boy will never have a name," her father said. "If you would give Matthias a smile, he might be willing to do the honorable thing."

"I gave my promise to Willem," Betsy said as she turned for her father to give her a leg up into the saddle. Her father couldn't know it, but Matthias was more than willing to give little Willy his name. She just would not let him speak yet.

Betsy turned the mare toward the road and let her make her slow, plodding way past the house. Mama and little three-year-old Willy were huddled in the doorway, and Betsy waved, but only Willy waved back. Ma's face was creased with worry. Betsy looked away, straining her eyes into the grayness ahead.

Sometimes deep in the middle of the night, when the moon shadows of the hickory leaves danced on the ceiling and she listened to the sounds of little Willy's breathing, she tried to bring Willem to her. She tried to let her love call to his spirit, needing to feel his caring surround her for a moment, even if it was only a dream, but he never came.

Did it mean he was dead, as Papa said, or just that her love wasn't strong enough? Some nights lately she could no longer bring his face to mind or hear his voice in her heart.

The mare stopped her even plodding, and Betsy awoke from her thoughts. They had passed the stand of sycamores and the patch of wild raspberries and were at Gorman's Creek. But the gentle, meandering flow was gone and in its place was a raging, muddy torrent.

For a moment she stared at the rushing water, worry filling her heart. If the creek was this bad, then the waters of Stony River would be a devil's cauldron.

Matthias's train from Chicago had to cross that river.

Betsy urged the horse forward. She was going to Stony Mountain, same as she did every Friday, to look to the east as she prayed for Willem. Then, as had been her wont since Matthias had started working as a brakeman, she would turn to the west to pray for his safety.

Once Betsy crossed the stream, she turned west, following the path that wove in among the budding trees to the river and the railroad trestle bridge. At the water's edge, she stopped the horse and stared across to Stony Mountain.

It was a wild and godforsaken island in the river, more a high, rocky hill than a true mountain, and accessible only from the trestle bridge that crossed it. But it was the highest point in the county, putting her so close to heaven that God surely listened to the prayers she uttered there. It was her link to Willem, the only link she had left.

Today, though, the plank walkway on the bridge looked slippery and treacherous as the river seethed in rage below. She looked over to the mountain. Should she risk the crossing? She dismounted and followed the tracks to the bridge.

To leave would be deserting Willem, deserting the bond she'd shared with him for a few moments each week. She stepped onto the walkway. Water splashed onto the floor of the bridge, washing around her feet, and she stepped back onto the solid ground.

Maybe this was God's way of telling her to let Willem go. Maybe God was telling her that four years of silence was enough and it was time to move on.

Time to move on to Matthias.

Her heart felt a strange certainty, as if truth had settled there and made her stronger. She closed her eyes, breathing a silent prayer into the storm for Willem, then opened her eyes. It was right. He was gone.

Betsy climbed on the horse, but rather than head back home, she headed the other way down the path toward town. Matthias's train should be in and she wanted to see him. He deserved to know that she was putting Willem to rest at last.

The town of Stony Mountain was only a mile or so from the mountain, and Betsy was passing the first few houses before her heart lost its resolve. The town was quiet, Main Street deserted. Even the new train station, its red bricks darkened by the rain, showed no signs of life. Only the addle-brained—or the dream-driven like herself—would be out in weather like this, but even so, the stillness ate at her. The train was not in yet.

Betsy stopped the mare in front of the station and hurried under the wide overhang. She would know her feelings when she saw Matthias. Her heart would speak its mind.

She hurried along the brick walk and into the station. A handful of people were inside. The Veldemans were there—Michael must be coming back from Chicago—and Mrs. Hilliard looked to be leaving. Jimmy Tuttle and Dave Forycki were playing cards in the corner.

Daniel looked up from freight he was checking near the door. "Afternoon, Miss Betsy. Didn't expect to see you here today."

She shrugged. Normally, she loved the smell of the new station—the mixture of freshly cut wood and plaster and paint—but today it seemed overpowering. "I thought the train would be in," she said. "I wanted to see Matthias."

"He was hoping to find that army doctor in Chicago, wasn't he?" Daniel asked.

"I guess."

"Many were hurt and died at Gettysburg. Too many to remember," Daniel said as he slipped his list into a back pocket so he could shift a crate. Betsy turned away, walking to the window that looked down the line to the east. Toward Willem.

"I've heard that men still lie in hospitals out east," Mrs. Hilliard said. "Willem could be in one."

"Maybe he can't remember who he is," Jimmy added.

"Or maybe he can't talk," Dave agreed.

Betsy just sighed. Although they meant well, they only stirred up doubts in her heart. "Matthias looked."

"But he could have missed him," Mrs. Veldeman said.

" 'Tain't likely," her husband snapped.

Betsy just kept staring out at the track. The rain blurred the trees, the track became a thick black snake, and she closed her eyes. She tried to see Willem in a hospital bed. She tried to see his face as she came closer to his bed, tried to hear his voice. But it was Matthias there instead, reaching his hand out to her even as he seemed to be pulled farther and farther away.

Betsy opened her eyes, wiping at the tear that was trailing down her cheek. Mr. Carmady had come into the station and was asking Daniel how much later the Chicago train would be. Betsy slipped out the trackside door and leaned up against the station wall. A damp chill ate into her.

The rain dulled not only the scene around her but also the sounds. The train would be coming any moment. Betsy turned to the west but there was nothing there, not even the hint of steam from the engine. There was nothing but the steady drone of the rain. On and on and on.

"What am I to do, Matthias?" she whispered into the grayness around her.

But no words were whispered back. She sensed a stirring inside the station and went to the door. The telegraph was clicking wildly. Daniel's face was ashen as he wrote out the message.

"Something's happened," Mr. Veldeman said.

"What?" Betsy looked at Daniel. But the stationmaster was too engrossed in taking down the telegraph message. Betsy turned to Mrs. Veldeman. "What happened? What is wrong?"

But the old woman just shook her head as footsteps rang across the floor. Mrs. Walsh and eight-year-old Mary came in. Carl Walsh worked as a fireman on this run.

"Papa is late," Mary announced. "And he is to bring ribbons for my new dress."

The child didn't sense the tension in the room, but her mother did. Mrs. Walsh's hand went down to cover her daughter's mouth. "What's wrong?" Her words came out in a whisper.

No one spoke as the telegraph key continued to stutter and stumble.

"Come on, lad," Daniel muttered.

Betsy felt her breath catch. She knew the train must be stopped, but Daniel's words told her that young Tommy Brown was sending the message. The conductor must have sent him up the telegraph pole to hook on to the line.

Slowly and painfully, Daniel wrote out the message. "There has been an accident," he finally said, his voice tight and full of pain. "At the trestle bridge."

"No."

"Pray God, you've got it wrong."

"I've been saying that bridge was weakening," Mr. Carmady said. "But none would listen."

Betsy closed her eyes, willing the sudden clutching of her heart to cease. She tried to see Matthias's smile again and take strength from his care, but he would not come. As if teasing her, he danced far out on the edge of her sight. Suddenly the telegraph started clicking again.

"They need help," someone said.

"We can take six, maybe eight, on the handcart," said another.

"Mary, run to the church and set the bells to ringing. We'll be needing all the help we can find."

Mary raced out the front door as the men dashed off to get the handcart. Betsy and Mrs. Walsh pulled medical supply boxes from the closet in the rear of the station and carried them out to the platform, piling them with tool boxes and slickers that were there also. It didn't seem much, though, once the men had loaded it all onto the handcart.

"What else will be needed?" Betsy asked.

"Draft horses for moving the cars out of the way," Mr. Veldeman said. "Some of you lads get out to the farms. And we'll be needing all kinds of supplies."

"Pray the train wasn't full," Mrs. Hilliard was saying.

But Betsy wasn't waiting about to weep with the women. While Dave and Jimmy ran back through the station on their way to the farms, she ran across the street to the Schillers' general store. The church bells began to peal as she entered.

"There's been a train accident at the bridge!" Betsy called out.

Mrs. Schiller looked at her husband. "Hitch up the wagon. Betsy and I will get the supplies." Once he was hurrying out of the room, she turned to Betsy. "Come, lass. There's much they will be needing."

With few words exchanged between them, Mrs. Schiller pulled out ropes and hitches, blankets, muslin for bandages and sheets of canvas, giving them to Betsy to carry out back to the wagon. By the time everything was loaded, Mr. Schiller had it hitched to their horse.

"Hitch your mare to the back and ride up here with me," Mrs. Schiller told Betsy. "They'll be needing us to make order out of chaos. Women's work, you know."

Betsy climbed into the wagon, feeling mild surprise at the woman's grudging acceptance of her. Mrs. Schiller had never hidden her feelings toward Betsy in the past—that she thought Betsy was a sinner and ought to be shunned. But then, Betsy had thought she was expressing the view held by most of the town.

Betsy looked away into wet shadows. Matthias had said that would change if she would stand with him for all to see. But that was not reason enough to put her hand in his.

Had her chance to do so passed?

The ride seemed to take forever, though Betsy knew the bridge was not that far. She wrapped her arms around her chest as if it would stop the shivering cold that had seized her. The rain continued to pour down on them, the branches along the path slapping wetly at her as the wagon forced its way along the narrow path. If only it wasn't Matthias's part of the train that went down.

But it seemed wicked to pray that Matthias would be saved, for it might mean others were lost. She couldn't help it, though, and tried not to think or feel or hope.

She had loved Willem, but she knew now it had been the wild, unhampered love of youth. Her feelings for Matthias were different. Deeper. Maybe even stronger. She had not wanted to look at the differences, afraid of betraying Willem and his springtime promises, but she knew the truth. She loved Matthias.

If only it wasn't a truth come too late.

"Ah, merciful God," Mrs. Schiller exclaimed.

The bridge was before them. Or what remained of it. The middle had collapsed as if stepped on by a giant, cars hanging from it. The massive steam engine was on the near bank, but derailed, looking as powerless as a fallen Goliath. Over the sound of the rushing water came the screams. People were clinging to bridge supports, and some were pressed against the windows of the cars still upright. Downstream, two bodies were caught in the branches of a fallen tree.

Betsy's stomach churned. She wanted to turn away from this scene of hell and wipe it from her thoughts forever. She wanted to hide in the trees and fight the awful twisting of her stomach. She wanted to find sunshine and laughter. But she could do none of those.

Mrs. Schiller called out to the men working at the river's edge as she jumped to the ground. They came rushing over, and Betsy climbed into the back of the wagon, giving them the ropes and hitches, all the while wiping the rain and tears from her face. Through it all, the church bells still rang.

More men arrived, some on horseback and some in carriages. And in the distance, Betsy would see the first of the draft-horse teams arriving—slow, plodding creatures of enormous strength.

Betsy climbed out of the wagon herself, carrying blankets for the few shivering folks already rescued. She led them aside, making a small shelter by stretching sheets of the

Schillers' canvas from branches and allowing the others more room to work. She comforted a small child and bound wounds as best she could, but her ears were always straining for the sound of Matthias's voice.

Carl Walsh was pulled from the water, ignoring the blood dripping from his forehead as he joined the rescuers. Tommy Hilliard was carried to the little shelter, his left leg mangled and bleeding. Then Ben Tuttle and Harry Kirkland were helped ashore, along with two women passengers and Mickey Kearns. But no Matthias.

Twice Betsy took the Schillers' wagon back to town with the wounded and rescued, and twice returned with prayers that Matthias would be there waiting for her. And twice was disappointed.

Her heart tried to keep hope, to call his spirit to her to give him her strength, but the gray afternoon turned into evening and the evening into darkness. Still no Matthias. Bonfires were lit to illuminate the efforts as the frenetic activity slowed.

The men were working now on the twisted wreckage of the train. The shouting and screaming had given way to a quiet seriousness. They were not bringing the living to shore any longer, but the bodies of those crushed by the debris. There was little for Betsy to do but tighten her hold on her heart each time they brought up a new body.

And so she waited, staring at the rain-swollen river and praying for Matthias to come bounding to her side, laughing at her worries and wiping her tears away. Beside her, Mrs. Veldeman was sobbing as she waited for her Michael to be found.

A chill crept up to Betsy's heart. Just as she waited for Matthias to return to her one last time.

No! Betsy's heart cried out. She wanted to scream out her pain. She wanted to push back time until she could laugh again in Matthias's arms. This could not be happening, her soul screamed. She had already lost a love. A merciful God would not let it happen again.

"I'm sorry."

Carl Walsh stood before her and Mrs. Veldeman. His face was smeared with mud, his eyes weary and hurting. "We just found Michael and Matthias," he said. "We'll be bringing them up shortly."

Matthias was gone. It was real. There would be no reprieve. Betsy could not speak. She could not even grieve aloud, for her silence toward Matthias did not give her the right.

"This will be hard for your boy," Carl said to her. "Losing his pa and now his uncle."

Betsy nodded, trying to swallow her pain. She could barely breathe for the knot of agony twisting inside her, but it hardly seemed to matter. "There's just a cousin left over in Little Fork now. He'll need to be told."

"The sheriff will be taking care of that." Carl started to turn away, but then stopped. "He never stopped trying to find Willem," Carl said. "He loved his brother as much as you did."

Betsy could say nothing, but just watched Carl walk away. This was wrong. This was all wrong. If only she'd crossed over the bridge when she'd come earlier, she might have sensed its unsteadiness. She might have been able to prevent this terrible tragedy.

Unable to watch the men bring Matthias up, she walked slowly along the tracks to the river's edge, keeping the derailed engine between her and the workers. If she kept her eyes to the north, the river raged on with no sign of the havoc it had caused. She could almost pretend nothing had happened. There was no fooling her heart, though.

Turning away, she caught a glimpse in the dim light of the bonfires of something growing from under the track. It was a rose plant, the shoots only inches long, the longest of them broken by all the trampling.

Sinking to her knees, she gently pulled the plant from the rain-soaked ground. She sensed it was a sign that life was stronger than death. A promise that Matthias's love for her had not died with him.

Silent tears streamed down her cheeks, her heart ready to break with sorrow as she stared down at the tiny plant in her hand. She loved him so. Why hadn't she grabbed at the chances love had offered her? Why had she been so afraid to let her hand rest in his? Why hadn't she crossed the bridge?

She sat back on her heels, seeing the bleak and dreary future ahead of her, then slowly wrapped the little plant in her kerchief before sliding it into her pocket. The thorns cut into her skin as her fingers stayed closed around it.

"We will have our chance," she whispered into the night. "Someday, Matthias, we will be together again, and I'll never let you go."

Chapter One

A gust of wind whipped around the corner of the train station and blew bits of dirt into Liz Michaelson's eye.

"Damn," she murmured. Sitting back on her heels, she took the gardening glove off her right hand and rubbed her eye. The weatherman had forecast April showers and high winds for the area, but had said the turbulence would hit Stony Mountain around midnight, not late this afternoon.

Another gust came up, stronger than the first, and scattered her pile of garden debris. Liz brushed at the front of her T-shirt. She could almost hear the moaning sound of the wind blowing through the building's eaves.

"Looks like old Betsy's crying already." Her sister Jan was in the doorway of the old train station, holding a cup emblazoned with the logo of their sandwich shop. "I can almost make out her *'Willem, Willem.'*"

"Jeremy prefers the more scientific wind-in-the-gables theory," Liz said.

Jan frowned and sipped her coffee. "Your son needs a ghost or two in his life. He's too serious."

"He doesn't get it from me. I like the story of Betsy waiting here for her love to return, crying her heart out when it storms." Liz went back to her gardening, digging up last year's mums from the cool earth.

She loved tending this patch of earth by the old train station each spring. Living in an apartment as she and Jeremy did, it was her chance to feel the rebirth, the promise of wonder and magic, that each spring held.

"Is that what you're doing—waiting for your love to return?" Jan asked.

Liz fell back on her heels again. The wind blew her hair into her face, creating a blond curtain through which she frowned at her sister. "What kind of question is that?" she asked. "I thought you were on my side." Jan was the one person in their whole family that wasn't always bugging Liz about finding a new husband, a father for Jeremy or just a date for Saturday nights.

"I'm not on anybody's side," Jan protested. "I was just curious."

Liz went back to her gardening. "I figure I'm in for it when we go to Mom and Dad's for dinner tonight. Think there's some way I could stop celebrating birthdays? You know, claim that since I'm thirty-one as of today, I don't have to acknowledge any more of my birthdays."

"Oh, Mom'll buy that all right," Jan said with a snicker, then glanced over her shoulder toward the corner of the old station where their sandwich shop was located. "Uh-oh. Looks like our horde is through with their snacks."

Jan disappeared back inside the building, leaving Liz alone with the garden and old Betsy's ghost up in the eaves. In spite of her mother's fear that Liz was going to spend her declining years with fourteen cats and a shelf full of African violets, Liz wasn't worried. Maybe she wasn't convinced that cats and African violets were all that bad as housemates. Or maybe she wasn't buying into the happily-ever-after routine.

She looked up to the rafters, where the ghost of old Betsy was said to be residing. "Or maybe I bought it too well," she told the shadows above. "Maybe I can't accept the fact that I didn't get what every fairy tale promises."

Her one foray into love had been a rousing failure, unless she counted Jeremy. And while she didn't think she was sitting around waiting for Bill to come back, she sure wasn't interested in having her mother play matchmaker. She dug up the last chrysanthemum.

"I think I'm just a poor sport," she told Betsy as she shoved the debris into a plastic bag. "If there's no guarantee I'll win, I won't play the game."

"Mom?"

Liz started and looked up. Jeremy had stepped out of the train station. He was standing with the sun at his back, but she didn't need to shield her eyes to see if he was wearing his stern look. She could feel it in his voice.

"You know it takes more muscles to frown than it does to smile," she said.

Jeremy ignored her motherly advice. "Who were you talking to?" he asked.

Liz could almost hear the frown lines circling his eyes, like a wagon train. Jan was right: he was too serious. Liz picked up her garden shears, giving him a teasing smile. "Betsy," she said.

He rolled his eyes in eleven-year-old exasperation. "Geez, Mom. What if somebody heard you?"

"Well, if that someone was Betsy, maybe she'd give me some advice."

"Mom! No one believes that old story. There's no such thing as ghosts."

He gave her such a look of impatience that she wanted to laugh, but then the sunlight caught his face in a way that made him look like Bill, and she was thrown back in time. Dreaming, scheming, brilliant Bill, who knew the world was his for the taking. Who knew his older brother Matt's harping on homework and studying and giving your all was for dummies and suckers.

Jeremy had his father's brains and some of his athletic ability, but a thousand times more grit and gumption. She didn't care if he never put Stony Mountain on the map for football or soccer or even his studies, so long as he wouldn't run at the first sign of trouble.

She threw off the past and began cutting the dead leaves from the daylily plants. "So what are you so grumpy about?" she asked. "Amanda give you a hard time on the way home?"

Her sister's three kids and Jeremy walked to the train station together after school, and as the oldest, Jeremy took it upon himself to keep them in line—a task that was neither needed or wanted. Stony Mountain wasn't exactly a bustling metropolis, and the school was only two blocks away.

But Jeremy believed in order. And taking charge. And accepting all responsibility up for grabs within a twenty-mile radius.

"You were supposed to bring the tax forms with you," he said.

Ah, the root of the problem. "I mailed them this morning," she said, cutting off another wad of dead leaves.

"But I got that tax program for the computer, and I wanted to make sure everything was figured right."

"Our taxes aren't big or complex," Liz said. "There really isn't any need to use the computer for it."

Jeremy sighed and rolled his eyes. "Mom, it's the way things are done these days."

"The computer doesn't add or subtract any better than I do with a calculator."

"But there are a number of ancillary benefits."

"Ancillary?" This time it was Liz's turn to roll her eyes.

"Yeah," Jeremy said. "You know, stuff that comes along even though you didn't ask for it."

"Thank you," Liz murmured. She had a degree in English, but lately it seemed that Jeremy felt she needed additional instruction.

"Using the computer would give us the chance to file electronically."

"Why would we want to do that?" Liz asked.

"It's faster," Jeremy replied. "And more reliable."

Liz could point out that if she wanted speed, she could have filled out the forms sometime before the last minute, or that in her sixteen years of filing income-tax forms, the post office had never lost hers. But she knew that Jeremy was just waiting for such a discussion. And had better answers than she did.

Two boys carrying a bat and baseball gloves walked around the corner of the train station.

"Hey, Jeremy," they chorused.

"Hey, Mike," Jeremy replied. "What's happening, Danny?"

The boys nodded at her. "Hi, Mrs. Michaelson. Can Jeremy come play baseball with us?"

"It's okay by me," Liz replied.

Jeremy paused for only a moment. "My stuff's inside," he said as he started toward the door. Then he stopped and made a face at the scrawny rosebush in the corner of the garden. "You ought to just pull that junky old thing out," he said. "It's dead."

She frowned down at the old plant. It wasn't the best-looking plant in town, but neither was it the worst. "It's not dead," she said, leaning over closer. "Look, it's starting to sprout down here near the ground."

"It's still ugly," he said. "And it never flowers."

He was right on both counts, but there was something about the rosebush, wild and untamed as it was. It seemed special. "Betsy's supposed to have planted it here," she said. "And if it's lasted this long, I'm not going to rip it out."

"Then put some nice things all around it and cover it up." A sly little grin flickered on his face. "I bet Leo could fix this strip up real nice."

"Get out of here before I think up some chore for you." Liz tossed some dead leaves at him as he darted into the train station.

Liz shook her head and returned to her gardening. He balanced her checkbook, managed her appointments, and now was trying to pick out a husband for her. But Leo Tuttle? Liz shuddered. She could hardly wait until Jeremy really got into his teen years and had girl troubles of his own. Then maybe he'd leave her love life—or lack of it—alone.

She moved around to the side of the little plot to loosen the dirt around the rosebush, her last chore for the afternoon. The bush was scrawny, but every spring it came back, green and living, if not actually flourishing. To be honest, Liz had to admit that she admired it.

Jeremy would think she really had gone off the deep end if he knew, but the health of this rosebush had become important to her. It was her talisman. They were two of a kind. Both had hurdles to overcome, and though not exactly blooming, they were hanging in there.

Sure, she was a single parent, but she lived in a comfortable little town where her son was safe. Her parents were healthy, and Jan and her husband, Hank, were nearby. She wasn't really alone, and Jeremy didn't lack for male role models.

She pruned off the last of the rosebush's dead branches, then got to her feet. "You know, Betsy," she said, looking back up at the eaves. "You don't need to bloom to be alive. And I don't need some love to come off that train to be happy."

A gust of wind swirled around her, but Liz didn't stay around to argue.

"Hey, old man, how are you?"

Matt Michaelson leaned on his cane and glared around at his welcoming committee. Looked as if every single detective from the day watch was there. His vision blurred for a moment. It seemed as if he'd been gone forever, but right now he wasn't sure whether that was good or bad.

"Your old man's walking stick goes great with the gray in your hair."

He grimaced. It had been just two weeks. He'd gone on a raid to pick up a hired killer. Scurvy mutt had been hiding in the closet and came out shooting. The perp went down, but the cross fire left Matt with a slug in his right knee. It wrecked his leg all to hell and he'd probably never walk right again.

"Get out of my way, you bums." Matt's voice had his cop snarl in it. "Before I whack your heads off."

"Right, Matt. Float like a butterfly, sting like a bee."

"More like float like a lead brick and sting like a baby kitty."

"Anytime, guys." He waved his cane like a baseball bat. "Anytime."

It took a bit of effort, but he forced a smile to his lips and endured the rough humor and backslaps of his fellow officers. Police work was dangerous, especially in a big-city department like Chicago. And, from his own experience, he knew that if cops didn't laugh at adversity, they would go out of their minds.

"Feisty little fella, isn't he?"

"Yeah, nurses probably been telling him he'll be as good as new."

"That ain't nothin'."

"Yeah, I heard he wasn't all that good when he was new."

"Ah, you know how those nurses are. They'll lie and—"

"Watch it, guys," Matt snapped. "My mother was a nurse."

There was a little pause, but before anyone could say anything, a short, nattily dressed man stepped into the group. "What happened?" Lieutenant Harding asked. "Crime take a holiday?"

With minimal mumbling, the detectives drifted back to their desks, leaving Matt alone with his lieutenant.

"They let you out yesterday, right?"

"Yeah." Matt put his cane to the floor and leaned on it. "Would've come in then, but I had a little business to take care of." He guessed you could call the funeral of your only relative a little business.

"Can you drive yet?" the lieutenant asked, staring at Matt's leg.

"Not this way. They got my knee all wrapped up."

The lieutenant stared at him for a long moment, and Matt returned it. Two old cops. Lieutenant Harding was in his late forties and Matt was rapidly approaching the big four-O. Not that that mattered much. Six months on Chicago's streets made a man old in every sense of the word. Old man, old cop, old everything. Tired in spirit, washed-out mentally, with a body full of more aches and pains than a computer could count. Old enough to just go through the motions every day of the rest of his life.

"Why don't we step into my office?" the lieutenant said.

"Sure."

Matt followed him through the maze of desks, back to a small room. Harding stood and waited until Matt had stiffly lowered himself into one of the guest chairs. Then the lieutenant sat down, straightened his tie and snapped out his hands so that the proper half inch of white cuff showed beyond the end of his jacket sleeves.

"Sorry about your brother."

A painful tightness seized Matt's stomach for a moment. "Yeah," he murmured, then looked away when he felt the need for words to come out. "It was crazy. I was always bailing him out of some escapade or other. He was eight and I was fifteen when our father died, but the old man had been going off on binges for years before then, so I sometimes felt more like Bill's father than his brother. But when I was in the army and he was in college, we lost touch. Then last week he's brought into the E.R. of the hospital where I'm laid up."

The kid'd caught his lunch last Saturday right here in the City of Big Shoulders. Crossing with the light and taken out by a gypsy cab with bad brakes. It wasn't something he could've protected his brother from, but still—

He saw the kid's laughing eyes and heard his list of excuses. *It was just a joke. I was sure I could make it. Want Lizzie to think I'm chicken?*

"You gotta have eyes in the back of your head in this city," the lieutenant said.

Matt nodded, but it was an attempt to push Stony Mountain back into the past. Back into the hollow barrel of history where it belonged. Friday night football, fishing in Gorman's Creek and bagging groceries at the grocery store on Main Street.

Matt swallowed the lump building in his throat. He'd caught the kid fishing off the rotting old trestle bridge about every other week when they were growing up. Gone with him to the principal's office all too often. And took him to the hospital emergency room more times than he could count.

And now? They hadn't sat down to a beer in more than a year.

"You guys keep in touch much?" Harding stared when Matt remained silent. The man was like a snake. He could stare for days without blinking.

Matt shrugged. "Sort of."

Sort of. Hell, that meant not really. He hadn't even known Bill's latest address, but it was obvious that Bill had known where he was. That next-of-kin card in his wallet had Matt's correct rank and office number.

Why hadn't Bill let him know where he was? Why hadn't the kid contacted him? A phone call. A letter. Something. Anything.

"You caught yourself a streak of bad luck," the lieutenant said.

"It happens," Matt replied with a shrug.

"Yeah." The lieutenant cleared his throat and tugged at his sleeves. "Any problems with funeral arrangements and that kind of stuff?"

"Nah. Everything's cool."

Bill had been cremated. A total of about eight people showed up at the service yesterday afternoon, partly because most of Bill's peers probably weren't into reading the obituary page yet. But Matt couldn't deny the fact that neither he nor his brother seemed to be touching many people. Now Bill's ashes sat in an urn at the undertaker's, waiting for Matt to make a decision.

They sat in silence for a long moment. Harding looked down at the desk and blinked. Matt figured the man's eyelids wouldn't see the light of day for another five, ten years now. He looked up at Matt, all business once more.

"So what do your doctors say?"

Matt shrugged. "They want me to lay off the dance contests for a while. I should be able to handle a fox-trot, but nothing fancy."

The lieutenant cleared his throat. "Gonna limp forever?"

"Nah, just until I die." Matt shifted in his chair. Funny how a bum leg gave you aches and pains even when you were sitting down. "Although I was thinking of having some mutt on the street shoot me in the other leg."

Harding's eyebrows went up.

"You know," Matt said. "Whack the left the same as my right. Make them both the same. That way I shouldn't have to limp."

Harding straightened his tie again. "Think you could handle riding a desk?"

"Don't know," Matt replied with a shrug. "Need to think on that."

Harding blinked—wow, twice in one day; that had to be some kind of a record—then thrust out his lower lip. "How about the 911 board?"

"No."

Matt looked away from the lieutenant's flat eyes. Ten years of street duty, of rushing in where the action was. Ten years on the front line, and they wanted him to go from that to sitting between a telephone and the chattering cop radios. Hearing the screams, the shouts, the sirens, the shots. Chewing his fingernails while he waited to see how things would play out. He'd die of a heart attack before he finished his first week.

"Absolutely not."

Harding nodded, looked down at his desk, and then up at Matt again. "Gonna have to think on what you want to do."

"Yeah," Matt replied. "I'll do that."

"You got three months," the lieutenant said. "Then it's disability or put on a pair of desk-jockey boots. Take your brother home and think on it."

"Home?"

"Yeah." The lieutenant blinked. "I know your parents are dead, but you probably got other relatives around."

Matt felt his body go into a state of shock as he stared at his lieutenant.

"You know—cousins. That kinda thing."

He'd never seen the man's eyelids work like they had today. Three blinks in less than an hour. It was obvious that something was wrong, and Matt knew what it was. The lieutenant was getting all sentimental on him. Matt pushed himself to his feet. It was time to get outta here.

"Gotta go," he said. "I gotta clean up my brother's apartment and stuff."

Harding nodded curtly. "Keep in touch."

Matt turned on his heel and hobbled out as fast as his three legs could take him.

"Oh, hell." Matt sank down into the torn, overstuffed chair and let his eyes glaze over. He saw, but didn't really see, the dinginess of his brother's apartment. "Looks like you and I had the same interior decorator, bro."

Bill's apartment was a single room; not even the kitchen was separate. The stove, refrigerator and cabinets were in an alcove in the wall and next to the kitchen stuff was an attempt at a clothes closet. Bill had to do everything in this one room except shave and shower.

Not that Matt's apartment was much better. His was a one-bedroom—living/dining room, bedroom and small kitchen, but as colorless as this place.

He'd like to believe that the bland apartments meant that neither of them were wedded to material things, but that was a joke. Both apartments were generic dumps, proof that their owners had no life. Were they both so afraid they were carbon copies of their father that they'd avoided relationships?

Matt'd tossed the apartment as thoroughly as a narc looking for drugs. He'd found no liquor, so apparently his brother wasn't drinking anymore, but there wasn't much else of interest or value, either. Losing lottery tickets, old copies of the *Racing News*—appeared Bill was still looking for the pot of gold at the end of the rainbow—and some old fishing gear. But no clue as to where Bill would want to be buried.

Matt's eyes went down to the small lockbox at his feet. This was all that was left—the personal stuff, he supposed. The kind of stuff he wasn't sure he wanted to see, but was hoping would hold some answers.

He sensed movement to his left and his eyes flicked toward the doorway. A tabby cat was standing there. Matt must not have shut the door all the way and the cat had pushed it open.

"Hi, kitty," Matt said.

The cat continued staring at him, not blinking even once.

"You any relation to Leonard Harding?" Matt asked. "He never blinks, either."

"Toby. Toby, where are you?" The door opened farther to reveal a young man in his early twenties, a single rose wrapped in green tissue paper in his hand. "Come here," he said to the cat. "This isn't your home any—"

He stopped, spotting Matt. A cautious concern filled his eyes. "I'm sorry," he said. "I didn't know anyone was here."

"Yeah," Matt replied. "I'm a quiet kind of a guy."

The man bent down, picking up the cat. "I was just looking for Toby." The cat purred and rubbed his head under the man's chin. "He's sort of my cat now. He used to be sort of Bill's cat."

"Sort of?"

"Nobody can own a cat," he replied.

Remembering back to the farm cats he'd known in his youth, Matt could agree with that. Dogs were always eager to please, but cats always let you know who ruled the roost.

"You're Bill's brother, aren't you?"

"How did you know?"

"He always talked about his brother the cop," he replied. "And you are definitely a cop."

Matt grimaced. When civilians could make you, it was time to move on.

"I'm sorry about Bill."

Matt didn't know how to respond. Sitting here in Bill's apartment, he felt strangely exposed, as if all the years of taking care of Bill were playing out on a stage behind him, under a neon sign proclaiming how Matt'd failed him in the end.

"That's the way it goes," Matt finally said with a shrug. "Life is hard, then you die." It was his grandfather's favorite saying, used whenever things didn't go your way. It fit all too well now.

The man shifted the cat in his arms. "He was starting to put things together, you know," the man said. "He was working days as a short-order cook and taking classes at Loyola at night. He wanted to be a social worker and work with kids."

A lump pressed up in Matt's throat and he turned away to look out the window. Through the grime of the brick wall of the apartment building across the alley, he could see into the past.

Bill had been a golden boy back home. Star athlete, first in his class, president of the student council. Everything he touched had turned to gold until he threw his knee out during his senior year. Then he'd wandered about aimlessly. Maybe Matt had rescued him too many times. For all his lectures about taking things seriously, maybe Matt had made it too easy for the kid back then.

He turned away from the past. "What's with the rose?" he asked gruffly. "Have an argument with your girlfriend?"

"Nope," the man said, laughing. "It's for my wife. We found out this morning that we're going to have a family."

Matt let himself go detached, like he did when he came across something exceptionally gruesome. After years on the force, a guy didn't want to be touched by anything. Good or bad.

"I ran out and got the rose after lunch." The man's face took on a hidden happiness as he looked inward. "I was going to buy her a dozen, but she'd break my neck if I spent that much money. I'm a graduate student and our budget is tight."

"Yeah." Matt just glanced away. The naked joy and contentment in the man's face made him feel as if he were spying. He shifted in the chair.

"We were all from small towns, but Bill seemed to miss it the most," the man said. "Used to talk about his home a lot."

"Is that right?"

"When you're a kid, you can't wait to get out," the man said. "But then something happens. You get older and all you can think of is going back."

"I wouldn't know," Matt said.

"You will."

His voice was filled with the obnoxious self-confidence of those who have the world by the tail. Matt considered telling him to get the hell out, but he pushed at the box with his cane instead.

"Do you want the cat?"

"Huh?"

"Well, it was sort of Bill's, and if you want it—"

Matt looked at the animal, content in the man's arms. "Nah, he seems to have adopted you."

"Thanks." The man turned to leave, but then stopped at the door. "He wanted to go home, Matt. He really did. We used to go fishing along the lakefront here, but he said there was nothing like the old trestle bridge back home."

"He never used to catch a damn thing off that old bridge," Matt pointed out.

The man just shook his head. "It's not that catching was the draw. It was the fishing." The guy turned and left, closing the door behind him.

If Bill had been so all-fired needy about going home, then why hadn't he? There'd been nothing stopping him. No Wanted posters. No angry citizens waiting to string him up when he reached the city limits. Sure, he hadn't fulfilled his youthful potential. But, hell, who did?

Matt made a face, then bent down and picked up the lockbox. Folks said people had a soul that traveled in the hereafter. Then Bill's soul could go back to Stony Mountain. Sure save a lot on transportation that way.

Matt pulled his Swiss army knife out of his pocket. It didn't take but a few twists with a knife to open the box.

Other than the faint smell of roses that floated up to greet him, there was very little in the box. Matt pulled out a handful of papers. A scattering of receipts, some canceled checks and a few legal-looking papers banded together. He tossed most of the stuff aside, looking at the last packet. The lease for the apartment, a car-rental agreement from a few years back and divorce papers.

Matt stared at them, the footing knocked from under him. Divorce papers?

He hadn't even known Bill had been married. Had they drifted that far apart that Bill hadn't told him he was getting married? The idea twisted his stomach, the papers in his hand mocking proof of that gulf.

A flash of color caught Matt's eye and he reached into the box for a school photograph that had been covered by the legal papers. Funny thing for Bill to save here—a picture from his childhood.

But then Matt froze. That kid in the photo who looked so much like a nine- or ten-year-old Bill wasn't. He couldn't be—he had blue eyes, not brown, and he was wearing a well-worn T-shirt that read Stony Mountain High School, Michigan State Football Champions. That was Bill's team.

Matt turned the photograph over, an awful, hollow feeling growing in the pit of his stomach. A childish hand had written *Jeremy William Michaelson* on the back. Swearing mightily, Matt threw the picture back into the box.

"Goddamn you, Bill," he said through clenched teeth. "You're always leaving some mess behind for me to clean up."

Chapter Two

"There goes the day's profit," Larry Veldeman said.

Liz stared at the plate she'd just shattered, the mocking words of Stony Mountain's expert mechanic ringing in her ears. Folks around the area always said that if Larry couldn't fix it, bury the damn thing, but she didn't think he could fix the plate or the dropsies she was afflicted with today.

"Are you okay, sis?" Jan asked.

Liz thought she was—except for that jumpy, tingly sensation just beneath her skin. She'd felt strangely on edge since she'd gotten up today.

"Liz?"

She started, realizing suddenly that Jan was expecting an answer. "Yeah, I'm okay." Her hand went up so her fingers covered her lips. "I'm fine."

"That's the third dish you broke this morning," Jan said.

"I'm sorry." Liz bent down to pick up the pieces, glancing over at Larry. "You're right. I have messed up our profit for today. Just splattered it all over the floor."

"Maybe it's one of those bad hair days," Larry said.

Jan was still staring at her. "You want to go home and lay down?"

"No." Liz was emphatic. She didn't know what was wrong with her this morning, but hiding wasn't going to help.

"It's probably Old Betsy," Jan said. "She's putting her hex on you."

"Jan, don't be ridiculous."

"Well it has to be something. As a rule, you don't go around throwing dishes on the floor." Jan picked up the coffee and went refilling along the counter. "There's something bugging you. And Betsy's just as likely as anything else."

Liz took a ham sandwich and chips off the serving ledge and carried the plate to the counter. "It's not fair to blame Betsy just because I'm a little edgy."

"Why not?" Chuck Harrington asked as he picked up the ham sandwich. "She's a mean one."

"That's right," Darci, their insurance lady, said. "We always get more accident claims after she's gone howling like she did last night."

"Maybe there are just more accidents after a storm," Liz said, turning to Larry. "How about a piece of cherry pie?"

He nodded, so Liz brought him the pie and a clean fork, and hoped the conversation would change.

"Everything's going fine with you these days," Jan said to Liz. "So it has to be something strange. And Stony Mountain ain't got nothing stranger than old Betsy."

"It's probably the atmospheric pressure."

"That's right," Chuck said. "My wife says the kids in school always go bonkers the day before a storm."

"The storm passed through last night," Darci said.

"Yeah," Jan said. "I bet the barometric pressure is back up to normal."

This was getting out of hand. "I really don't want to hold a public analysis of my mental health," Liz said loudly. "So, people, end of discussion."

"Are you girls bickering again?"

At the sound of the gruff voice, Liz snapped to attention and bet Jan did likewise. "Hi, Daddy," they chorused.

"They're not bickering, Mr. Kelleher," Larry said. "Liz just has a bad case of the dropsies."

"And we were trying to decide if old Betsy was spooking her," Darci added.

Her father grimaced as he sat down on a stool, and Liz brought him a cup of coffee. "You and old Betsy have a lot in common," he said.

"Dad." If she didn't want a public discussion of her mental health, she sure didn't want one focusing on her emotional state. Especially since she and her father had had this discussion a few hundred times already. The only thing she and Betsy had in common was that they were both named Elizabeth. Betsy had found true love, but fate, in the form of the Civil War, had taken it away. Liz had put all her money on the wrong horse, trying for that prize, and now was content to hoard her emotional reserves. She was not waiting for anyone.

Her father sipped his coffee, leaving it black and unsweetened, as always. After swallowing, he made another face and put his cup down.

"Mom said to give you decaf when you come in," Liz said. "Besides, there's no difference in taste."

"Shows what you know," he grumbled.

She ignored his grumping. "Want your usual lunch?" She didn't know why she bothered asking. Her father had had a cup of soup and a bacon, lettuce and tomato sandwich for lunch every working day of his life.

"Old Betsy spent a lifetime mourning her lost love, and so are you."

"Hank," Liz called back to the kitchen, "a regular for Dad." Then she turned back to her father. "Anything else?"

He shook his head, so Liz went over to fix his soup. There were times when her dad was just a bit too much, but she didn't know where she'd be without him and her mother. Or Jeremy, for that matter.

When she'd gotten married in her sophomore year in college, they'd stood behind her. They'd thought Bill was a kid who hadn't grown up, not husband material, but they never said 'I told you so' when Bill had left before Jeremy was even born.

She filled a small bowl with vegetable soup and placed it in front of her father. "Anything else?"

He just sat there, looking at her. She knew something was on his mind.

"Dad, I'm fine," she insisted.

"You got a letter from Bill, didn't you?"

She frowned at him for a long moment, both surprised and annoyed that his mind always ran along the same lines. "I did, but it was six months ago. I think Betsy's a more convenient excuse for my dropsies than Bill."

Twisting his face, her father looked out the window toward the tracks outside. "You're still expecting him to come back," her father said. "After all the hurt he caused you, you're still waiting for him. You wouldn't spend all your time here, if you weren't."

"Dad," Liz said with a sigh in her voice, "we're ticket agents. That was the deal when Jan and I got the contract for this sandwich shop. The rent is low, but we have to sell tickets and take care of any other paperwork for trains stopping here."

"Yeah, but—"

A whistle sounded off in the distance. The Chicago train. "Dad, I have to go. The twelve-thirty-three is coming in."

"It's late," he muttered, looking at his watch.

It usually was, but she didn't want to listen to a lecture on the decline of American industry any more than she wanted a discussion on why she still wasn't dating. Liz ducked under the counter and hurried toward the platform outside.

It wasn't as if she held her breath each day as she scanned passengers getting off the train. She'd cut her emotional ties to Bill long ago. She did harbor a slight hope that he would come back someday, but that was for Jeremy, not for her. And that was the reason she answered the letter that had come out of the blue about six months ago. He wanted to come see Jeremy. She'd been surprised at the request, then annoyed, then afraid. Jeremy had copies of newspaper clippings, game programs and all kinds of souvenirs of Bill's athletic career. What if Bill came this once, then disappeared for another eleven years? How would Jeremy take that?

Liz sighed as she watched the train round the bend and chug into the station. It hadn't taken her long to realize that Jeremy needed *any* contact with his father, even if it was only one short visit. So she'd written back, sending Jeremy's school picture from last year, but, true to form, they heard no more from him.

The train stopped, and she stepped away from the wall, the scent of roses suddenly washing over her. She frowned for a moment and looked around her. It was too early in the season for anyone's garden to be in bloom, but there had to be one hell of an air current to bring the scent over from Myers Florist Shop on Second Street.

Liz shook off the eerie feeling the scent had awoken in her and stepped forward as the train's doors slid open. She had no passengers today, but she had to trade some forms with the conductor. He got off first, then turned to help a passenger down the steps. Based on his solicitous manner, Liz figured it was an elderly woman. Probably coming back to visit relatives.

But to her surprise, a man descended. A not quite middle-aged man, around forty, or maybe younger. He looked reasonably fit and athletic, but his cane and stiff gait explained the need for assistance. When he turned, Liz saw that he was—

"Oh, my God," she gasped.

There were streaks of gray in the hair now and the face looked harder, but—

The man, limping toward her, suddenly stopped. They stared at each other.

After a long moment, Liz found herself breathing again. Nobody could deny the resemblance, but now that the man was up close she could see how foolish she was. The man wasn't Bill at all. Maybe her father was right. There were some things still hanging in her life.

"Afternoon, Mrs. Michaelson." The conductor had come over to her side.

Liz gratefully turned her attention to him. "Good afternoon, Mr. Connors," she said. "How are you today?"

"Tolerable, ma'am," the conductor replied. "Tolerable."

They exchanged their paperwork, then Liz turned away. The man who'd gotten off the train was still standing there, watching her.

"You're Liz Michaelson."

She wasn't sure whether it was a question or a statement. The man's manner was so...so hard. So aggressive. So take charge.

"Yes, I am."

"I'm Matt Michaelson."

"How do you—" She stopped, interrupted by her own laughter. Matt Michaelson. Now it all made sense. It was Bill's older brother. "Matt. Welcome home."

"Yeah," he replied, not looking as if he wanted to be welcomed *or* home. He looked around them. "You run the sandwich shop."

Question or statement? Maybe statement. She was surprised that he knew, though it certainly wasn't a secret. "Yes. How about a cup of coffee?"

"Sure."

"This is a real surprise," Liz said as they walked slowly toward the station. "You'll create quite a stir here in town." He'd been way ahead of her and Bill in school, so she hadn't known him very well, but she'd thought he'd been well liked and respected.

"Great."

"Though I think you'll find things have really changed," she went on. Now that her initial shock at seeing him had passed, questions were flooding her thoughts. Why was he here? Was he staying? Should she ask him about Bill?

Rather than say anything, Liz just hurried a few steps ahead of him and pulled the door open.

Her father was still at the counter, and sitting next to him was Jeremy, who'd had only a half day of school today. He would be thrilled to meet his uncle Matt.

"Jeremy," Liz called as they stepped through the door. "Look who's—"

Her son turned around, then his eyes grew as wide as saucers. Liz could see his hands begin to shake.

"Dad?"

"Oh, Lord," Liz murmured, her heart stopping.

"Damn," Matt muttered under his breath.

There was a definite quiver in Jeremy's boyish voice, and his eyes were shining. A look of hunger filled his face, a look so intense that Liz almost cried out. For the first time, she had to admit to herself straight up that her son wanted a father. No, not wanted. More like desperately needed.

Matt paused a moment to lean against the storefront. Oh, Lord, but he hurt. It was enough of a problem being a cripple, but having been laid up for the past two weeks wasn't helping him any, either. Along with being a gimp, he was out of shape.

Damn, but this trip wasn't going as planned. Not the least bit. First person he runs into when he gets off the train is Bill's Lizzie, except she isn't the cute little kid she'd been back in high school. She'd turned into a beautiful woman, and he'd found himself staring at her like some randy junior high kid. Then, when he was finally able to take his eyes off her, he was confronted with Bill's kid, thinking Matt was Bill, as if the kid didn't know what his own father looked like.

"Damn." Matt pushed himself away from the wall and crested the hill, where he stopped again and smiled slightly. Fortunately, some things didn't change in this world. A cluster of little cabins stood on the river side of town like they had when he'd been growing up here. And the same sign still beckoned—Kearns' Kabins.

Matt crossed the street and climbed the low steps to the motel office. A tinkling bell on the door announced his entry.

"Be right out," a voice called from a room behind the counter.

Old man Kearns had passed away years ago, but it sounded as if his daughter Maude Carmady were still running the place. Mrs. Carmady had grown up with Matt's mother, but where his mom had gone into nursing, Maude had become a teacher, quitting to run the motel when her father had gotten sick.

The curtains over the doorway parted and a short, stocky woman stepped up to the counter. Gray hair had succumbed to a henna rinse and the story in her face had added several chapters, but her eyes still twinkled.

"Hi, Mrs. Carmady."

Her mouth opened. Closed. Then opened again, letting out a shriek that probably woke some bears in the Upper Peninsula. "Land sakes alive. Matt Michaelson." She ran around the end of the counter and advanced on him. "Come here, boy, and gimme a big Michigan hug."

Matt bent down so Maude could grab him around the neck. Bracing himself on his cane with one arm, he tried to hug her as best he could with the other.

"Oh, let me look at you." She stepped back, putting her hands on her hips, and stared at him a moment. "You're looking more like your momma every day." Maude's face fell for a moment. "Bless her soul. Ain't a day goes by I don't think of her."

Not sure how to reply, Matt just nodded.

"So how is Billy?" she asked. "Ain't seen him since the elephant got his trunk."

With all the emotions flying around that train station, Matt had never gotten a chance to break the news to Liz. And until he did, he certainly wasn't going to tell anyone else.

"Uh." Matt cleared his throat. "We don't see each other all that much."

"That happens," Maude said. "Billy always was a fast mover. I imagine he's jumping around more than a bridegroom waiting for his mail-order bride."

Matt coughed into his free hand, thinking of the urn tucked into his suitcase. "He's quieted down a might." He felt his stomach squirming as Maude gave him one of her patented eagle-eye stares. "I mean, for Bill."

"He was a fun kid. Everybody liked him." She paused to look out her window. "But you were your mother's favorite. She always said she could give you any kind of a load and you'd carry it without complaining and without dropping anything."

He took a turn at studying the scene outside, but things didn't look all that clear. Memories scuttled around at the edge of the mist. A younger brother—handsomer, smarter, more talented—laughed and gamboled about, strewing the path with toys and other items. An older brother followed, picking up after him. The elder one wasn't laughing, but he knew his duty.

"So what are you doing back here?"

Matt quit breathing for a moment as he tried to rearrange his thoughts into an orderly whole. He was still cleaning up and he still wasn't happy about it.

"Just visiting?"

"Yeah." He started to breathe a sigh of relief but quickly choked it off. "Yes." He finished his sigh, now that he'd spoken properly. "But just for a few days."

"Want a room?"

"Room?" He felt totally dumb even before the word was completely out of his mouth.

"Yeah," Maude replied. "One of those things with four walls, floor and a ceiling. Mine are a tad on the drafty side, but they sure beat the hell out of a cave."

He stood there, tongue-tied, feeling dumb. Just like the days when Maude was trying to pound the elusive concepts of long division into him. He shook his head, rattling his brain and hoping sense would follow. "Yeah. I want a room. A single."

Maude pushed a registration card toward him. "All my rooms have double beds, and I charge one flat rate. What you do with your social life ain't none of my business."

Matt filled out his card, thinking that the years sure hadn't changed Maude all that much.

"Number fourteen," she said, handing him a key. "Just go on out back. A smart fella like you should be able to find it easy."

"Thanks." He picked up the key and turned to leave.

"Didn't you bring any baggage with you? Stay here more than a couple of days and your underwear is gonna get kind of ripe."

Matt felt all his muscles slowly tensing up and knew he had to get out of there. His imagination was dragging him back to fifth grade again. Only this time, Mrs. Carmady was discussing the excessive number of erasures on some paper he had handed in.

"I left my bag at the train station," he told her.

"Did you see Liz?"

"Yeah."

"Too bad things didn't work out with her and Bill. She's such a sweet thing. Girl like that needs a man around the house."

Liz's face danced on the periphery of his consciousness. He saw the softness of her face, the deep blue of her eyes and the fullness of her lips. *Sweet* wasn't the description he'd use for her. Sensuous. Irresistible. Certainly somebody who could fire up a man's kindling.

But he was also sure that Maude was right. There was something else about Liz, a gentleness, a vulnerability that said she needed a man, a tough guy to protect her from the meanness in this world.

But that wasn't his problem. He wouldn't let it be. He turned to go again.

"I imagine you met your nephew. That boy's the spitting image of Billy."

Again Matt stopped, but not out of respect for his old fifth-grade teacher. This time he froze, his stomach twisting in pain.

Up until now Jeremy had just been a boy. A kid with some problems, but just a boy. Maude's words had changed all that. They changed Jeremy into something belonging to Matt.

"Although his personality is more like yours than Bill's," Maude was going on. "You know, more on the serious side. He's a hard worker, too. Just like you were."

A lump grew in Matt's throat. Jeremy was a relative, blood kin. And the cool professionalism Matt had acquired in his years as a cop was no defense against a blood tie. Matt's only blood tie.

"I'm feeling pretty tired, ma'am," he told Maude. "I think I'll lay down for a while."

He limped off toward cabin fourteen. He would have run, except he knew even without a stiff, useless excuse for a leg, he'd never outrun the responsibility Bill had laid on his shoulders.

The cab listed sharply to port as the driver got in. "Here you go, Matt." The man turned slightly as he handed Matt a bag. "Grilled chicken sandwich and a diet cola."

Matt hesitated before taking his food. He still couldn't believe a cab without a bulletproof shield between driver and passenger. Had life as a big-city cop rendered him unsuitable for life in Small Town, America?

"Thanks, Luke," he murmured.

Luke Schiller and his wife ran the combination gas station-convenience store out on the edge of town. Apparently it wasn't enough to keep Luke busy since he also ran a three-vehicle cab company out of the location.

"We'll chow down," Luke said around a mouthful of burger. "Then we'll head back to town. I'm sure Liz'll be home by then."

"I can always see her tomorrow," Matt said.

Although he wasn't all that anxious to tell Liz about Bill, he didn't like putting it off, either. Maybe he should just let fate decide when he would perform his duty.

"She'll be back," Luke said. "Probably just out dropping Jeremy off someplace."

"It's Friday night," Matt pointed out. "She could be out on a date."

"Liz don't date."

Matt couldn't believe that, not after seeing her, unless all the men in Stony Mountain had gone blind. But he wasn't going to pursue the matter. "Well, I don't want to interfere with any plans you might have."

Luke let out a loud guffaw. "Me and Cindy got the business and two kids under three. We don't date, either."

Kids, a wife, a home. Visions, like sugarplums, danced in Matt's head and he chewed his food thoughtfully. He'd gotten caught up in things. Became a garbage man, hauling away a city's human waste, most of them losers from the get-go. But Bill, like Luke, had gotten dealt a different hand, a different set of opportunities.

"So how is old Billy making out?"

Luke had inhaled his sandwich with no more effort than he breathed in air. Now they had reached the point that Matt didn't want to be at—discussing his younger brother.

"Okay," Matt murmured.

The cabdriver said nothing, and for a while Matt wondered whether the man had heard. He didn't want to talk about Bill, but he didn't want to be rude, either. Luke was staring out his front window, maybe seeing private scenes from his own past with Bill.

"He was a high flyer back in high school."

"Yeah," Matt agreed.

"Makes you wonder why no one's heard hide nor hair of him all these years. Almost like he dropped off the face of the earth."

Luke let his right arm rest on the back of the seat as he stared down his memory lane. Maybe this would be someone to have an honest discussion with, Matt thought, staring at Luke's fingers, which were all bent and twisted from years of playing on the offensive line. Here was someone who'd also spent time protecting Bill. Bill had been the quarterback, while Luke, if Matt remembered correctly, had played right tackle.

"Billy was really something else. You know, he played our championship game with a separated left shoulder."

"He was right-handed," Matt said.

"Yeah." Luke chuckled. "He said afterwards that it was a good thing he was. Otherwise he wouldn't be able to pass no better than old Maude Carmady." He shook his head and sighed. "I'll always remember Billy. He's at the top of my list."

Matt turned to stare out at the night. Damn Billy. He'd always been a lucky bum. Never did nothing for the town. Yet, once he'd led the high school football team to the state championship, he went from Friday night hero to near saint.

"Maybe we should see if Liz is back," Matt said.

Luke nodded and started the car. They made the trip back downtown in silence.

"Light's on," Luke said as he rolled to a stop in front of Hilliard's Hardware. "She's in."

Matt looked up at the shaded second-story window. He could see the glow of the light through the shadow.

"Stairs are off to the left," Luke said.

Matt struggled out of the cab and hobbled over to the driver's window, but Luke waved him off before he could reach into his pocket.

"You don't owe me nothing," he said. "I owe Billy more than I can ever pay back." Luke put his car in gear. "Give me a call when you're ready to go."

Matt stared at Luke's taillights until they disappeared around the corner, then he turned to go up the stairs. Might as well get this damn thing over with.

Even with his stiff leg, he did well on the stairs. He didn't make too much noise, but was breathing a bit hard by the time he reached Liz's door. No doorbell and no peephole.

Shaking his head, he knocked. People in small towns lived in their own strange little world.

There was only a slight pause after his knock before the door was opened. It didn't make Matt any happier to see that Liz didn't have a chain on her door. Or that she swung the door wide open without calling out to see who was there.

"Matt." Her soft voice demolished the stone wall around his heart as if it were made of straw. "How nice to see you. Won't you come in?"

He stepped into the living room gingerly, as if he were stepping onto thin ice. "You know, I could have been some kind of weirdo."

Closing the door, she laughed. It sent sparks flying through the night like the sparklers they used to play with on the Fourth of July.

"Maybe that would make my Friday nights interesting," she replied.

Grimacing, he hobbled over to a straight-backed chair by the window. No need to get too comfy.

"Can I get you something to drink?" she asked.

"No, thanks."

"Good," she said, as she dropped herself on the sofa. "I'm not sure I have anything. My entertainment schedule isn't very full."

The only thing Matt felt like entertaining right now were thoughts of running away. Looking into Liz's eyes, he saw the harsh outlines of his own loneliness. His brother had left this woman and their child, choosing a life of loneliness over a life of love. Had he ever regretted it? Had he come back here often to see his son?

He looked away. "Jeremy around?" he asked.

Liz shook her head. "Birthday party sleep-over at Eddie Coulter's."

Great. Looked as if the fates had set things up for him.

"So what brings you to Stony Mountain?" Liz asked, tucking her feet up under herself on the sofa.

He looked her in the face, his eyes searching hers for any excuse to avoid the revelation he had to make. She just gazed back at him, her eyes so calm and serene. Would they stay that way?

"You," he said simply.

Her eyes frowned. "Me?"

He leaned forward, resting his arms on his knees and staring down at his hands for a moment. Then he looked up, holding her eyes with his. "Bill was in an accident last week," he said. "He was killed."

Chapter Three

Liz leaned back against the upper stadium wall, bringing her feet up onto the seat so she could wrap her arms around her knees. The stadium was deserted, except for a few early risers who were more intent on jogging along the track down below than jogging down memory lane.

She looked out over the field, at the scoreboard shrouded in the misty morning. This was where Bill had worked his magic, had woven the tapestry that the town still talked about today. From the moment he stepped onto this field his freshman year, he was working up to that moment of pure magic when he won the state championship his senior year. Everything he'd touched became perfect.

What had gone wrong?

She'd been unable to sleep after Matt had left last night, her mind bombarded with memories. Bill as a grade-schooler, accepting every dare and challenge with a wicked grin—and winning most of them. Bill in high school—everyone's friend, everyone's hero—and with that same streak of recklessness in him. Bill after that automobile accident late in his senior year, proven suddenly as vulnerable as the rest of them.

He'd never been the same after that. Along with his torn-up knee, he had torn-up scholarship offers. He'd turned into just regular folk and hadn't liked it. The mundane was something he never had any patience for, things like working day in and day out, without any spotlight, like picking new dreams away from the cheering crowd. She'd probably been crazy to give in to his plea to marry him—he'd been searching for stability and purpose, or maybe just a cheering audience that wouldn't leave him. In the end, he'd been the one who had left, walked out when she was seven months pregnant, and he hadn't been back since.

Liz wiped a stray tear from her cheek and got to her feet. All through the night she'd tried to figure out how she felt about Bill now, but all she came back to was that same sense of disappointment. She'd stopped loving him ages ago; she only felt a sense of sadness that he'd never found happiness. But when she thought of Jeremy, she got angry that Bill should have stayed so immature and selfish as to deny his son a father.

But that anger didn't do anyone any good. She climbed slowly down the risers, her hands jammed into her jacket pockets to hide her fists. Telling Jeremy wasn't going to be easy.

She drove across town to the Coulters' small frame home, where the boys were just getting up. "What's wrong?" Jeremy asked as soon as he saw her. "Is grandpa sick? Is something wrong with his heart again?"

"Nothing's wrong," Liz said. Though it wasn't strictly true. It was just that the worry on his face scared her. He was supposed to be happy and carefree—that was what childhood was. "I just wanted to have breakfast with you."

"Mrs. Coulter's making us eggs."

"You hate eggs. Why don't you come have breakfast with me?"

He stared at her. Hard, probing eyes. "We're gonna have a talk, aren't we?"

She looked at her son and a picture floated up before her eyes, the one they took at Jeremy's birth. Even then he'd looked so serious, like a little old man, thrust into this world against his will.

"Yeah," she replied. "We're going to have a chat."

His eyes darted to the ground. "Great."

He trudged back to get his things, then came out to the van with her. Neither spoke as she drove back downtown and parked by the train station.

"Why we eating here?" he asked.

"I had a taste for a banana split," she said as she unlocked the side door of the station. Their sandwich shop was closed on weekends.

"That's no kind of breakfast."

"Who says? Ice cream's full of vitamins, and fruit is very healthy."

"You're stretching it," he said, following her inside. "Mothers are supposed to make you eat stuff you hate."

"So you can eat eggs, then."

But he didn't push the issue, choosing instead to get out two banana-split boats, then slicing up a banana. She scooped out the ice cream while he got the toppings out of the refrigerator. She wished they could go on making these things forever, so that she'd never have to find the words to tell him his father had died. But all too quickly they were done and sitting side by side at the counter. She suddenly had no appetite.

"I don't know how to begin this, Jeremy."

A spoonful of whipped cream hovered halfway between the dish and his mouth. "You said everyone was okay."

Liz rocked her head slightly. "Everyone in Stony Mountain."

"I don't know anyone else," he said with a shrug. The spoon finished its journey to his mouth.

Her eyes roamed around the room for a moment, finally settling on a mounted fish on the far wall. The thing had been there so long it looked fossilized. It was Jeremy's father who had died, and Liz didn't know which was sadder—the death, or the fact that the son never knew his father. She opted for the latter.

"I know that you didn't know your father all that well." His chewing slowed, and she paused to take a deep breath. "But he died last week."

Jeremy swallowed and stared at her.

"He got hit by a car."

There was still no reaction from her son.

"It wasn't his fault. He had the green light."

He took another spoonful of the ice cream, carefully keeping his eyes on his food. "Like I said, I don't know nobody that don't live in Stony Mountain."

A lump sat heavy in her stomach. Liz wasn't sure what it was she was feeling. Fear? Anger? Pain? She wanted some emotion from Jeremy. Tears. Anger. Anything. Some admission of human feeling.

"I know it seems like he forgot all about us, but I don't think he had," she said, taking a moment to quiet the tremor that wanted to fill her voice.

Jeremy dug into the chocolate ice cream.

"He wrote to me a little bit ago, wanting to come see you," Liz said.

But her words didn't seem to be stirring any kind of reaction in her son's soul. His eyes remained shaded. Either he didn't want to show any emotion or, worse, he didn't have any.

"I wrote back and told him to come. I sent him your picture from school last year, but I guess maybe he couldn't get time from work like he'd hoped." It was a lame excuse, with about as much substance as the whipped cream they were eating, but maybe Jeremy wouldn't poke holes in it.

Fat chance.

"In more than six months, he couldn't find one day?" Jeremy said. "Nobody works every day. It's against the law."

"I never said it was six months."

He just gave her the look. "If you'd gotten the letter after September, you would've sent this year's picture," he pointed out, then went back to his eating.

Damn kid and his logic. "Maybe it wasn't that simple," she went on. "Sometimes it's hard to own up to something when you've done wrong."

"It doesn't get any easier if you wait."

"No, but not everybody thinks about it that way."

"Nope. Chickens don't."

"Jeremy! Your father wasn't a coward."

"Oh, no?"

His banana split was disappearing as fast as those talent scouts after Bill's accident, but Jeremy's emotions still stayed buried. Or maybe they just weren't there. It had always been hard to tell with her son. He kept things inside, closing everyone off with his hard stare.

"So how do you feel about him?" Jeremy asked. "You still love him?"

"No," she said slowly, not certain how much she should admit. "But I'm sorry that he died leaving so much undone. Getting to know you is part of it, but also just finding something that made him happy. I don't think he was avoiding us because he was having so much fun someplace else. I think he was a lonely, unhappy man."

"I wouldn't know."

There was a hardness, a distance about Jeremy that reminded her of no one so much as Matt. Maybe he could talk to Jeremy, have one of those man-to-man talks. On the surface, the two seemed a lot alike. Besides, Matt had to have stories about Bill that Liz knew nothing about, especially something more recent.

She pushed her uneaten ice cream away. "Let's drop in on your uncle Matt," she said.

"Why?" Jeremy asked.

"I just want to see how he's getting along. He can't drive or get around very well with that bum leg of his."

"Where's he want to go?"

"That's what we need to find out."

Jeremy gave her an odd look, but helped her clean up the dishes in silence.

The knock on the door brought Matt out of his chair as if shot from a cannon, and the newspaper he'd been reading fell to the floor. He reached into the nightstand, pulling his gun from the drawer.

"Yeah?" he shouted.

There was a long moment of silence. He held his breath and counted the beads of sweat as they slowly popped out on his forehead. What the hell was going on? No one knew he was here.

"Matt?" The voice was female. It sounded young and definitely of the gentle and sweet variety. It was—

"Oh, God." Suddenly feeling shaky on his legs, Matt fell back against the wall. He closed his eyes and dropped his head back. His gun hand dangled at his side. "I've been a cop too long. Too damned long."

"Matt? Are you all right?" The murmur of voices on the other side of the door seized his attention.

"Hell!" he exclaimed. That was Liz's voice and, most likely, she thought something was wrong with him. She was probably sending the kid for help. That would bring ambulances and God knew what else.

He lunged toward the door and pulled it open. "Good morning," he said in his best Officer Friendly voice.

Liz and Jeremy just stared at him. The kid had looked slightly pouty, but that quickly changed to dumbfounded. Liz looked like a spring flower blooming up through the slush of winter. She took his breath clean, clear away.

Matt looked away for a brief moment, trying to push his common sense back into place. "How are things?" he asked.

Still no reply. They just kept staring. Damn it. He was giving this cheerful bit all he had.

"Are you going to shoot us?"

He looked at the kid, at the gun in his own hand and then at Liz. "What kind of stupid TV shows do you let your kid watch?"

It was the wrong thing to say. Her mouth snapped shut and anger sparkled in her eyes, bringing them alive with such fire and depth that they wanted to consume him. And he wanted to let them.

"Are you on the run?" Jeremy asked.

"How the hell am I going to run on a bum leg?"

This wasn't like him at all. He'd met all sorts of women in his work, from drop-dead-gorgeous model types to eager sweethearts in spandex, yet none of them had touched him like this. Why was this small-town girl in jeans and no makeup igniting his fuse? He didn't like the sense of not being in control.

"What's the matter, kid?" He hoped anger would burn off the mist in his head. "You use your brains for a seat cushion?"

"Excuse me," Liz said, sounding like an angry schoolmarm.

He had the grace to be slightly apologetic. "Well, what kind of a question was—"

"I'm speaking, and I think it's rude to interrupt."

Matt glared at her but kept his mouth shut. How could she be so pushy when she looked so soft and cuddly?

"Number one." She held up a small index finger. "We were just being neighborly. You know, that's how us small-town hicks are."

He started to open his mouth, but she raised a second finger and pushed right on.

"Number two. We aren't at all accustomed to having our friendly advances met with a gun."

He sighed. He'd been a jerk and knew it. "Look, I'm sorry," he said. "But I'm a cop and I'm supposed to—"

"You're a Chicago cop," she snapped. "This is Michigan."

All right, he didn't have jurisdiction in this state, but he couldn't put a lock on his reactions. If he could, he wouldn't react to her like a moth to a flame. "What do you want?" he finally asked.

Frown lines violated the smooth sweetness of Liz's face, but her eyes seemed more filled with hesitation than anger. He fought back the need to ease that uncertainty from her blue depths.

"It's such a beautiful day," she said with a shrug. "We thought you might like to take a ride. Just to see if much has changed since you've been away."

She wanted to spend time with him? Why? She couldn't be interested in him, could she? The idea was too ridiculous.

"My knee still doesn't bend." Matt indicated his leg. "Makes it hard for me to get in and out of cars. That's why I took the train."

"We've got an old VW van." She looked at him for a long moment.

Her eyes seemed to be pleading, and his heart turned to marshmallow. Real tough cop he was turning out to be.

"It's got plenty of room for you to stretch out in."

The kid was busy giving her the fish-eye, and suddenly the light dawned. Matt felt like a fool. She wasn't harboring some secret passion for a gimpy old cop. She wanted him to do something for the kid, probably tell him Bill stories, all sorts of little details about his life. Details Matt couldn't give them.

He looked away down toward the river, an unidentifiable quiver growing in his stomach. How could he admit to those blue eyes that he'd barely ever seen his brother these past few years?

Matt turned back toward Liz and Jeremy. "Thanks, but—"

"The next train to Chicago doesn't come until Monday morning."

Monday morning. Damn. Those eyes played havoc with his heart again. Oh, what the hell. It wasn't as if he had anything to do but sit around here. If nothing else, he could make up stories about Bill. His hand went up to his jaw. Should he shave?

"You look just fine," Liz said.

Matt gave her a hard stare. What the hell? Was she a mind reader?

"Lots of the guys around here don't shave on Saturday," she said. "The van's over by Maude's office. We'll wait for you there."

Matt watched as her petite figure swung up the gravel trail. Potent, but not dangerous, he told himself. He could handle an hour or two with her without any problem. And with a little maneuvering, he probably could get them to tell him Bill stories. After all, it was why he'd come here—to tell them about Bill's death and mourn his brother.

As soon as they were out of sight, Matt took out his electric razor and gave himself a quick once-over. Not a real shave, just enough to top off the bristles. Then he put on his clean shirt and took a moment to stare at his gun. One part of him said leave it, but another said a cop without his piece is like a beached whale. He put on his shoulder holster, jammed his pistol into it and put on a light jacket to cover the whole thing. Then, grabbing up his cane, he hobbled up the path.

Liz and Jeremy were already in the van, but they'd left the sliding door open. He pulled himself up and dropped into the middle seat, pushing the door closed after himself. The van was actually rather comfortable. Easy to get into and, as promised, had a lot of space to stretch out in.

"Got any druthers on where you want to go?"

"You're in charge," Matt said.

"Yeah," Liz replied, "but you're the guest."

They were sitting at the entryway to Kearns' Kabins. Left would take them north of town. Right would take them south into the downtown area of Stony Mountain.

"How about north?"

"Yes, sir," she replied as she turned left.

He stared out the window, looking at, but not really seeing the houses on the edge of town. It was really strange being here again. He hadn't been back since Bill's freshman year in college, when their mother had died. Matt had been in the army, stationed in Germany at the time and had only had a short leave. Wake, funeral, burial next to Dad and condolences accepted. Bill had tried to sell the farm; neither of them had wanted it.

Matt saw himself and Bill as kids running through the long grass, the wind at their backs and the world at their feet. They were all gone but him.

"Do you remember where we used to live?" he asked, surprised at how quiet his voice was. "Bill and I?"

"Sure. Want to see the old homestead?" Liz asked.

He shrugged. "Yeah, sort of." He coughed into his hand. "I just want to take a quick look."

Liz knew where she was going, and they rode in silence. Over Gorman Creek and down past the place where he and Bill used to pick wild raspberries in the summer so their mother would make her special sweet jam. Then by the stand of sycamores that Matt used to long to climb, back in the days when he'd thought touching the sky was not only possible but a challenge he wanted to take on. Jeremy seemed to be staring out his side window as if the places they were passing were dull and ordinary.

"What grade are you in, Jeremy?" Matt asked.

"Fifth."

"How are things going?"

"Fine."

"You in any sports?"

"Basketball. Little league, when it starts."

Kid would make a good prisoner. Name, rank and serial number—and he didn't offer even that unless asked.

But Matt would starve to death if he had to make it as a talk-show host. His mother had been a precise person just like him. Bill, on the other hand, took after their father—the silver-tongued orator of the family.

"The place is empty again," Liz said. She had pulled the van over to the side of the road and was slowing to a stop. "I think the last renters moved out in the fall."

He looked out the window. The place had been for sale since their mother had died, but had attracted only a series of renters. The old farmhouse stood back from the road, looking even more weathered and worn than in his dreams. Its walls might have gotten a new coat of white paint since he'd last been here, but it was no more than a distant memory. The rest of the farm looked just as shabby. The barns needed repairing. Trees needed trimming. And some rusty old equipment needed to be dumped.

"A lot of the land was sold off," Liz said. "I think there's only about twenty acres left with the house."

"Enough for a horse," Matt said.

"Or even a couple of horses," Liz said.

The past played before his eyes again. "Each of us had a horse when we were kids."

Silence greeted his news.

"Did your dad ever tell you about our horses, Jeremy? Mine was a black one and I called it Midnight. Bill had a—"

"My father never told me anything." Jeremy had turned around in his seat and glared at him.

"Huh?" Matt was confused.

"I never met him."

Matt just stared at the kid for about three thousand aeons, trying to make sense of his words. "You never met him? But—"

"He dumped my mom before I was born and never came around again."

Matt felt stupid. Dense. Like his mind was stuck in the mud with its wheels spinning. "How—" He bit off his words. "What—" He ran his fingers through his hair, letting his breath out slow and easy. The fog started to fade slightly.

Bill had abandoned his family, not just divorced Liz. He'd been one of those spineless jerks who left a trail of hurt behind them. It wasn't just Matt who Bill had ignored. He'd brought a life into the world, then tossed the kid adrift without so much as an occasional guidepost.

"Damn worthless bum," Matt snapped. He felt like punching someone—something—and settled for smacking the seat back next to him. "What a worthless excuse for a man."

He saw the lifetime of fatherless kids who had paraded in front of him as a cop. Kids needing a father's guidance, support and sometimes a kick in the butt. Deadbeat fathers who took no responsibility for anything. His own brother had been one of them.

"I shoulda beat the hell outta him years ago."

How could Bill have done that? Hadn't he suffered enough each time their father had left on one of his binges? Hadn't he felt the emptiness when the old man had died? How could he choose to do that to his own kid?

Matt looked up, or rather looked out of himself and away from his anger. Jeremy was staring openmouthed at him. Liz was turned around, watching him. Matt stared back, trying to pull his control around him once more.

"I didn't know," Matt said slowly. "I hardly saw him, but I just assumed that he was in contact with you two."

"He wrote last summer about coming to see Jeremy," Liz said. "I told him he could, but he never came."

Matt nodded. "He kept Jeremy's picture."

Neither Liz nor Jeremy seemed to feel this atoned for much, but Liz turned back around and drove the van farther up in the drive. As if by mutual agreement, Bill was dropped off their conversational cliff.

"Why don't we walk around?" Liz suggested.

"I'm tired," Jeremy said. "I'll stay in here."

"Oh, no you don't, kid," Matt said as he pulled open the door next to him. "If I'm going to be walking all over this bumpy ground, I need a point man ahead of me."

Jeremy frowned. "What's that?"

"The guy who trips the mines," Matt said.

Jeremy only looked more confused.

"The one who warns me when there's a bumpy patch ahead," Matt said. "Hey, look at it this way. It'll be easier than having to drag me back to the van if I turn my ankle."

Jeremy seemed to accept his new responsibility without any more persuading, and jumped down from his door, checking the ground around the van's side door. "I sometimes play point guard," he said.

"Like to be in charge, eh?"

"My coach says I see the court well."

Matt hopped down on his good leg, then limped toward the house with Liz. Jeremy went ahead of them, swishing the matted brown grass with a stick he'd picked up.

"I'm sorry about that crap in the car," Matt said quietly.

Liz shrugged. "He's got very mixed feelings about his father," she said. "He used to idolize him, even made up stories that Bill was probably off someplace training to get back into football. Like he was so busy, so important, that it was understandable that he had no time for his kid."

"You think he really believed it?"

"Of course not," Liz said. "But sometimes we need to play games with ourselves to get by."

He watched her as she leaned forward to look in a kitchen window. What games had she played? Did she still love Bill and try to rationalize his abandonment?

"I always liked this house," Liz said, stepping back. "Your mom hated it, but I always thought it could be fixed up real nice."

Funny Liz should remember his mother always complaining about the bad wiring and leaky roof. Maybe if she'd thought their dad wouldn't drink up her housing fund, she'd have tried to put something aside to get the place fixed up. Matt looked inside, too, but the kitchen was all shadowed and dreary-looking. They left the house and walked toward the barn.

"There's a big rut here in the grass," Jeremy called out suddenly.

Matt skirted the area that Jeremy had pointed to. "He seems like a good kid," Matt said to Liz.

She nodded. "He is, but it's hard for him. His grandfather and Uncle Hank are great, but—"

"They aren't the same as a father," Matt finished for her.

"And then, all over town he hears what a great guy Bill was."

"Not exactly what he thinks."

"No, not exactly."

She shook her head, tossing her short blond hair so that the sunlight fell on her face. Her hair glittered and shone, inviting his touch while the sunshine seemed to make her lips fuller, more tempting. He looked away.

"Maybe it would help if he could visit Bill's grave," she went on. "Maybe he could yell or scream at him and get down to the business of mourning him."

Matt stopped walking, staring down at the short sprigs of springtime grass around his feet. "Actually, that's one of the reasons I came to see you," he admitted. "To see if you knew where Bill would want to be buried. Would he have wanted to come back here? Would Jeremy want him buried here?"

"Hey, there's about a million bushel baskets in here," Jeremy called from the barn door. "You gotta see this."

Liz glanced toward the barn, then back at Matt. "I have no idea what Bill would have wanted, or what would be best for Jeremy," she said, her gaze drifting away. "The only place Bill seemed really happy was on the football field."

Matt made a face. "Well, I doubt we can bury him there."

"Hey, you two," Jeremy called.

Liz waved and took a step away before she looked back at Matt.

He just shook his head slowly. "I think I'll take a pass. I've seen a million bushel baskets already."

She nodded and turned away.

Matt watched, hypnotized by the slow rhythm of her walk as she met Jeremy at the barn door, then disappeared inside. Freed of the spell she cast over him, Matt sighed and walked slowly past the barn. The river lay ahead of him, but he wasn't up to such a trek. He stopped, instead, at a wide patch of weed-choked ground. His mother's rose garden.

Bending down, he pulled at a few of the dead weeds. The bushes were still there, some in urgent need of pruning, but he could see little red shoots of new growth near the ground.

"They're love turned into a flower," his mother had told him one evening as he'd helped her weed. "You water and prune them and all they do is tease you with little buds that dry up and fall off. You feed them and keep their beds weeded and they just cut you with their thorns. But you keep coming back for more, because when that one flower opens, it's worth all the pain and toil."

He stood back up, leaning heavily on his cane and letting the softness of the spring air surround him and ease the pain from his wounds. Was there such a thing as a love like his mother had talked about? Was it only saved for a special few or was it like a fruit growing in an orchard, ready to be picked by whomever came along?

Everywhere spring was budding, that soft green replacing the dark death of winter, and Matt was suddenly glad he'd come. It was a beautiful day. Bright sunshine, gentle breezes, sweet smells of the earth reborn, birds dashing about building their new homes. There had been a lot of days like this when he'd been growing up here; it had been a good place to spend his youth. The farm provided a good balance of work and fun, a place to make men. Except, had it?

A lump came to his throat, and he pushed away from the garden. Had they both become carbon copies of their father? Bill had fallen off his mountain into a valley of loneliness. And Matt wasn't any better, steering clear of relationships for fear of repeating the past.

Not that Dad had been all bad. Aside from his week-long binges a couple of times a year, he could be great. You just never knew if he'd be around when trouble hit the next time. Matt remembered going down to the river with him some summer evenings and lying on his back in the grass, watching the clouds while his dad fished. They'd talk and plan and dream, as if all things were possible. As if it were possible to touch the sky.

"Tired?" Liz had come back, though he hadn't heard her.

Matt just shrugged, and the three of them drifted back down the driveway to the van.

"How come nobody'll buy this place?" Jeremy was asking. "It's kind of neat."

"It's also Betsy's house," Matt said.

Jeremy looked astonished. "You mean, the Betsy from the train station? What was she doing out here?"

"She lived here," Liz said. "This was her family's farm. Hers, once her parents died."

"Really?" You could almost see the gears moving in Jeremy's mind. He turned to face Matt. "You mean, you're related to crazy old Betsy?"

"And so are you," Matt said, patting him on the shoulder.

Jeremy's face fell, his eyes reflecting a horror that Matt could relate to. As a kid, he'd endured all sorts of teasing because of living on Betsy's farm. Bill had laughed it all off, later even playing up to it, but Matt had never been able to. It had seemed wrong somehow to laugh at the story of love lost.

"Actually, you're related to both sides of the story," Liz said, mussing Jeremy's hair as she laughed. "You're Betsy's great-great-great-great-great-grandson or something like that. Then, on my side of the family, you're something like a tenth cousin once removed of Will, her true love."

"Jeez."

Jeremy looked as if he were going into shock, and Liz just laughed. The easy sound floating on the spring breeze brought an answering smile to Matt's face. Jeremy climbed into the van as if it were the tumbril that would take him to the guillotine. Liz went over to her door.

Matt turned to look around him before he climbed into the van. Some things he'd found here before were still to be had—the peace and tranquillity, the clean, fresh air, the idea that some things were possible, if not all.

He climbed into the van, an idea starting to open like a leaf on a tree. He was tired of cleaning up after people. Tired of fighting the garbage, of taking care of people who wouldn't take care of themselves.

All he wanted was to be left alone. He wanted to watch the sun set, smell the sweet country air and not be hassled in any way. And maybe even write a little. Cops could always tell good stories.

Hellfire. Why not?

He had a reasonable amount of money saved, plus now he had his disability pension. He could get out of that rat race of a city. The damn rats were winning, anyway.

He glanced ahead of him and saw the soft curve of Liz's cheek, then darted his eyes away as if his soul had been stung by the sight. Maybe he could even undo a little of the hurt his brother had left in his wake.

"Liz," Jan said softly, "you got company."

Liz was refilling sugar bowls while her mind was on Jeremy, but Jan's words brought her head up. Matt was in the doorway, shaking the rain from his coat. He made his way to the counter, and the gloominess of the stormy morning seemed to lift a bit. Even Betsy's crying in the eaves seemed to lighten.

"Hi," Liz said. "Brave of you to come out in this weather."

He shrugged. "This is the first train to Chicago since Saturday. Besides, a little rain never hurt anyone."

"Boy, we need your attitude around here," Jan said with a laugh. "And your touch with Betsy." She looked up toward the rafters. "How'd you turn the old girl down?"

"She likes me," Matt said with a short laugh, but Jan shook her head at him.

"Mustn't laugh. Liz here believes in old Betsy."

Liz didn't know why, but she felt the need to explain, to make Matt, of all people, understand. "I don't know that I believe in her exactly," she said. "But sometimes when I'm alone, it seems like there's someone else here. Or maybe it's more of an overwhelming sadness in the air."

Jan rolled her eyes, but Matt's face almost said he understood. Not that it mattered. He didn't have to understand about Betsy or feel that lost love was a tragedy or anything. He was going his way, and she hers.

"Can I get you anything?" she asked.

"Coffee," he said. "And put it in a throwaway cup. I want it for drinking on the train."

Liz picked up a disposable cup and put it on the counter in front of him. "I'm sorry to see you go," she said, pouring the coffee into the cup. Her voice was cool and businesslike, one casual friend to another. "There's so many things we've never talked about."

"Well, actually—"

"Cream? Sugar?" she asked him, offering both.

He shook his head. "I take it black."

"That's the way my father drinks it," Liz replied.

"Actually, I'm not leaving for good," he admitted, clearing his throat as if preparing for a long speech. Or a difficult one. "I'm going to move back on the old farm."

"You are?" Liz said. The day seemed suddenly sunny. "That's wonderful. Jeremy will be thrilled." She stopped then, pulling her kites back to earth. It was fine that he was staying here, and Jeremy would be thrilled, but there was no reason for her heart to be dancing.

"How is he coming along?" Matt asked.

"Hard to say." Liz went back to the sugar bowls. "He's not exactly a talker."

"My mother was like that," Matt said, nodding.

And so was Matt, Liz suspected. "Bill wasn't."

"He was a lot like our dad."

Which was better—glib charm or silent steadiness?

"You had this business long?"

Liz was grateful for the change of direction. "About five or six years," she replied. "We're open for breakfast and lunch. It's enough to earn a comfortable living, but it doesn't chew up so much time that we can't do anything else with our lives."

"Like take care of your kids."

"Yeah." She leaned down, putting her elbows on the counter. "But we do other stuff. Jan runs an accounting service."

"Oh, yeah?"

"And Liz teaches a writing class," Jan volunteered, leaning closer.

He looked up. "Really? Where?"

Liz felt a wariness in her stomach at his interest. She was reacting too much to him already. She needed to ease away, get back to leading her own life. "Just at the local high school in the evenings. It's an adult-education class."

"Is your class full?" he asked.

"The session's half-over," she said. "We started in January."

"Why?" Jan asked. "Are you interested in writing?"

"I'm sort of thinking about it."

Liz felt flustered, unsure of herself for some reason. "I don't know if my class would work for you," she said. "It's mostly older women who want to write the history of their families." He almost looked disappointed, and she sighed. "Although they're very nice. And I'm sure they'd be glad to have you join us."

"I'll think about it."

"How long are you going to be gone?" Jan asked.

"Couple of days. Three at most."

"Her class meets Thursday evenings," Jan said. "You should be back in time for that."

He nodded, then suddenly his head came up. "The train's coming."

"It is?" Liz looked up at the clock. Damn. The train was almost in the station and she didn't have any paperwork ready. What was the matter with her? She'd never lost track of time like this before. "Would you excuse me, Matt. I have to—"

"I've got it," Jan said as she walked by and waved a packet of papers at her.

Liz gave her sister a sharp glance. There'd been something in Jan's voice. Later, she promised herself, turning her attention back to Matt.

"Here." She snatched the cup from his hand. "Let me warm it up."

"You don't have to do that," he protested.

She just dumped the coffee down the sink and poured him a hot, new cup. After putting a cover on, she started to hand him the cup, but took a look at his cane and the door out to the tracks. Carrying his cup was the least she could do. She came around the counter.

"I can carry that."

"That's okay," Liz replied. "Service is our motto."

They walked in silence out onto the platform where they stood, watching as the train pulled slowly into the station. She turned toward him, finding his eyes already on her. There was something in them, almost like a message he wanted her to read.

Sure, and the Easter bunny really laid chocolate eggs. She glanced away. "Are you bringing a car back?" she asked.

"No, I don't have one. A friend of mine has a used-car lot and lets me use one when I need it. Besides, I can't drive until they take this cast off my knee."

"Right, I forgot about that." Jeez, her mind was on vacation. She glanced back up at him and found her gaze captured by his. Her heart smiled and disconnected her brain once more. "I can drive you around," she said slowly. "You're going to need some furniture. And there's grocery shopping."

"I guess." His voice was slow, as if the words were hard to find. "As long as it won't be too much trouble."

"All aboard," the conductor shouted.

"I'll call you when I get in."

"I'll be here." She smiled up at him. "I'm the ticket agent."

The conductor was making impatient noises, and Liz knew Matt needed to get on the train, but for some reason he didn't move. It was as if her gaze were holding him prisoner. A crazy idea, but nonetheless she took a step backward.

"Listen," he said, his voice suddenly urgent. "Are you still in love with Bill?"

She stared at him for the longest moment. She didn't know what she'd expected him to ask her, but that sure wasn't it. "No, of course not," she said. "You know, you'd better get on the train."

"Are you sure?" he asked. "You're not still carrying some torch for him? I mean, would you walk the trestle bridge for him?"

Liz laughed at the reference to the almost forgotten test of true love—crossing Stony River on the ruins of the trestle bridge. Matt was joking. He had to be. "Never." She laughed again. "You'd better get on or they'll leave without you."

"Yeah," he said.

He took a step, but then was back. Ever so gently, he let his lips brush hers. It was a quick, darting touch that she almost thought she had imagined, except for the racing of her heart.

He looked slightly embarrassed, sheepish even. "Thanks for the extra coffee," he said, holding up his cup as if it were why he'd kissed her.

"Sure," she said.

Maybe it was.

She felt, rather than saw, him move toward the train, so she turned to go back into the station. Three days he'd said he'd be gone. That meant she had three days to get her heart back in line.

Chapter Four

Chicago was the pits. Everywhere Matt went, people acted as if he'd gone crazy, until he began to wonder if they were right.

"You're becoming a farmer?" his ex-partner asked him.

The guy who lent him his car practically laughed in his face. "You've got to be kidding. You're moving to the sticks?"

"Mark my words, you won't be able to sleep for the quiet," was his landlady's response.

Even the cabbie who took him and his luggage to the train station had an opinion. "You'll be back," he said as he dumped Matt's luggage on the sidewalk outside Union Station. "Only so long you can watch the corn grow."

This was absurd, Matt told himself. He probably would be back in a few weeks, and not just for his doctor's visits. What had seemed like a great idea back in Stony Mountain, standing in his old backyard and looking at his mother's rose garden, now looked like what it was—lunacy. Sheer, idiotic lunacy.

Just because he was tired of dealing with society's messes, tired of cleaning up after everyone, it didn't mean he had to run away. He could be left alone—he could find his silence—in Chicago, too. All he had to do was look.

But his doubts slowly slipped away as the train rumbled closer and closer to Stony Mountain. It wasn't thoughts of peace or tranquillity that took center stage in his mind, but Liz's smile and her soft fragrance of spring that had clung to him after they'd parted a few days ago.

It didn't mean anything, he told himself as the train left the Gary, Indiana, station and headed north for the Michigan state line. They were just friends.

They both had been close to Bill, and both closed out of his life in his later years, he told himself as the train sped past muddy fields awaiting spring planting. It was natural that they should feel a bond.

He needed change in his life and she just represented that, he thought as they roared over Stony River. To the south he could see the old trestle bridge. His old life had been like this concrete-and-steel bridge—fast, efficient and cold. His new life would be like the old trestle bridge—hurrying nowhere with time to look around.

Matt got off the train with renewed energy, ready to react with nothing more than simple friendliness to a certain smiling blonde. But Liz wasn't at the sandwich shop.

"Hi, stranger," Jan called. "How was Chicago?"

"Crowded," he said, trying not to look around too noticeably. Trying not to feel absurdly disappointed. Where was Liz?

"Liz is grocery shopping," Jan said as if reading his mind. "Sit down and have some coffee. She should be back soon."

And have it look like he had nothing in his life? "I think I'll just go on over to Kirkland Realty and pick up the key to the house," he said. "If it's okay, I'll leave my stuff here and have Luke come round and get it as soon as he can."

"Sure, no problem."

He limped from the station as quickly as he could. He was a man with a lot to do, a man who had more on his mind than saying hello to a friend. The sun seemed to have hidden behind some clouds, but that didn't matter. He headed down the block to the Realtor.

He'd pick up the key, then call Luke to take him out to the house. Once there, he'd be so busy he wouldn't think of another person for weeks.

"Oh, Liz picked up the key the other day," Mary Kirkland told him. "It's been almost six months since the last renter left, and she wanted to get the Merry Maids in to clean it up."

"I see." He didn't mind, not really, though it ruined his plans for this afternoon. He'd have to find her and get the key and—

"Hi, there," Liz called out.

Matt spun to find the sun had come back out. Liz was in the Realtor's doorway, her smile lighting up the room and his heart.

"I was just telling Matt that you had picked up the key to the house," Mary told Liz. "Did you get the power turned on, too?"

"Should be on by now." Liz stepped aside, holding the door open for Matt. "I got back to the station and found out you had arrived."

"Jan told you?" he guessed as he limped over to the door, drawn by her smile and the laughter in the air around her. "Or did you trip over my luggage?"

"No, old Betsy told me." She led the way to the van. "I've got your luggage. Want to make the rounds?"

"What rounds?"

"Furniture, linens, groceries." Liz went around to the driver's side while he climbed in the side door.

"I just thought I'd go out to the house." He was suddenly afraid of her, afraid of her power to make his knees go weak.

"And do what? You can't even sit down. There's no furniture." She started the van and pulled into traffic. "Unless you're tired out from the trip, we should at least get you a few basics."

Unless he was tired out from the trip? What did she think he was—some old man? "I just didn't want to take up too much of your time," he said. "You know, there's no reason for you to go to all this trouble."

"Hey, I'm your ex-sister-in-law," Liz said. "Or something like that. We're practically related."

"No, we aren't," Matt snapped. The whole idea was annoying to him. Preposterous.

"Okay, so we aren't."

Liz didn't seem bothered either way. A fact that annoyed him even more. He glared out the window at the kids playing on the jungle gym at the park.

All right, so he wasn't the youngest guy around, or the most fit at the moment. He still wasn't her big brother or an uncle figure. Not with the kind of feelings that churned through his body every time he looked at her. He had the almost uncontrollable urge to sweep her into his arms, to kiss those tender, pouty lips until she moaned with passion, to make those blue eyes of hers burn with the fever that seethed through him.

"Here we are," Liz said suddenly.

Matt forced back the dreams that had raced across his consciousness. They were in the lot of Tuttle's Furniture, parked with the van's sliding door opposite the building's front door. Great, now she thought he couldn't walk a few feet.

"You know, I'm not a crippled old man," he snapped, waving his hand at the almost deserted lot. "Look around, would you? This is a No Parking area. You're not even in a handicap space."

Liz just got out and opened the sliding door. "Out."

"You're blocking the doorway," he said. "You're going to get a ticket."

"Our police officers have better things to do than hand out stupid parking tickets."

"What? They're too busy to enforce the law?"

"They're probably rescuing sweet little cats out of trees. Now get out here before I bounce you out."

"Okay, okay."

Matt pushed himself up and jumped out onto his good leg. They walked into the store in silence. Liz was at his side, her soft scent attacking his senses so that he could barely think straight. He was due to get his cast off in a couple of weeks and could hardly wait. He'd show her he could take care of himself, that he was a real man.

"Hi, Liz." A tall, slender woman with a touch of gray in her dark hair approached them. She looked vaguely familiar, but so did just about everybody in this whole damn town. "Hello, Matt."

Matt just nodded while Liz broke into a smile. "Hi, Tina."

"I'm sorry about Bill," Tina said. "It's such a shock not to hear from him all these years, and then he's gone for good."

"Yes, it is," Liz replied, nodding.

"How is Jeremy taking it?" Tina asked.

"Okay." Liz turned to Matt. From the look on her face, it was obvious that she wanted to change the subject. "This is Tina Doran. I don't know if you remember her. She used to be Tina Bucknell." Liz turned back to Tina. "You were what—four or five years ahead of Matt in school?"

Tina gave a hearty laugh. "Let me jog his memory. When you were in sixth grade, I was a junior in high school."

Matt shrugged. Something in the woman's eyes told him this story wasn't going to raise his manly standing with Liz.

"That was the year we had that wham-doozer of a snowfall the weekend after Thanksgiving," she said. "Some friends and I were walking to church one Sunday and you and some of your more dweebie acquaintances decided to bombard us with snowballs."

"Boys will be boys," Matt murmured.

"Oh, yeah." Tina snorted. "Well, girls will be girls, old buddy. Me and my friends ran you guys down. Washed your

faces and stuffed snow down your shirts and in your pants.
You guys had to sit through services on frozen butts.''

The two women snickered while Matt tried to remember
those words by Thomas Wolfe. Was it you couldn't go home
or you didn't want to?

This was the trouble with small towns. Nothing much ever
happened, so the old stories just lived on and on and on.
Taking on a life of their own, long after anyone was interested. A person couldn't come in and impress anybody because there was always some busybody with some stupid old
story to relate.

"Excuse me, ladies," Matt said, putting a street-tough
tone in his voice, "but can I buy some furniture?"

Tina brought herself under control, but just barely. "Only
on Wednesday afternoons," she replied.

He debated telling her she wasn't funny, but thought better of it. Sure, it was the middle of April and there wasn't an
ounce of snow outside, but it was best not to tempt fate.
Especially since he was trying to convince Liz he was wor-
thy of notice.

"I need a bed, table and a couple of chairs," he said.
"Just a few things to keep my can off the floor."

Tina nodded. "How about appliances?"

"There's a built-in stove," Liz said. "It's not too great,
but it'll do for now. There's no refrigerator, though."

"A refrigerator, then," Matt said.

"What kind?" Tina asked. "Color?"

He shrugged. "Small. In anything but black."

The two women exchanged raised eyebrows.

"Hey," Matt protested. "I'm just going to eat and sleep
there. I've got other things planned besides sitting around,
staring at the walls."

"You have any idea what kind of style you want for the
other furniture?" Tina asked. "Colors?"

"Dark," Matt replied. "So it don't show the dirt. And
built solid. Something that won't fall apart if a football
lineman sits on it."

Tina made a face. "Well, we're certainly making progress."

Oh, hell. He'd show Liz he was in charge of his life. "I'll take one of those," he said, pointing at a bedroom set in the window.

"That's a boy's bedroom set," Tina said.

"The dresser and everything looks regular size," he said.

Tina nodded. "The bed does come in double as well as single."

"Great. Wrap it up. I'm one of the young at heart." He went back to his mental list. "How about a kitchen table and chairs? And throw in a refrigerator. Pick whatever you have handy."

"You really should get a microwave," Liz said. "They're very nice when you're alone and just cooking for yourself."

"One microwave," he said to Tina.

"Yes, sir."

"And deliver it all today. I don't want to sleep on the floor."

Once Tina realized that he seriously didn't care what the stuff looked like, she was pretty efficient. She showed him the basic models of refrigerators and microwaves, while Liz tossed in a few opinions about what features she thought he would need. Selections were made in no time, payment was exchanged and arrangements were finalized for delivery in an hour.

"That was relatively painless now, wasn't it?" Tina said as she handed Matt his receipt.

"Not bad at all," he said. "I don't know why women make such a production out of shopping."

Liz just rolled her eyes while Tina laughed.

"Better show him who's boss, Lizzie," Tina said. "He's gonna get in a lot of trouble if you don't take him in hand."

Liz looked surprised, then seemed to fold back inside herself like a flower closing at the end of the day. He felt suddenly bereft, as if the sun had fled. What had happened?

"Thanks for your help, Tina," Liz said. "Say hi to Ted for me."

Matt wasn't sure what was going on, if anything. Liz looked the same outwardly. And Tina didn't appear to feel anything was strange as she waved them out the door. Maybe his imagination was working double time. It wasn't as if he knew Liz so much better than anyone else that he could judge if there was less bounce in her step.

"We'll go to the mall down on the edge of town," Liz said, once they were back on the road. "We need to get you some linens."

"Linens?" he asked. "What the hell do I look like? Some kind of a duke or something?"

"You need towels, sheets."

Oh. If she had said that in the first place, he wouldn't have sounded so stupid. He slumped back in his seat. How'd she know he wasn't bringing all that stuff from his home in Chicago? Did he look like the type that barely had two sets, and both were worn to paper-thin? He didn't like the image she seemed to have of him.

"Don't you have to look in on Jeremy?"

"He's at Jan's," Liz replied. "Baby-sitting his cousins for a couple of hours."

She drove in silence until the end of the block. "He likes earning the money." For just the smallest moment, he saw her mouth turn down in the rearview mirror. "And it takes his mind off things."

Matt turned away, his crazy preoccupation with Liz washed away by a rush of anger at his brother. How could he have left such pain in his wake? Matt wished he knew what to do, how to make it better for Jeremy. And Liz, too.

Liz had such a strength in her manner, but Matt wasn't fooled. He could see that she was hurting badly, that she was only pretending to have everything under control. She needed someone strong to lean on, someone to take over some of her burdens.

"Matt."

They were in another parking lot, and he hadn't even noticed that they'd stopped. "Yeah?"

"I said, what about dishes?"

He rubbed his eyes with his fingers. Jeez, it was just a little move. He was coming from a dumpy little apartment to a little house in the country. There was no reason for him to be taking up so much of her time. She was supposed to be leaning on him, not him on her. "We can get some paper and plastic stuff at the supermarket."

"Okay for now," she said. "But that's not very smart economically or environmentally."

"I'll reuse them until they disintegrate," he promised, hoping to see a smile come to her lips, but it stayed elusive.

Did he know her well enough to ask her if something was wrong? Maybe it was just everything. Maybe it was nothing. Maybe he was addicted to her laughter and couldn't get enough of it.

They went into the linen shop in silence. Surrounded by towels and shower curtains and ceramic swan soap dishes, he didn't regain his urge to joke and tease. Talk about a bull in a china shop—he felt clumsy and awkward and about the last thing that any sane woman would rely on. Liz picked a few things out for him, and he gave the money to some older woman who clucked at Matt's limping gait as he came around the end of the counter to get the package.

Instead, she handed it over the counter to Liz. "Maybe you better take it, honey. Give your man a rest."

Great, Matt thought as they trudged back out to the van. Now even little old ladies were warning Liz that he wasn't much of a bargain. Those lips seemed to grow farther and farther away, his dreams some strange, unreachable fantasy.

Matt sagged into his seat, feeling drained both physically and emotionally. He just sat there like a lump of clay while Liz drove to the supermarket. He didn't know how to convince Liz he wasn't some washed-up old piece of garbage and didn't know if it was even possible. She'd probably gotten all quiet because she saw what a burden he was.

"Why don't I just run in myself?" Liz said as she parked at the grocery store.

"Hey, I'm fine," Matt protested. "Just getting my second wind."

She made a face at him. "It'll be faster," she said. "I'll just grab the basics. Nothing fancy, I promise."

Then she was gone before he had a chance to protest. Maybe it was for the best. He was just a crippled old cop, too damn big to ride around in the grocery cart. Maybe he was useless and his hormonal surge was making him fool himself into thinking he could get her to see him as a man.

He watched her slim figure hurry across the parking lot. Why hadn't she remarried? From lack of chance or lack of interest? He sat up a little straighter, scolding his heart. He wasn't interested in that way. No matter how attracted he was to her, he was just dreaming. He wasn't looking for a relationship. He was no better a bet than his brother or his father had been, just a bit more up front about it.

He closed his eyes and leaned his head back. Once he got settled in, he'd change her perception of him, though. He'd start helping her and Jeremy. Maybe have them over for dinner to pay her back for all the trouble she'd been going to. Show Liz that he was a man.

The sound of the back door opening brought Matt out of his reverie. Damn, Liz was loading the groceries by herself.

"Hey, you should have given a yell," Matt said. "I can help, you know."

But she had already put the bags into the back and slammed the door shut, rushing to come around to the driver's side. "Don't worry about it," she said. "There were only a few packages." She turned on the ignition and slammed the van into gear, causing the transmission to grind slightly.

"What's your hurry?" Matt asked. "Got a hot date tonight?"

Her smile flashed in the rearview mirror and his heart sank. Of course she did. He wouldn't be the only guy around who couldn't keep his eyes off her. He suddenly forgot about his resolve that he wasn't interested in a relationship with her himself.

"Your furniture is supposed to arrive in about fifteen minutes," she said. "We want to be there when it does."

"Oh." The relief that washed over him was stronger than he'd expected. Stronger than it should have been. "Wouldn't hurt them to wait a few minutes." He watched the scenery dash by. "I take it your cops don't give out speeding tickets, either."

"Don't be such an old nag."

The sunlight bouncing over her golden hair radiated springtime wonderment, and he found his heart wallowing in mud and muck. She thought he was an old nag.

He thought she was springtime laughter caught in a crystal glass. She vibrated with an energy that was contagious. Just to be near her was to be alive. To hold her in his arms would be...

Dangerous.

Matt looked away, but could still sense her. "How about dinner tonight?" he asked. "I owe you for all your help."

"I really can't tonight."

"Jeremy's invited, too."

"I need to go over my notes for tomorrow's class," she said.

Holding his facial muscles stiff, Matt continued staring out the window. The old "I gotta go over my notes" excuse. No big deal. He'd come back to Stony Mountain for the privacy, anyway. He'd just get started on it a little sooner than he'd planned, that's all.

Liz fought indecision all day and it got no better as she drove to her class. She was getting too tied up with Matt. Like yesterday, when she came back from the store and suddenly found herself tossing his luggage in the van and going out after him. Why? Jan said he'd been going to call Luke.

There was something about his eyes, about the way he held himself so separate, as if he wanted to be included in

the game but was afraid to ask. She saw a depth of loneliness and pain in his eyes, mirrored from his soul but certainly not magnified. If anything, she'd caught just a glimpse of his inner pain and had this insatiable need to ease it.

She was crazy. A Florence Nightingale she definitely wasn't. The last one she'd tried to heal had been Bill, when he'd been sure that marriage would bring him the stability and sense of belonging that he so craved. And look how well she had done then.

Liz scanned the faces in her class, then let her gaze flash over to the clock on the side wall. She was just as glad Matt hadn't come. She was not about to show him who was boss, as Tina had instructed. Neither was he *her* man, as the woman in the linen store had implied. She had her own life, completely separate from him, and that was the way she wanted it.

The minute hand finally made it to the hour. "Okay, class," Liz said. "Let's get going."

But before she could get started, the door was opening and Matt was walking in slowly. Her heart warmed to him in spite of her insistence that it behave.

"Sorry," he said, flashing a smile at her. "Luke was late."

The smile wormed its way down into her soul, leaving a warm and welcome trail along the way. Liz tried to keep an echo of it from showing on her face. She feared she was failing as she felt a slow flush ease over her cheeks, but then everybody had turned to watch Matt come in, so maybe she was safe.

After a moment to pull her wayward stirrings back into their respective corners, she faced her students. "Class, I'm sure you all know Matt Michaelson. He's going to be sitting in with us for a while."

She wanted to say he'd be there for the rest of the semester, but that would have sounded so presumptuous. Heck, one class might be enough for him. He might take a look at the ten women and two elderly men and say the hell with it. Or he might find out that he just didn't like writing.

Or maybe he wouldn't feel she had anything to offer as a teacher.

Shutting the lid on her rambling thoughts, Liz found the class was clustered around Matt. From the snatches of words reaching her ears, she could see that they were expressing condolences over the loss of Bill and trying to jog Matt's memory to see if he could remember them. He looked like he would have preferred to have sneaked into the room.

"Ladies. Gentlemen," Liz said briskly. "We have a lot to do tonight."

The murmuring quieted down as people returned to their seats. She waited while Matt found a place in the back where he could sit with his leg outstretched.

He was just one man, husky but not that large, yet he seemed to dominate the room. Both brothers had that facility, but where Bill did it with his athletic physique, Matt did it with his personality.

Not that he wasn't handsome. With his muscular physique, thick brown hair and piercing dark eyes, he'd rate an extra look from any woman still breathing, but it was his brooding personality that seemed to envelop the room.

"Liz, I have a question."

Liz turned quickly to Maggie Alwine, glad to get down to business. "Great, Maggie," Liz said. "Does it concern the use of first person that we discussed the last class?"

"No." The woman turned around to face Matt. "Are you really a homicide detective?"

It wasn't what Liz had expected, but part of her didn't really mind. Maybe a little detour would be good for her. Let her get used to the sight of him back there.

"Not anymore, ma'am," Matt answered. "But I used to be."

Liz tried to draw the class back to her. "Okay," she said. "Now let's get started."

"What happened to your leg?" one of the men asked.

Liz raised her voice just a touch. "Today we want to continue our discussion of point of view." The class stared

at her, their eyes pleading like little children begging for one more bedtime story. "Okay, fine," Liz said. "Matt can answer this one question. Then we're on to point of view."

Matt gave her an apologetic smile before turning back to his questioner. "I was shot in the leg."

"How?"

"It was on a raid."

"What kind of a raid? Was it a drug bust?"

There was a scraping sound as students turned their chairs to face Matt, rather than the front of the room. Matt looked at her for guidance.

She shrugged. How could she blame them for their interest? Wasn't there a similar fascination in the way she looked at him? "Tell your story," she said. "Then we'll go on."

Except that they never really got there. Her students, like kids around a star athlete, were constantly on Matt with questions. Everyone had something they wanted to know, and then something else. By the time the evening was over, Liz was exhausted, but not from teaching.

She felt like she'd been sparring with her emotions for hours. She was fascinated with Matt's stories, found herself watching the way his eyes darkened at certain parts and the way his mouth tightened with unspoken memories. He was so patient with his questioners, and so gentle in turning away from areas he didn't want to discuss. Through it all, she'd been conscious of his strength, of the way he was willing to put himself in danger to keep others safe. Yet he also seemed so alone.

"I'm sorry," he said as he limped toward the front of the class. The last of the other students had finally left.

"That's all right," she said. "Verbal storytelling is good practice for writing." And he'd had quite a lot of practice. Normally the class was released at eight-thirty, but it was past nine-thirty now. "And you brought exciting things into their lives."

"I didn't want to mess up your class."

His voice could melt the polar ice caps. She could listen to it forever and never stop being amazed at the way it slid so smoothly over her defenses and into her heart. A dangerous idea. She turned away to pick up her papers. "You didn't mess anything up. I could have stopped the questions if I'd wanted. Everyone was interested." Her among them. "And it was really nice of you to offer to talk to Marilyn's grandson. She's been at her wit's end trying to keep him in line."

"No big deal. I've given that speech about a hundred times now."

"Oh, yeah? Maybe you should get involved with the youth center the local churches are trying to start."

"I don't think so. I'm moving onto new ground." Matt seemed to move a step closer. She felt his nearness though she was facing the other way. "You look tired."

She shrugged. She didn't need—didn't want—him getting too close. She hadn't had much practice in throwing up her defenses lately and there were places in her heart she didn't want seen. "Things have been a little hectic."

"Because of Bill?"

There was a depth, a hardness to Matt. Even in asking the simplest of questions, she could sense it in him. He wouldn't run when things got tough.

"Come on," she said, slinging her bag over her shoulder. "I'll give you a ride home."

"That's okay," he said. "Luke is waiting outside."

She stopped, disappointment rising above all other emotions. "You're taking a cab home?" She'd thought she'd drive him.

"Yes, I'm taking a cab home. I don't want you driving alone at night."

Who was he to make those decisions for her? "This isn't Chicago," she pointed out.

"Crime is just as much of a problem in Stony Mountain as it is in Chicago."

She felt like a kid who'd lost the promise of an ice-cream cone. It was a crazy, stupid feeling. Why should it matter if it was Luke or her who drove him home? But it did. "I'm driving home alone from *here*."

"It's only a couple of blocks," he replied.

"Oh," she said. "And how many blocks are required for something to happen, Mr. Super Duper Expert on Crime?"

"Look, you're close to home here. There are people around. The streets are well lit. The odds are—"

What was she getting so annoyed about? she asked herself. If he wanted to have Luke drive him around, fine. It meant less time for her away from Jeremy. And hadn't she spent enough of her evening trying to treat Matt as an acquaintance, a casual friend? Well, great. Casual friends could take cabs and she could go home.

"It's getting late, Matt, and I'm not up to this kind of a discussion. Take your cab."

She started to walk away, but stopped and turned back, fearing she'd been more abrupt than she'd meant to be. "Good night."

His eyes seemed to pierce through her, sneaking between the chinks in her wall and hitting her squarely in the heart. There was so much in his gaze—hunger, fear, need and loneliness—that her feet almost took her back to his side. Her unsettled spirit wanted to touch those lips and bring warmth to his soul, take the bleakness from his eyes and the chill from his features.

She should never have turned around. "Good night," she repeated, and practically fled out the door.

Liz looked at Jeremy's science exhibit and tried to concentrate on the ants running around all the little tunnels. "It's very nice, honey," she told her son.

"It's just some stupid kit that I put together," he snapped. "Any dummy could do it."

Liz sighed, wishing she could just go home. Go home, jump in bed, curl up under the covers and hope that sleep would come, like it had in her childhood.

She hadn't slept well last night. Part of it was a childish wish that things could go back to the way they used to be— with Bill out of their lives, except for the old newspaper clippings and the pictures in the high school's athletic hall of honor—but mostly it was her childish irritation at Matt.

It had been so silly to get upset because he wouldn't let her drive him home. After her little display, he was probably relieved—probably would have feared for his safety.

And why had she done it? God only knew. She must be overly tired. Or afflicted with spring fever. She'd never gotten upset before when someone saved her a little work.

"Hello, Liz."

Liz turned to find her landlady at her side. "Oh, hello, Mrs. Hilliard."

"I'm so sorry about Bill," the older woman said. "It must be such a shock for you and your little one."

"We're doing fine," Liz replied.

The woman patted Jeremy on the head and then murmured some things that Liz couldn't make out before moving on down the tables of exhibits.

"That's really stupid," Jeremy hissed by her side.

"People are just trying to be kind, honey."

"Aw, come on, Mom. The guy wasn't around for like ten years." Bill had gone from "my father" to "the guy" in the few days since Jeremy learned of his death. "Did anybody come around and say how sorry they were when he was missing all that time?"

"No, Jeremy. They didn't."

"Then why are they bothering now? And, anyway, I'm glad he's dead. That way I don't have to wonder if he's ever coming to visit."

Liz felt a stinging in her eyes and didn't know whether to hug Jeremy or shake him.

No matter what Bill had or hadn't done, he was still Jeremy's father, and in Liz's book that meant he got respect. But she also knew where Jeremy was coming from. His pain was her pain. Why couldn't everyone just forget about Bill?

"Mrs. Michaelson." A young, red-haired woman had stopped by them. "I'm Edith Jones, Jeremy's science teacher. He's doing very good work in class. It's a joy to have him."

"Thank you." It was so nice to talk about normal things. "Science has always been one of his favorite subjects."

"I just found out about your husband today," the teacher said, then turned to Jeremy. "I'm really sorry about your father."

"I'm not," Jeremy snapped. "I mean, like I never saw the guy in my whole life. What do I care if he's dead?"

"Jeremy," Liz gasped.

"I don't care," Jeremy said. "I just don't care."

Then, before Liz could do anything, he turned on his heels and ran out of the room. Liz tried to follow but found a hand on her arm. Miss Jones was looking quite miserable.

"I'm so sorry," she said.

"It's nothing you did." Liz took a deep breath. The poor teacher had a look of absolute anguish on her face. "Bill and I were separated before Jeremy was born. He had some personal problems and he went off to try and fix them. Jeremy wasn't even a year old when the divorce was final."

"I'm really sorry," the teacher said. "I just moved here and there's so much I don't know. I mean, everybody knows everything about everyone else. There are times that I feel like I've come in at the middle of a movie."

"That's okay," Liz assured, edging away. "Really, it's all right."

She was able to escape at last and hurry out to the parking lot. As she expected, Jeremy was nowhere in sight. She got into her van and slowly drove around the neighborhood, heading toward her parents' house. Her father came out onto the porch when she pulled into the drive.

"He's in with your mom," Liz's father said. "They're having chocolate doughnuts and milk."

Liz felt so weary all of a sudden. "Is he okay?"

"Better than you, I'd guess," her father said as he put his arm around her shoulder. "Why don't you let him spend the night? He doesn't have school tomorrow, and you could just go home and pamper yourself."

It sounded like a great idea, but once she got back in the van, she just sat there. She felt as if she were the last person left in the world. She didn't need to go home and be alone; she needed somebody to talk to. Somebody who wasn't about to break into a song and dance about Bill.

Without really making a decision, she started the van and drove through town, across Gorman's Creek, past the wild raspberries and the stand of old sycamores to Betsy's old farm. There was a light on in the kitchen, so she pulled into the drive.

Matt must have heard the van, for he stood in the open door, the warm welcome of his home spilling across the porch and down the steps to her feet.

"Liz?" he said.

"Yep, just me." She suddenly felt silly for coming over. She should have just gone home and taken a bubble bath. There was no reason to impose on Matt. But his arms seemed so strong and his shoulders just right for leaning on. "I was just driving by and wondered if you needed anything."

He didn't say a word, and with his face in the shadows she couldn't read his eyes. She slipped her hands into the pockets of her skirt. "You know, since you're here all by yourself with no car..."

"Want to come in?" He came to the edge of the porch, reaching his hand down for hers.

This was crazy. It was so silly. But her heart was practically in her throat as she placed her hand in his and came up the steps. His touch was so gentle, surprisingly so since he seemed so gruff most of the time. Maybe it was just the night, or the almost summerlike breeze that carried the hint of a sweet, flowery scent.

God, it had been so long since she'd felt as if she needed someone. Since she'd felt the need to lean on another for just a moment and let them carry the burdens. She felt silly, craven, weak, but mostly glad to be under the gaze of those brown eyes.

"Can I get you something?" he asked. "There's coffee, soda, water, orange—" He started to laugh. "Hell, you know what I've got. You bought it."

She just smiled and walked slowly around the kitchen. Her heart was still fluttering and uncertain, not sure if it wanted to admit why she'd come. "Your furniture looks nice," she said.

"It'll look better once I get the place fixed up. I need to get a contractor in here and decide what needs to be done."

She nodded and sat down at the table. The local newspaper was open to the editorial page.

"Just reading everyone's opinion on the youth center," he said as he folded the paper up.

"No one agrees on anything about it," Liz said, then sighed as his eyes rested lightly on her. "Jeremy blew up at one of his teachers at the science fair tonight."

"A science experiment gone bad?"

She just stared at him, totally lost.

"You know," he coaxed. "Jeremy exploded. A science experiment on explosives that didn't work." He sighed. "It was a joke."

She shook her head, trying to laugh or smile or show that she was alive. It was too much work. She played with the edge of the newspaper, folding the corner down and creasing it over and over again. "She offered him her condolences on Bill's death."

"Ah."

"He said he didn't care that Bill was dead." She ran her fingernail along the crease.

"He probably doesn't," Matt said.

"But he was his father."

"A lousy one."

"But his father nonetheless." Liz tore off the small triangle she creased on the edge of the paper. "It's just that—"

"It's just that his anger's not very polite." Matt pulled the paper away from her, capturing her hands in his. "It's hard to pretend that you're strong and tough and don't need anybody when he's shouting out just the opposite, isn't it?''

''This doesn't have anything to do with me,'' she protested. One part of her was telling her to take her hands from his, but another part wanted to lean on him, let him protect her.

Habit came to her rescue, that and common sense reminding her how dangerous leaning was. She wasn't depending on anybody.

''I mean, it has to do with me because I'm Jeremy's mother,'' she said, slowly drawing her hands from his, then standing up. ''I don't know how to help him.''

''Maybe you have to let him be angry.''

She walked to the back window and stared out at the yard. Moonlight had turned it to magic, hiding all the weeds and dead branches and old equipment. Dreams and promises could live out there. Pain and loneliness would have to wait for the harsh rays of daylight.

She turned back. ''Letting him be angry is all fine and dandy, but what then? I need to help him through this, not let him muddle along on his own.''

Matt came over to her side. ''Be patient,'' he said. ''Expect him to be courteous, but let him vent his anger to you, just not *at* you. Then help him move on.''

''I guess.''

''Give Jeremy a little time, then we'll have some sort of service for Bill. Maybe in June, around Bill's birthday. Bury him alongside the folks, and then we'll all be able to move on.''

''Sounds reasonable.''

Up close to him, she found it harder to concentrate. And her problems seemed suddenly less serious. Matt's eyes were so dark, yet she could see the caring and concern there. She could see the willingness to ease her worries from her shoulders, if she'd let him. And she wanted to let him.

Hadn't she learned anything from the past?

''If you want, bring Jeremy around tomorrow or Sunday,'' Matt offered. ''I'll find some work for him to sweat some of the anger out of him, and maybe we can do a little talking, too."

"Okay." That wouldn't be leaning, would it? It would be for Jeremy, so it would be all right. "He's really a good kid."

"I know."

There didn't seem to be anything else to say, though Liz's crazy heart was suggesting things they could do. They could dance to that slow waltz that seemed to be hanging in the air. They could let that soft scent of roses surround them and ease all their restraints away. Matt's eyes seemed to be agreeing, to be inviting her to stay a bit longer, but fear had a stronger hold on her heart than she'd thought. She took a few steps toward the door.

"I'd better be going," she said.

He nodded and followed her to the door. Out on the porch, bathed in the moonlight, her steps slowed. Her resolve was melting away under the sweet spring breeze that swirled around them. Desire was in the air, and the warning of long loneliness. Her imagination was working overtime, seeing a desperate sadness lurking in the shadows, waiting to claim her as its own. He was closer to her suddenly, and his hand found hers. She turned to him, moving into his waiting arms.

They had kissed before, but when his lips touched hers this time, it was like a beginning, like being born all over again. There was nothing but the two of them, their hearts racing into the unknown and the heavy scent of the night. Their lips clung as their arms tightened.

She'd never felt so safe, so protected. It was as if she'd been lost and had suddenly found her way home. A small, secret flame began to flicker deep in her heart, a need for something she'd been without for so long now. She leaned closer into him, letting his arms imprison her and reveling in the sensation. His mouth whispered into her heart; her soul spoke back into the night.

She didn't have to be alone, she didn't have to fear the darkness and the night. It could be a time of magic and

wonder, of love and belonging, if she'd just reach out for it.
Her heart yearned for the fire of passion and the searing
pain of desire. She wanted to be alive, to feel free as the
birds on the wind.

Then somewhere in the distance, a night animal called out
and the spell was broken. Liz pulled away, relieved that
sanity was returning and slightly embarrassed that it had
fled for even a moment.

"I'd better be going," she said quickly, pulling her heart
back in place.

Matt didn't try to stop her as she hurried down the steps
and found the sanctuary of the van. He waved as she pulled
out of the drive, but she refused to watch any longer to see
how long he stayed out there.

Everyone was entitled to slip once in a while, she told
herself. That was all this was—a minor slip.

Chapter Five

Matt sat down on the porch and watched the sun punch through the clouds left over from the morning's rain. Just as Liz was punching holes in his neat and ordered plan for his life. He felt as if he had as little chance against the power of her smile as those wispy old clouds up there had against the heat of the sun.

He glanced at his watch and grimaced. It would be another twenty minutes before Liz and Jeremy got here.

Time sure moved a hell of a lot slower here. He'd had some breakfast earlier, then, after cleaning up the dishes, he'd gotten started on his writing. Well, not right away. He'd had to get the kitchen and his bedroom cleaned up. Just because a man lived alone, it didn't mean his home had to be a pigsty.

But once he'd gotten his chores out of the way, he'd jumped feetfirst into his writing. He'd never been one for dillydallying, but he hadn't been as productive as he'd have liked. He had learned a lot, though. For one, he knew now that he couldn't write on his kitchen table. It just wasn't right. He'd have to turn one of the empty bedrooms into an office. And he needed to get himself a computer.

Words looked different on paper than they sounded in his head. This morning, he'd been writing out a few lines—writing his own letter to the editor about the youth center to tell them the right way to do things—then ripping the sheet off the pad when the words were wrong. He wasn't a computer expert, but he knew one would enable him to go back and rewrite forever if he wanted to. All the modern writers used one—that's how their words came out so good.

Maybe Liz would know something about computers and could help him find one. The rumble of her muffler drew his attention. He smiled as the rest of the clouds drifted away and the day grew brighter.

The orange of Liz's van skipped through the trees. He took up his cane and walked slowly down to the driveway. Hopefully, it wouldn't be too long before he could ashcan this damn stick.

Liz smiled through the window and waved as she drove up, bringing the sun and spring and the promise of tomorrow with her. Jeremy just sat there, not giving off cheery vibes of any kind. The kid must still be nursing his grumps. Liz stopped the van and hopped down.

She looked even better than he remembered, her cheeks flushed with the warmth of the day. He could suddenly taste again those lips that had so captured him last night, and felt again those stirrings of male hunger. He groaned inwardly. Time to derail those thoughts.

"Welcome to Matt's acres," he said.

Jeremy remained seated in the van.

"Jeremy." Her voice was its usual soft, but there was no mistaking the firm undertone it carried. "Come out and say hello to your uncle Matt."

The kid opened his door and climbed out. Matt could see a touch of petulance to his face as he rounded the front of the vehicle, but all things considered, it wasn't that bad. And it would certainly keep Matt's eyes from drifting off after Liz.

"How you doing, Jeremy?" Matt shook the boy's hand. "And my name's not *Uncle* anything. It's Matt."

"Hi, Matt," he said softly.

"I just thought the title was a form of respect," Liz said.

"I'd rather earn my respect," Matt said.

"Okay," Liz said before going around to the back of the van and pulling out a large paper bag. "I made us lunch."

He fought a quick flash of disappointment that wanted to swallow him up. It wasn't as if he could take them anyplace for lunch, or that *he* could have provided them with something great. Still, he didn't like Liz taking care of everything. That was his job.

"I'm going to take you two out to dinner one of these days," he promised. "How about Monday night?"

"We'll see," Liz said as she started up the porch steps. "I'll put the ham and turkey and condiments in the fridge along with the soda. The bread and potato chips and doughnuts should be okay left out unless you've got mice."

"They're on a low-fat, low-cholesterol diet. Anything you leave will be okay." What could he have offered for lunch? Peanut butter and apples? He needed to get back on his feet and start acting like a man. "Sounds like you brought the whole nine yards," he said.

Her brow wrinkled. "What does that *whole nine yards* thing mean? Guys are always saying that."

"It's a guy thing," Matt said. "It's hard to explain."

"You don't know what it means, either."

"I told you it was a guy thing. Have a little decency. Leave us guys with a few secrets."

"I don't know what it means, either," Jeremy said.

"That's because you're too young," Matt said.

The kid's eyes tightened up, like Bill's used to when he thought someone was trying to pull a fast one on him.

"When is someone going to tell me what it means?" Jeremy asked.

"No one has to tell you," Matt replied. "You discover it. It's like a universal truth."

"You're right," Jeremy said to his mother. "He doesn't know, either."

"Why don't you put the grub inside?" Matt told Liz. "And I'll march this smarty-pants down to the barn."

"Yes, sir," Liz said, snapping him a reasonable facsimile of a salute.

He should have looked away then. He shouldn't have tried to test his willpower where she was concerned. But the sight of her slender body walking away from him was too much for any mortal man to turn from. Her blond hair was holding the sun's brightness captive; the sweet rhythm of her walk could keep the poets busy for the next hundred years.

"Why don't we go down to the barn?" Jeremy said, a smirk evident in his voice.

Startled, Matt turned. Damn kid made him feel as if he were caught peeping in Liz's bedroom window. Hell, he was just looking at one of the beauties of nature. That was all.

"You're kind of slow," Jeremy said, looking pointedly at Matt's bum leg. "So we should get started now. Mom will catch up with us easy."

"Yeah, right." There was nothing wrong with enjoying the beauty of nature, whether it was a bird in flight, a flower in bloom or Liz in motion.

Matt started off, trying for a snappy pace that would keep Jeremy huffing a bit, but didn't quite make it. He'd forgotten just how much energy kids had. And how much he'd slowed down in the past few weeks. He'd have to start exercising or he'd have even farther to go once he got his cast off.

Liz caught up with them just as they'd reached the building. "Okay, Captain. What are your orders?"

Her eyes were sparkling, her lips just barely containing her laughter. A sudden and strong need to hold her washed over him. He wanted to hug her to him, to have her laughter join with his. He wanted those smiling lips beneath his and feel the laughter change as other worlds took over. But her kid was at his side.

Matt tried to block out those distracting thoughts. "Mostly I just want to sort through this junk," he told them. "The Buckleys are taking the bushel baskets, or the ones that are still good. And I'll have most of the rest hauled away. I just want to make sure there isn't anything valuable here."

"Okay," Liz replied.

They sorted through stacks of old tools, throwing out rusted shovels and bent pitchforks and broken hoes. Odd pieces of canvas went also, as did scraps of wood and worn harnesses. Not that Matt could do much more than make decisions—he was about as useful as some of those tools they were tossing—but he pitched in on the little stuff.

He tried hard to keep his eyes from following Liz everywhere she went, but that would have taken more willpower than a saint possessed. She was just so damned beautiful, even in jeans and a T-shirt, even in the dim light of the old barn. Her laughter floated on the air, bringing a lightness to his heart that he'd never remembered feeling before.

"Was any of this stuff Betsy's?" Jeremy asked.

Matt felt confused, startled, as if he'd been woken from a sound sleep. He stared for a moment at the kid, then said slowly. "No, I don't think so."

"The barn's relatively new," Liz said.

She wiped some stray hairs back from her forehead, a movement that captured his gaze again. Her skin shone with a glow that echoed the heat in his blood.

"Anybody else getting hot?" she asked.

Matt's mouth went dry. He couldn't answer.

"Yeah," Jeremy said.

"How about if I make us some lemonade?"

"Great," Matt managed.

Liz went back to the house, while Matt and Jeremy slowly followed her out of the barn. Matt refused to watch her, refused to let her have that power over him. He sat down on an old bench near the overgrown garden. Jeremy sat down next to him.

"You think my mom is pretty?" Jeremy asked.

Matt turned to look at him, suspicion reigning, but Jeremy's gaze reflected only curiosity. "Yeah," Matt said carefully. "She's real pretty."

Jeremy said nothing, just looked away toward the house. They could see Liz moving around in the kitchen as she made the lemonade. For the moment, though, Matt was more interested in what was going on in Jeremy's head than in watching Liz. The kid didn't seem angry or jealous or even smirky. Either he was a better actor than Matt had ever run across before, or he was playing a game Matt wasn't in yet.

"Mom says you used to be a homicide detective in Chicago," Jeremy said, changing the subject.

"Yeah." Matt heard Liz's steps on the porch, but kept his eyes on Jeremy.

"Did you like it?"

Matt shrugged. "It was okay, but I liked the task force better."

"What's a task force?"

"We were regular patrol officers," Matt answered. "Only we got to dress in plain clothes. We drove in beat-up old cars and we harassed the mutts before they had a chance to beat up on the regular citizens."

"What are mutts?" Jeremy asked. "The bad guys?"

"Yeah."

"Isn't it dangerous to be a homicide detective?" Jeremy asked.

"Only on television," Matt said. "Most of the time you come in after the crime is done—it's usually one poor mope killing another poor mope that he knows—and it's a hell of a lot of paperwork."

Jeremy nodded as if he understood.

"The task force was more dangerous," Matt said. "But I got shot on a routine homicide bust. Just goes to show you that life is dangerous."

"Not in Stony Mountain," Jeremy said. "The only new thing around is that Mexican restaurant on Third Street."

"Oh, yeah? I'll have to get me some of their tacos one of these days."

"Hope you don't want more excitement than that," Jeremy said. "Life is dull here."

"That's when life is the most dangerous. Because that's when you get careless. And careless is dangerous anyplace in this world."

Jeremy nodded as if he'd already learned that, then pulled up a piece of grass to chew on. Matt gave up the struggle and turned to watch Liz come across the yard. Her hair, catching the sun, sparkled as if it were strewn with diamonds, and her soft curves were enticing even from this distance.

He looked away. He'd better listen to his own words about carelessness being dangerous. He wasn't looking for anything but peace and quiet out here, not for someone to set him a place at their table. He was a loner.

Always was and always would be.

"Hello there," Matt said.

Liz stopped inserting tomorrow's specials into menus and looked up. Matt stood in the doorway of the lunchroom, dressed in slacks and a sport coat for their dinner out. He looked rather dapper, even with his cane, but she didn't let herself linger on those lines long.

"You didn't walk here, did you?" She'd been expecting a call to come get him in a half hour or so, and something close to disapproval made her voice come out sharply. Neither she nor Jeremy were ready yet.

"I took a cab," he said. "So sue me."

"You're not all that far from here," she said. "Why didn't you call?"

"I don't like to be a bother."

"You don't like being dependent," she retorted, not certain why she was so irritated. He just looked so handsome there in the doorway, so in charge, that it started a fluttering in the pit of her stomach. He was looking less like an ex-brother-in-law and more like a hunk.

He stepped into the room and took a seat at the empty counter. "Same thing," he said.

"You're too proud for your own good."

"Since when does concern for others become the sin of pride? You better get your money back from Sunday school."

"Kiddies," Jan called out as she came in from the kitchen. "You two aren't playing nice."

Jeremy was close behind her. "Are they bickering again?"

"Yes, they are," Jan replied.

Liz frowned at her son. Jan always had to take someone else's side against Liz, but when had Jeremy become so jovial? "We're not bickering," she snapped.

"At least, I'm not," Matt said.

Liz didn't think Jan's smirk was any more necessary than Matt's remark. They just fed on each other. "I have a few more things to do," Liz said to Matt. "Do you think you can sit there and behave yourself while I finish my chores?"

"I always behave myself," Matt said.

Jan laughed. "Poorly or nicely?"

"Hey." Matt raised his hands in surrender. "I'm not qualifying or fudging in any way. I just said I always behave, and I do."

Liz shook her head and went back to stuffing the menus with tomorrow's specials. Maybe she shouldn't have agreed to this dinner out, but then Matt had been so insistent. They had done so much for him, it would just be his way of repaying. A man had to pay his debts. And Jeremy would be along, so those few kisses she and Matt had shared had nothing to do with this. He probably didn't even remember them.

Jeremy pulled the menu inserts gently from her hand. "I'll do that," he said. "Why don't you just go home and clean up?"

"How can you do this?" Liz looked at him quizzically. "You need to change, too."

"No, I don't. I mean, I can't go."

"You can't?" Liz repeated, fighting off the panic rising in her heart. "Why not?"

"Yeah, why not?" Matt asked. "I already made reservations at Hannah's over in New Buffalo for the three of us."

Hannah's? Liz stopped, forgetting Jeremy for the moment, and turned toward Matt. "That's an hour's drive from here."

"I know," he replied with a shrug. "But the food's good. And I thought it would be nice to walk on the beach."

"Can you walk on the sand with your leg?" she asked.

"Yes, I can," he snapped. "I have no intention of babying the damn thing."

Tension appeared in lines around his eyes. Boy, he sure was sensitive about giving even the slightest appearance of needing help. Must have been all those years he spent playing macho cop.

Jeremy moved slightly, drawing her attention again. "Anyway, young man," Liz said, "why aren't you coming?"

"Me and the guys have to work on our science project."

"The science fair is over." Liz frowned. Why did she feel she was being manipulated?

"We got ribbons," Jeremy explained with what sounded like infinite patience. "That means we advance to the district show."

She still wasn't buying this. "So you haul your portable anthill to Grand Rapids."

"I know, Mom. But I have to coordinate my exhibit with the other kids."

"Coordinate? In what way?"

"Liz," Jan said, coming up next to her and gently pushing her around the counter, "go get ready. We'll finish up here."

But she'd be alone with Matt the whole evening. She didn't know how to be alone with a man anymore. "But what's Jeremy going to do about dinner?" she asked.

"Oh, he's eating with us," Jan replied.

"Yeah," Jeremy said.

Liz frowned at them both. They were making this up on the fly. "He's having dinner with you guys?"

"Yes," Jan replied. "And he's staying overnight. So don't worry about getting home early. Just stay out and dance until the cows come home." Her sister looked at Matt. "I forgot about your bum leg. Maybe you better forget the dancing."

"Thank you," Matt said.

"Do something that doesn't involve walking," she said. An innocent grin filled her face. "Maybe something with lying down to it."

Liz could feel her cheeks warm and she didn't even want to look at Matt. What had gotten into Jan? This was supposed to be a family dinner, and now she was turning it into some sort of liaison.

"I'm sorry," Jeremy was saying in his supersincere mode. "I thought I told you."

"You didn't," she said, trying to give him a stern look. She must have looked more scared to death if the gentleness of his gaze was any indication.

"I'm really, really sorry. Things have been so hectic lately. I sort of lost track of time." He took her hands, looking so much like Bill when he was trying to talk her into something absolutely crazy. "But, hey, no harm done. You guys can still go."

Liz stood there looking at her son, not saying a word. He'd given up getting her to date Leo Tuttle and was now pushing Matt. This was all a setup. But how could she get out of it? And did she really, really want to?

No, down deep in her heart, she wanted to put on that red dress that had been hanging so long in the back of her closet. She wanted to wear her dangly gold earrings and feel like a woman. It was just that it was so scary.

"Well, you better get going," Jeremy said.

"Right," Jan added.

Liz didn't move. Did she have the nerve? Matt didn't say anything. The silence stretched out to the ends of the earth and back again.

"You're not going to let a reservation go to waste, are you?" Jeremy said.

Liz looked over at Matt. His eyes were waiting for her answer. They promised her fun. They promised her gentleness and conversation. They promised her the blessing of the stars upon her.

"Are you?" Jeremy repeated.

Matt was waiting. "I hope not," he said, his voice carrying the softness of the spring night.

Liz let out a long breath. "Okay, we'll go." A tremor went through her body and whipped around her soul. It felt almost like excitement, but it could have been fear. She turned to Jeremy. "We have some things to discuss tomorrow."

"Sure, Mom." His face spilt in a wide grin. "Have a nice time."

"Don't worry and have a good time," her sister said. "Everything's under control."

Under control? It might be, but just *who* was running the show?

The waitress put a glass of wine before each of them, then pulled out her pad and pencil. "Are you folks ready to order or would you like me to come back?"

Matt looked over at Liz. She smiled her readiness, and his heart sucked in its breath. Damn, but she had the sweetest smile in all creation. He wanted the waitress to go away and let him savor the pleasure of the moment, to bask for years in the glow of that smile. Except that it probably wouldn't last all that long if he refused to feed her.

"We'll order now," Matt said.

It didn't take very long, and soon the waitress had left. Liz's smile grew tighter, more hesitant as the silence built again between them. He ought to be used to it by now. It had ridden the whole way to New Buffalo with them, so that he'd been tempted to tell her to pick up that hitchhiker because he'd looked like a chatty fellow.

But what was Matt supposed to talk about? His cop stories weren't fitting topics for dinner conversation, not with a gorgeous lady, and he had nothing else. He guessed he could always bring up the walk along the beach, and how he'd proven after about two steps that, no, he couldn't walk on sand yet. That would be the ticket, all right. Remind her what a dud he was as a man.

"A penny for your thoughts," Liz said.

"Make it a dime," he said. "And I'll throw in the shoes."

Her brow wrinkled prettily. She was the only person he knew that could make a frown a work of art and beauty.

"That doesn't make any sense."

"Most of what people say doesn't."

She smiled at him—a soft, gentle smile, the kind that would melt kryptonite—then she sipped at her wine before speaking. "I'm sure once you get rid of the cane, you'll be able to walk along the beach just fine."

Matt felt the back of his neck grow warm. Wonderful, she was feeling sorry for him. Just what every guy wants from his date. "Sorry." He gulped a swallow of his wine. "I'll have to bring you here in the summer when my leg is all healed. Then we'll walk the beach up to Traverse City and back."

Liz laughed. A pretty laugh. A laugh that reached in through his ears and massaged the soft spot in the brain where contentment lived. Maybe he wasn't doing all that badly.

"I told you I could handle the beach," Matt said. "Well, I was wrong, but I'll do it right the next time. I take my promises seriously."

Her eyes dimmed and she looked away. Damn, that was stupid. She'd had enough broken promises to last a lifetime. She'd probably sworn off any guy who made a promise, without even waiting to see if he'd break it or not.

Matt breathed a sigh of relief as the waitress came over with their salads and a smile. "Would you like any more wine?" she asked.

Matt looked at Liz and she shook her head. "Not right now," he said.

The woman nodded and left. Matt grabbed his fork and attacked his salad. The silence still floated in the air around them, but it was normal to have silence while eating.

"Looks like you're hungry."

He looked up. Liz had just started nibbling the edges of her salad. Maybe he should slow down. He wasn't one of those courtly, gentlemanly types, but he could fake it. Pretend he was undercover, infiltrating a gang of classy types.

Liz turned to stare out the window near them, and a tremor of worry shot through him. A fear that he was losing her, that she would just drift away like a branch caught in the river's current and he'd never get her back.

"Jeremy looked in reasonable spirits." There, that wasn't too bad. Mothers always liked to talk about their kids. Unless she thought he was prying. "I mean, he seemed to be when I came to pick you up."

Liz turned back to him. "These past few days have been hard on him, but he's a tough kid. He'll get through it."

"That's good."

They fell back into their silence and, for the life of him, he could not think of a single thing to say. She was so lovely that somehow he feared she'd be scared away by his clumsiness, like a bird frightened by movement.

"Anytime he wants to talk, he should just come on out," Matt said. "I mean, he's blood kin."

"I'll tell him."

They finished their salads and, several aeons later, their main course arrived. Liz ate like a bird as Matt tried to put a rein on his own appetite. Eating alone or on the run with other cops, he'd picked up a number of nonsocial dining habits over the years. Like gobbling his food and talking with his mouth full. If he hoped to salvage any bit of good feeling from this evening, he'd better start working at it now. He slowed down his eating to half speed.

"Do most cops drink the blush-type wines now?" Liz asked.

He stared at his glass a moment, then shrugged. "I don't know. I do."

"There's this image people have of cops," she said. "You know, rough-and-tough beer types."

Matt shrugged. Would she like him better if he drank beer? He was willing to give it a shot.

"I take it you don't like to put people in boxes," she said. Her voice was so soft and gentle.

Matt noticed his glass was empty, he cleared his throat. "Just two."

"Two?"

"Yeah. I put people into either of two boxes. Good guys and bad guys."

"Is it that simple?" she asked.

He thought back over his years in police work, remembering the perpetrators, most of whom were just as miserable as the victims. Many times it was hard to tell one from the other. "Nah," he replied. "Only in a few cases."

"Did you like police work?" she asked.

"Some of it." He cut a piece of meat, chewing and swallowing before speaking. "I liked the task force. I liked being able to stop things before anybody got hurt. It was a good feeling."

She nibbled at her fish. "Did you like being a homicide detective?"

"Not really." He dipped a dumpling in the gravy. "You just went in and played cleanup. The damage was done and there was no going back to undo it." He stopped, taking his turn staring out the window at the coming night. He saw the past, though, and row after row of miserable people. "Nine times out of ten the killer was somebody the victim knew. Wife, husband, drinking buddy. You just took their confession and built the paper case against them, but nothing ever changed."

Did anything ever change, though? Could he? He was saying he wanted peace and tranquillity, the solitude of the country, but was he trying to change his nature? Was he like some of those poor mopes he arrested time after time, unable to break away from the maze that led them over and over again to destruction?

He looked at Liz and saw her softness, her warmth and gentleness. There was so much more to be had from life. Was it only for the lucky, or was it there for anyone brave enough to try for it?

The waitress finally came by to clean up their dishes and ask about dessert.

Liz just shook her head. "I'm full." Those wonderful blue eyes turned to him. "But you should have some if you want."

He thought a moment, then shook his head. "Nah, I'm fat enough."

"You're not fat," Liz protested.

He shrugged. "Yeah, but it's an easy trip from where I'm at."

"You don't need to worry about that," she said. "You're a good-looking guy. Trim and tight."

The warmth in his neck crept up into his cheeks. "I bet you say that to all the guys," he said. One minute she was sweet and innocent, the next she was a temptress. Was she just being polite or—

Fortunately, the waitress came by with the check before he had a chance to let his imagination run wild. That wouldn't do at all. Matt paid the bill and they exited the restaurant into the beginnings of a beautiful evening.

"Care for a little walk?" he asked.

Liz laughed. "Maybe next time."

"I meant a stroll down the street, not—" Her words hit him. Next time? She wasn't going to give up on him because he couldn't keep a conversation going for a half hour straight? This move back to Stony Mountain might not be all that bad. He gave her his free arm and they crossed the street to the lot where her van was parked.

He'd had it with this front-seat/back-seat arrangement and slid the front passenger seat as far back as it would go. It gave a reasonable amount of room to stretch his stiff leg out. And gave him the chance to watch her as she drove, to feast his eyes on her beauty.

Liz headed north out of town, staying off the interstate as they had on their trip in. Soon they were heading east, away from the setting sun, so the trip was easier on his eyes. Of course, if he'd wanted to be kind to his eyes, he would have ridden sidesaddle and simply stared at Liz. He turned to look out his window, more to hide his thoughts than to see anything. He couldn't stay turned away long.

"How come you stayed in Stony Mountain?" he asked.

"It's home."

It was a simple answer, but it was what most people did. Stayed near the familiar, near family, near old friends.

"Got any dreams?"

"Yep," she answered.

He waited, but she maintained her speed and her silence. Liz played her cards close to the vest. "Do you write at all?" he asked.

"Some."

"Want to become a famous writer?"

She shrugged. "I want to write what I want to write. Whether I become famous or not isn't really in my hands."

He'd heard true happiness came from being satisfied with oneself. Liz seemed to have found the combination.

The silence grew again, but Matt did nothing to push it away. Had she really meant it about next time? She had to have her pick of livelier dinner companions, even in a little burg like Stony Mountain.

"I'll drop you off at home," she said. "Save you the trouble—"

Of being a man and seeing his date home? "Nope."

She made that sound in her throat again, the one that showed she was getting aggravated with him. "You are one stubborn—"

"Part of my charm," he said, hurrying before she finished her sentence and said something he didn't want to hear.

"We're almost passing your place," she insisted. "One little jog and I can have you in your front yard."

"I don't want you driving alone at night."

"It's just gotten dark. Technically speaking, it's still evening."

"Call it what you want, but I don't want you driving alone in it. I wasn't raised to treat my dates that way."

She made a little sound of aggravation and he didn't know if it was because of his insistence that she not drive him home, or because he'd called her his date. He wasn't about to ask for clarification.

"I'll just go with you to your place." Jeez, that sounded even worse. "And you can go up and call Luke for me, if you will."

They arrived at Liz's apartment with the frost lingering slightly in the air. She pulled up to the curb and turned off the ignition.

"Are you sure I can go upstairs by myself to call Luke?" she asked. "After all, the sun has set. And one never knows what can happen on Stony Mountain's dark streets."

"Go call Luke," he growled.

She exited the van and slammed her door, hard. So much for a relaxing end to their evening. And probably goodbye to next time. Damn it all to hell. Why was she being so stubborn?

Matt got out of the van. He made sure all the doors were locked, then leaned against the side of the vehicle and waited. Across the street, the train station sat in darkness. The wind had picked up slightly; he could hear its moaning in the old building's eaves. Liz was back down the steps in a few minutes.

"Luke says he'll be here in two shakes of an old dog's tail."

Matt nodded. "Thanks."

Liz came over and leaned against the van next to him.

He could feel the soft scent of her flowery perfume surround him. Like bands of iron, they drew him to her. Would her hair have that same scent or would it hold the taste of the lake breezes that had buffeted them on their walk?

He shouldn't be thinking along these lines. "You don't have to stay out with me," he said.

"Hey," she replied. "You never know what might happen on these mean, dark streets."

"You're a real smart mouth."

"I'm only repaying in kind," Liz replied.

Matt gave into temptation and put an arm around her shoulder. "Why don't you try being nice?" he asked. "My mother always said that you could catch more flies with honey than you could with vinegar."

"Well, I don't really care for flies." She moved up closer into him, slipping an arm around his waist. "But I do like nice."

He felt a shortness of breath, a fullness in his throat as he bent down close to her. Her eyes took the beams from the streetlight and returned them a thousandfold. "I ain't got nothing against nice," he said huskily.

Their lips reached for each other and the night danced. It was magic and he was young as a new colt. Stars sparkled in the heavens, but the fire growing in his heart made them seem dim and pale, weak imitations of the fire in Liz's eyes.

Her touch was everything. Soft, warm, gentle, hungry. He echoed that same need with his lips, trying to tell her of that longing that was consuming him, eating him alive with the promise of more wonder and sweetness. His arms closed around her, pulling her into a haven that he'd never release her from, that she'd never want to leave, if only—

A blaring horn caused them to jump apart.

"Hey," Luke shouted from the window of his cab. "You guys want to do stuff like that, do it inside your car like everybody else."

Chapter Six

"Good afternoon, dear," an elderly female voice said.

Liz felt her heart take a nosedive. All she wanted was to putter happily in her little strip of dirt alongside the train station, ridding her heart and mind of those lingering images from last night. She needed to convince herself that the sweetness she'd found in Matt's arms had been a temporary weakness on her part, that she wasn't violating every law she'd set down for herself. But everybody and their cousin was out to wreck her plans.

Sighing, Liz rocked back onto her heels. "Hi, Mrs. Tollson. How are you?"

"I'm fine, dear. The more important question is, how are you?"

"I'm just fine, ma'am. In fact, I couldn't be better."

Mrs. Tollson, like every single person in the town and surrounding five counties, had already expressed their condolences on Bill's death. Now they were into the *tsk, tsk* stage, exclaiming how pale she looked, how she should go home and rest. Treating her like a little girl who'd lost her puppy.

"You're being so brave, my dear."

She wasn't being brave, Liz wanted to shout. She wasn't being anything but stupid. She had a perfectly good life and she was putting her happiness in jeopardy just because some handsome man came into town and smiled at her. But that wasn't what she was supposed to be feeling or saying. She was supposed to be wounded and brave.

Liz hacked at the ground with her trowel.

"What are you planting, dear?"

"Marigolds, ma'am," Liz replied.

"Might be a tad early."

"Yes, ma'am." Liz kept right on working the dirt, unable to stop for fear that she'd explode with rage at herself. Hadn't she learned anything in those long years alone?

"Just the first week of May," Mrs. Tollson said. "Still could get a frost."

"If I have to, I'll cover the flowers at night." Hadn't she figured out that you just didn't let your happiness rest on someone else's shoulders?

"Don't pay to go looking for extra work, dear."

"No, ma'am."

There was a long moment of background street noise, then Liz heard Mrs. Tollson's sensible oxfords thump their way down the street toward the bakery. She breathed a sigh of relief and quit her digging. Leaning back, she glumly stared at the dirt.

What would people here think if they knew just what was occupying her thoughts these days? Would they be shocked that she wasn't overcome with grief as they all seemed to suppose? Well, she was pretty shocked at herself.

It wasn't as if Matt were the first good-looking guy to come to town. She'd been able to avoid the temptation of the others. Why was Matt able to touch her when none of the others had?

There was a tap on her shoulder. "Earth to Liz. Yoo-hoo. Earth calling Liz."

Liz shrieked as she sat up to look into her mother's face. "For heaven's sake, Mom. You practically scared the life out of me."

"I said hello. You didn't respond."

"I was working."

"Oh, yes," her mother said. "You've always been such a serious little farmer."

There was definite sarcasm in that voice. "What do you want?"

"My goodness," her mother said, scolding lightly. "Have you forgotten your manners, young lady?"

No. Liz had just overdosed on them. She took a long breath, willing Matt and all his attendant feelings away. "I'm sorry, Mom. I'm just a little tired."

"You ought to date more often, then. It'll help build up your stamina."

Warmth crept up and filled Liz's cheeks. So now the whole darn town knew that she and Matt had gone out to dinner. Great. "It wasn't a date."

"I see."

Liz really hated it when her mother said that. It was such a know-it-all remark, guaranteed to turn a Quaker into a mass murderer. "Jeremy and I helped Matt clean out one of his barns," Liz explained patiently. "He wanted to take the two of us out to dinner for that."

"I see."

Liz held her breath for a second to get a tighter grip on her patience, then went on. "Jeremy had some last-minute work on his science project, so he couldn't go. Since Matt had already made the reservations, the two of us went instead."

"But to go traipsing all the way to New Buffalo?" her mother asked, a touch of the certainty still in her voice. "In my day, that was a date."

Liz was not going to fall into the "in my day" trap. She leaned down to resume her planting. "Matt picked the restaurant. I just drove."

Her mother said nothing for a long moment, but Liz refused to look up, refused to let her gaze with those mother's eyes and read something Liz wanted kept hidden in her soul.

"Bit early for marigolds," her mother said.

"I know," Liz replied. "We could still get a frost, but the days have been pretty warm this year."

"True," her mother said with a nod. "But you never know around here. Weather will turn on you if it has half a chance."

Liz relaxed a tad, though she knew her mother wasn't really finished with her favorite topic, Liz's social life. Her parents worried about her, she knew. Worried that she was alone and would remain so, but they had to understand it was her choice. She was happy this way. She didn't need a man to be complete.

"Matt is a nice man," her mother said.

Liz looked away, watching images dance in the afternoon sun. A tall, husky guy with brown hair just lightly touched with gray. Brown eyes that could go from cop-hard to puppy-dog-soft in the blink of an eyelash. A quiet strength emanated from that image. Sure, Matt was nice enough. And he seemed steadier than Bill ever was, but she wasn't getting involved with anybody.

"Hi, Grandma." Jeremy walked out of the train station.

"Hello, Jeremy," her mother said.

"Going to play baseball?" Liz asked.

Since he was carrying a baseball glove on his left hand, it was pretty obvious where he was going. But he was tolerant of her for once.

"Yeah," Jeremy replied.

"Be home by five-thirty," she called after him.

"I will." Before he had gone two steps, he stopped and turned. "Oh, Mom. Matt called. He wanted you to bring him some tacos."

"He *what?*" She must have heard him wrong.

"You know," Jeremy said. "From that new restaurant in town."

"He wants me to bring him some tacos?" Liz was totally confused.

"That's what he said." With a quick wave and a grin, Jeremy hurried down the street. "Gotta go," he said over his shoulder.

Liz stood there and glared at her son's rapidly disappearing back. What was this? She was a delivery service now?

He didn't call and talk to her. Didn't ask how she was, if she'd had a good day, or if she had time to do him a favor. Just called up and placed an order like he owned her.

And after only one date.

"Can you imagine that?" Liz sputtered.

"I know, dear." Her mother shook her head, her voice filled with understanding. "He didn't say whether he wants chicken or beef."

Matt leaned back against the chair, glaring at the blank sheet of paper on the pad. No matter how hard he glared, it stayed empty. And his mind stayed blank. Well, not blank, exactly. Visions of a certain blond nymph kept creeping in. He remembered the taste of her lips beneath his and the softness of her gentle curves pressed against him.

Damn. This was getting him nowhere. That article he'd read in the writers' magazine said to treat writing like a job. So he'd gotten dressed like he did on the job—a pair of slacks, knit shirt and loafers.

When he couldn't even produce a simple letter to the editor, he put on his shoulder holster and pistol. After all, he'd been a cop and that's how he'd dressed for work.

Unfortunately, it hadn't helped. Fresh country air wafted in through his window, bringing visions of Liz back to play in his mind. Some damn birds were singing an accompaniment. And some pea brain was plowing a field nearby.

Matt considered firing a few warning shots out the window, though he knew the problem was in his head. He shut the window instead, but that didn't help. Now it was getting stuffy in the old house. And, as any fool knew, if you couldn't breathe easily, you couldn't work well.

"Oh, hell." He groaned and put his hands to his face. "I gotta get me a computer."

He had plenty of room in his house and it was spilling over with atmosphere. No reason why he couldn't write here. No reason at all. And it would be easier to concentrate if he had the proper tools. His mind wouldn't be able to wander all over creation.

A loud rapping at the door brought his head up and put a smile on his face. Liz? No one else ever came out here.

But the smile faded as quickly as it came. If it was her, she was knocking on his door with a baseball bat. No, it had to be somebody else, somebody big and strong. Either way, it didn't sound like some little friends who wanted him to come out and play. Patting the piece in his shoulder holster, Matt eased himself to the door and jerked it open.

"Yo, Matt." Luke Schiller stood there on the porch, a big grin on his face and a brown paper bag in his hand. Then his eyes slid down to Matt's armpit and the grin fell off his face. "You expecting company?"

Matt shook his head.

"Like somebody you maybe don't like?"

"I said no," Matt snapped. "Now what the hell do you want?"

The grin returned to Luke's broad face. "Forgot what a friendly fella Billy always said you were."

"Luke, I'm busy. What do you want?"

"Busy?" The big man peered over the top of Matt's head into the kitchen. "Whatcha doing?"

Matt gave him his patented cop stare, filled with menace. It wasn't too hard to work up, seeing as he'd had his heart set on finding a blond little lady at his door. Finding a three-hundred-pound, ugly old lineman set his mood on edge.

"Stuff that I want to do," Matt replied. "Now why don't you tell me what you want?"

"Brought out some brew," Luke replied, opening the bag to show Matt the cans. "Thought we'd sit out on your porch, spit and watch the world spin."

Matt let out a long sigh. There really wasn't any reason for Liz to come traipsing out here. She had a kid, a business, a whole life of her own. And his writing had hit a bump in the road, so he might as well join Luke. Refresh himself creatively, as it were. "Yeah," Matt said with a short nod. "Nice day for it."

They walked over to the edge of the porch, where Luke watched Matt lower himself to a sitting position. He appreciated the big man standing back, not offering any help unless he needed it. Like if Matt fell on his face and, after three tries, couldn't get up.

"How's the leg coming?" Luke asked as he lowered his bulk down onto the porch floor.

"Getting there, I guess."

While Luke opened a can for each of them, Matt shifted around until most of his body was comfortable.

"Gonna be able to walk okay once the cast comes off?"

Matt shrugged as he accepted an open can from Luke. "Better than I do now. But I doubt it'll do me as well as it used to."

"Got me some parts that work like that," Luke said, nodding.

Matt glanced at Luke's crooked football player's fingers. And he knew they were just the tip of the iceberg. Luke was barely into his thirties, but Matt would have bet his last dollar that Luke had the joints of a man twice his age. Yet Luke appeared content with his lot in life, accepting of the aches and pains that were the price he paid for his moment of fame in college and the few years he played in the pros.

"You all alone out here?" Luke asked. "You ought to get yourself a dog."

Matt sipped at his beer and looked out over the yard. "A little company would be nice," he said. "Although I wasn't thinking of a dog."

Luke shrugged. "I guess cats are okay, but I'm a dog man myself."

Feeling that he'd already said too much, Matt just stared out over his yard to where the river winked in the distance. He wasn't thinking of any kind of an animal. What he was thinking of wasn't something he wanted to admit even to himself.

"'Course, you ain't entirely alone out here. You know that, don't you?"

"I guess you can say that," Matt said. "There's all kinds of critters in the woods and fields around me. And I'm sure the house has mice."

Luke laughed. "I was thinking of old Betsy."

Matt scowled at him before taking a sip from his can. He thought that that kind of teasing was reserved for the young.

"She may howl around the old train station during a storm," Luke said, "but I hear she spends most of her time out here."

"Don't look like I need to get any kind of a pet, then," Matt said. "Old Betsy's a lot less trouble. Don't need to feed her or clean up after her."

"Still rather have me a dog." Luke drained his can and set it by his side. After clearing his throat, he squirmed around to lean against the porch post and face Matt square on. "I got something I want to air," Luke said. "So, if I put my size fifteens somewhere personal, you just tell me to back off. Okay?"

Matt nodded, but his heart took a flip. Damn. He'd forgotten how small towns were. How everybody took care of everybody else. How everybody would look after a pretty, sweet little widow woman like Liz. Especially if that somebody was a three-hundred-pound former lineman who used to play with Matt's brother.

It was stupid of Matt to have been caught kissing her in the street last night. He should have known better. Everybody saw everything in these parts. Worse still, they talked about it.

"You know, old Billy done a lot for this town," Luke began.

Matt's tension stayed high. Liz and Bill had been divorced for almost ten years now, but he wasn't always sure the town's folks saw it that way. "So have a lot of other people," he said.

Luke ran a paw over his lower jaw. "I think the town ought to do something for old Billy." He stared hard at

Matt. "You know, sort of an even-up kind of an exchange."

Matt felt his tension escape rapidly, like air from a pin-pricked balloon, leaving him an emotionally shapeless pile of relief. Luke wasn't concerned with what he and Liz were doing last night.

"What do you think?"

Matt cleared his throat. "Well." He cleared his throat again. "I don't know."

"For one thing," Luke said, "he ought to be buried here in Stony Mountain."

Matt nodded. He wondered whether he should tell Luke that, at the moment, Bill was sitting on the fireplace mantel. Old Betsy's ghost and Bill's ashes. Were they in there exchanging ghost stories?

"And I think the town should put up some kind of memorial for him. You know, to honor old Billy for all that he did for us."

What all had he done for them? Matt wanted to ask. He led the local high school to a state championship and he abandoned his wife and child. Which one did Luke think was deserving of a memorial? Did he think one outweighed the other? But Matt just stayed silent.

"So?" Luke asked. "What do you think?"

Suddenly the roar of a tiny engine blasted out over the fields. Luke paused and turned toward the road. "Lizzie needs a new muffler."

"Yeah." Matt pushed himself up off the porch. "I told her that."

They walked down the driveway and waited by Luke's cab.

"Women ain't that mechanically inclined," Luke said.

Matt didn't bother to argue. He was more concerned that Luke might stay and push his memorial idea at Liz. Matt wasn't sure, but he didn't think it would make her jump for joy.

"You know," Luke said as they watched Liz swing her old van into the drive, "a lot of the guys from our championship team still live around here. How about I get them together and we kick around this memorial thing for old Billy?''

To be perfectly honest, Matt would have preferred that Luke just forget about the whole thing. What kind of feelings would get stirred up if Bill's every exploit was recounted? Would Liz relive the pain of the rejection and Jeremy the agony of being abandoned by his father? Or would they see Bill once more as the conquering hero, the exalted one the town was determined to keep on a pedestal?

And just where would that leave *him?*

Matt watched as Liz brought the van to a stop and turned off the ignition.

Luke was still talking. "Maybe we'll come up with some plans and programs. Stuff like that. You know?''

"Yeah, sure,'' Matt replied.

What was wrong with a simple burial service? He should have had it in Chicago, instead of fooling around with what Bill would have wanted. Matt watched as Liz dropped lightly down to the ground. He'd never thought anybody could outdo spring for freshness, but that was before he'd really known Liz.

"I'll let you know what we come up with,'' Luke said.

"Fine,'' Matt said.

Liz walked up toward them, a package in her hand. She was like springtime come alive. Her brightness, her beauty, took his breath away. His sense, too. Nothing else existed around her.

"See you later,'' Luke said.

"Great.'' But Matt was barely listening. Liz looked as beautiful as ever, but something was wrong. That smile that could rival the sun wasn't there and her eyes reflected a coming storm, not the placid warmth of the summer's day.

"Hi, Lizzie,'' Luke said as he passed her going to his cab. "How ya doin'?''

"Just fine,'' she replied, giving him a glimpse of a sweet smile. "How are Cindy and the kids?''

"Super.''

The storm warnings returned as soon as she passed Luke. Hell. She was mad at him. What'd he do? His mouth opened to ask, plead, beg for forgiveness, whatever his transgression. But before the words came out, she thrust the package in his face.

"Here are your tacos, sir."

"Tacos?" He stared dumbly at the bag hanging at the end of a shapely little arm.

"I didn't know whether you wanted beef or chicken so I got you both."

"Tacos?" He could feel his head shaking.

"Here." She thrust the bag into his chest. "Take them."

But his hands stayed at his sides. The only thing he could do was repeat the word. "Tacos?"

"Would you stop being such a dimwit? You ordered the damn things. Now eat them, freeze them, throw them out. I don't care. Just take them."

He stepped back and raised his hands. What the hell was going on? He felt as if he were back in high school and had fallen asleep in geometry class, only to wake up in world history. "Why are you trying to make me eat tacos?" he asked. "Did you make them yourself?"

"I bought them at the new Mexican restaurant in town. Just like you asked me to."

"I didn't ask you to do anything for me." He had a whole string of things he'd like to ask her to do—whisper sweet words in his ear, make him feel young and alive again, let him catch her if she should fall. Getting him tacos didn't even make the top hundred.

"Yes, you did."

"But I didn't. Honest."

"Jeremy said—" She stopped. A gentle rose flush spread over her cheeks as the irritation fled. "Omigosh."

A smile touched Matt's lips. "Yesterday he couldn't go out to dinner with us," he said.

"And today he—" She was still holding the bag of tacos up against his chest, but somehow had moved away. "I just want to find a hole and fall into it."

"It'd be more comfortable to sit on the porch."

Her face was still flushed, but delightfully so. He took a step over to put his arm around her waist and lead her over to the porch. She felt so good against him, so soft and so in need of his strength. He wanted to tell her that she could lean on him anytime, anywhere. She didn't even have to ask.

But he didn't. Promises that came from the heart weren't to be relied on. They sat down on the porch, and he let her lean against a post, away from him. It was safer that way.

"I'm sorry," she murmured, but slowly her embarrassment was replaced by suspicion. "Did you put Jeremy up to this?"

"Me? No way. I had nothing to do with it. Today or yesterday."

He could see her suspicion building, stiffening her spine. "You better not be involved," she warned.

Involved in what, though? He wasn't involved in any plot with Jeremy, but something was definitely happening here, something Matt didn't understand at all. No amount of cop training had prepared him for the assaults on his heart that had occurred since he'd come here. He forced himself to look out over the fields surrounding Betsy's old house and down to the river. A gentle spring breeze danced around them like a merchant showing off his scented wares. A bit of newly plowed dirt, fresh-cut grass, the clean water of the river. Maybe it was too late to fight back.

"You know," he said, "it is getting close to dinnertime."

"So?" Her tone wasn't the least bit gentle.

He took more of a chance. No pain, no glory. "Shame to let these tacos go to waste."

Liz didn't reply, so he slowly turned to sneak a look. Her face was stern but there was a smile inside, struggling to get out.

"If I ever find out that you were behind this—"

"I am absolutely and totally innocent," he said.

"You'll be able to audition for soprano in the church choir."

"Luke left some beer," Matt said, indicating the cans by his side. "Ain't no reason to let that go to waste, either."

Finally her defenses fell and a smile came out on her lips like a daylily opening up to the morning's sun.

Or was it him opening to her sun like a flower hungry for the warmth and brightness?

"I want the chicken," she said. "You can have the beef."

Liz looked at the computer and monitor on display. "This one is supposed to be pretty good."

Matt just frowned. "It's not like the ones we had at the station."

"No, it's newer. Look, it comes with a word-processing program."

His frown deepened. "I don't know how to use that."

"So you'll learn. I think it's the one that Jeremy's using at school."

Matt waved the hovering clerk over. "At least I'll have an expert close at hand, then."

Liz moved to the side and watched as Matt paid for the computer. She envied how quickly he was able to make decisions. This computer looks okay, he takes it. This bedroom set looks fine, he takes it. She spent aeons agonizing over those kinds of purchases, and some decisions—like dating again—she never made at all.

Except somehow she seemed to be getting involved with a man, anyway.

Liz's gaze found Matt's hands, so strong and safe, so sure. Bill's hands had been different, strong and sure, but in a different way. Matt's were for pulling weeds as well as picking flowers. Bill's were for throwing passes and accepting awards.

"You ready to go?" Matt asked, waking her from her thoughts. "We're supposed to drive around back to pick up the equipment."

"Sure. Great." They walked out to the van. His nearness bothered her, made her feel tongue-tied and silly. "That's a nice system you bought."

"I'm going to be a writer," he pointed out. "I didn't want junk."

"You don't need a computer to be a writer," she said. "I didn't even have a typewriter when I first started."

"Yeah, but you just write poetry."

"Just poetry?" She stopped walking, her keys in her hand. "What is this *just poetry* nonsense?"

"Poetry is short," he replied. "It's no big deal to write out longhand. You need a computer for the long stuff, like books."

"And you're going to write a book?"

"Want to stop for a hamburger on the way home?" he asked.

The old change-the-subject-because-I-don't-want-to-talk-about-it-anymore ploy. Jeremy did that a lot. Men. Their voices grew deeper and they started to shave, but their tricks didn't change. Not one little bit.

But it was just as well to change the subject. She unlocked the van, and they drove around to the back of the store where a teenager loaded up the equipment.

"I didn't mean to put down your writing," Matt said as they drove away from the store. "All I meant was that it was shorter. Fewer words."

"It's okay. I wasn't mad."

She cast a quick glance his way, though she ought to have known better. Those eyes could win over the hardest heart. And it wasn't because he was so good at pleading or looking sad, but because he wasn't. She saw something so bleak and lonely in his eyes when she looked, as if he'd been on the outside all his life and didn't know how to come inside.

"I thought maybe we could stop up here," Matt said, pointing to an ice-cream parlor up ahead.

Liz glanced at her watch. "I don't know. We've got a half hour's drive to get back to Stony Mountain."

"Which will put us there after dinner either way." He turned in his seat to face her more directly. "You said Jeremy would go home with Jan. What's the matter, won't she feed him?"

Liz glared his way. "Of course she will. It's just—"

"That you don't want to eat with me twice in one week."

"That's not it, either." She sighed as she found herself pulling into the ice-cream parlor's parking lot. How did she explain to him that she was enjoying his company too much? That she was liking being part of a couple again and that worried her?

She parked the van and they walked slowly toward the building, Matt gazing around as they did so.

"They used to have carhops here," he said. "I guess times have changed." He looked at her, his feet slowing suddenly. "Did you and Bill ever come here on dates?"

"A few times." She pushed ahead and pulled open the door, which only seemed to deepen his mood.

"I hadn't thought of that." He took the door from her and waved her inside.

"Thought of what?"

"That it would bring back memories." He was standing just inside the door as if not wanting to find a booth.

She just laughed and took his arm, leading him over to the corner booth. "Everything and every place around here brings back some memory or other. If I couldn't take that, I would have moved away."

Somehow he moved his arm so that her hand was in his. It felt good there, right there, as if they'd been holding hands through all eternity.

"I don't want to remind you of Bill," he said.

Liz just looked away, seeing the past flash before her eyes. Her and Bill here after a movie. Her and Bill here after a game. Her and Bill here after a dance. But it had never been just her and Bill—it had been her and Bill and a horde of friends and well-wishers and hangers-on. Bill's audience.

Liz let go of Matt's hand to slide into the booth. He got in the other side a little awkwardly, but not too badly. He took her hand back right away, though.

"I don't know what I want," he said. "But I know I don't want to remind you of Bill."

"It's not bad that you do," she said. "A lot of my memories of you are tied in to him."

"Then maybe it's time to make some new ones," he said.

They stared at each other for a long time. She tried to read in his eyes what he meant since her heart was too chicken to ask. Was it a simple, joking comment or an invitation to a deeper relationship? And, God help her, which did she want it to be?

"You guys know what you want?" a gum-chewing teenager asked them.

A loaded question if ever there was one. What did she want? A home, happiness, someone to grow old with.

"Are you game for a Mount Everest?" Matt asked Liz.

"That's the two-person sundae," she said. "I thought we were having dinner."

"Who says dinner can't be a huge ice-cream sundae? Why always live on the safe side?"

"I don't," she protested. "Jeremy's the one that always wants the right and proper and nourishing thing."

"And you're the one who's always taking the risk," he said, his eyes telling her he knew better. "And here I had you pegged as the conservative one."

"Well, you were wrong." Wasn't she taking a risk just being here with him? Wasn't her heart in danger every time she looked into his eyes? She looked over at the waitress. "Make that one Mount Everest."

The waitress went away, leaving Liz to stare at Matt, wondering just how far this new boldness would take her. How far did he intend it to?

"How come you never remarried?" he asked her.

"I'm not sure." She nodded her thanks at the waitress, who brought water glasses and silverware before departing again. "My mother thinks I want to end up with fourteen cats and a shelf full of African violets, but I just never met anybody I wanted to risk being with."

He looked ready to pry a little further, but she wasn't sure she wanted him to. "Why haven't you ever married?" she asked. "Or have you?"

He shook his head. "Never found the right person." He shrugged. "Besides, cops don't make great husbands."

"A lot are married."

"A lot more are divorced."

"Did you ever get close?"

"Not really." He looked away, his gaze turned toward the window and the passing cars, but Liz doubted that was what he saw. "Maybe it's one of the reasons for moving back here," he said. "To see if I could have a real life."

Their sundae came then, a monstrous concoction of ice cream and fruit and nuts and whipped cream. It ought to serve ten or twelve, Liz thought, not just two. But they started in, and it gave her something to focus on while her heart danced around Matt's words about wanting a real life.

Was he saying he wanted a relationship with her? Or was it just casual talk? Her spoon dug through the whipped cream and found chocolate ice cream.

"So what's your idea of the perfect woman?" she asked.

He stopped eating and looked thoughtful. "I don't know. What do you look for in a man?"

She was going to argue that she'd asked him first, but it wasn't a contest. And if he didn't want to share his thoughts with her, it was all right. Maybe there was a reason he felt she didn't need to know. Her heart seemed to sink a little, but she ignored it.

"Dependability," she said. "It's easy to find somebody who'll be with you during the sunshiny days of summer. I think it's more important for a man to be there when the snows start to fall."

"Yeah, I can see that," he said.

She wanted to tell him that it wasn't just Bill, it was something deeper than that. But she couldn't explain in rational terms the terrible fear that crept over her in the middle of the night and froze her heart. Bill was a moment in time, a passing crush that had hurt her, but he hadn't shaped her indelibly. No, this seemed to have been with her forever, yet she had no idea where it came from. All she knew was that in some distant moment, she'd felt the awful pain of having her heart wrenched from her. And though she sought to be whole again, she wasn't sure she could be. Not if it meant risking the fire again.

"I guess, for me, a sense of humor is really important," Matt said. "And I don't mean just laughing at jokes. I mean a relaxed attitude toward life. You know, accepting things you can't change."

"But not a grudging acceptance," she said.

"No, real acceptance."

She watched for a moment as he worked on his side of the mountain of ice cream. What in his life had shaped that need? Was it something in his childhood or the misery he saw every day as a policeman?

His gaze caught hers suddenly. "What else?" he asked.

Her mind skittered about for a second, unsure what he was talking about. "Independence," she finally said. "I like a guy who can do things for himself. Like cook, wash his own shirts."

"Drive his own car?" Matt said, his voice a touch bitter.

But she shook her head. "No, that's leaning and that's okay. We all need to do that sometimes. I'm talking more about an overall attitude."

His eyes probed hers, seeking to find the hidden pockets of truth in her soul. "I have a hard time seeing you lean on anyone."

She laughed, short and with a trace of bitterness. "I lean all the time. Like leaving Jeremy with Jan. Asking my dad's advice before getting new tires."

"Those are trade-offs," he said, dismissing them with a wave of his spoon. "I do something for you and you do something for me. I'm talking about real leaning. When you're so tried emotionally that you need someone else to be strong. When you just can't fight off the demons of loneliness anymore and need someone to hold you. That's what I can't see you doing. I can't see you ever letting yourself be weak for even a moment and letting someone in."

There was an echo to his voice in her own heart, as if those words had been lying dormant there only to awaken when he'd said them. She didn't like the way he seemed able to see inside her, though, to put words to the vague feelings that she'd lived with over the years. He barely knew her. How could he know what secret thoughts were hiding deep within her? Yet he seemed to. She tore her eyes from his, staring down at the pitiful headway she was making in the sundae.

"I don't know what you're talking about," she said. "I'm the town's biggest mooch." She sat back from the mound of ice cream. "I think I've eaten all I can."

He didn't argue her words, though she half expected him to. The conversation turned mundane as they paid the bill and got back on the road. She was relieved, or at least convinced herself she was. She didn't need a magic man who could divine her innermost thoughts and feelings and fears. It was bad enough to admit them to herself, let alone have another put them into words.

Chapter Seven

Matt sat back and glared at the computer screen before him. It was filled with words, colors and stupid symbols. He'd wanted a computer to write with, something on which he could produce great stories that would impress Liz. This looked like some science-fiction game, and he didn't have the slightest idea how to use it.

"Okay," Jeremy said. "Now, this is the mouse. It's used to direct the arrow. So when you want to do something, you point the arrow at the proper icon and..."

Matt looked at the little rectangular thing that Jeremy held in his hand. When the kid pushed it around on the table, an arrow bounced across the screen. Icon-schmicon. Liz would forget how to read before he figured out this stuff.

This whole idea of moving here was stupid. The idea that he could be a writer was even dumber. And the most inane thing of all was wanting to impress a woman.

Yet he did. And the prospect of certain failure made him want to start a fight.

"Why do they call that thing a mouse?" Matt asked.

Bewilderment filled Jeremy's face. He stared at the gadget for a moment, then shrugged. "I don't know."

"A mouse is a little animal," Matt said. "It has fur, four legs, teeth, and it runs around going squeak, squeak."

Jeremy sat there staring at him.

"What's the matter, kid? You never saw a real mouse?"

"Why do they call this a shoe?" Jeremy asked, raising his left foot.

"Because that's what it is." Why was the kid arguing? Didn't he know enough to admit defeat?

Jeremy rolled his eyes. "Everything's got to have a name," he said. "So the people that designed this computer named this thing a mouse."

"Mouse was already taken," Matt said. "This thing should be named something else."

"Why? Is that some kind of a law?"

"Yeah," he said. "Natural law. That's where God says how things should be."

"Why does God care what people call some computer thingamajig?"

"Hey," Matt snapped. "What are they teaching you in Sunday school these days? God cares about everything and everybody."

Jeremy returned to his non-reply mode, choosing instead to stare at the computer screen. Matt decided the kid was right. It would be best if they got off theological issues and concentrated on computer operations. He took a deep breath and leaned forward again.

"So go ahead. Show me how to work this thing."

"I think I hear my mother calling me," Jeremy said.

"Your mother's back in town. You couldn't hear her way out here if she had a bullhorn."

This time it was the kid's turn to glare at him for a long moment before turning back to the screen. "When you want to get into your word-processing program, you just pull down this menu and double click."

"And then?"

"Start writing," Jeremy said. "Oh, and don't forget to save often."

"What are you now, my banker?"

"This surge protector's not going to help much if you blow a fuse."

Matt just sighed and ran his fingers through his hair. Picking a fight with the kid was stupid. It wasn't Jeremy's fault that Matt was suffering from a bad case of self-doubt.

"Why don't we pack it up for the day?" Matt said.

"Mom said I was supposed to help you."

Mom said. Right, Liz sent her eleven-year-old over to guide Matt. Showed just how capable she thought Matt was. And knowing he wasn't being fair to either Liz or himself didn't help.

Matt got slowly to his feet. "Don't worry about it. I'll go at it my own way. Read some of the manuals and play around with the thing. It'll come." He slapped Jeremy on the back. "You thirsty?"

The kid nodded.

"Okay." He shifted his cane to his right hand. "I'll grab a few pops and we'll go out on the porch."

"What are we gonna do out there?"

"We're gonna sit, spit and watch the world spin."

"We can't do that."

"What?" Matt asked. "You can't spit?"

Jeremy made a face. "We're standing on the world," he said. "So we can't see it spin because we can't watch it and a point of reference at the same time."

"Can you handle the spitting?"

"And the world spins so slow we wouldn't notice it, anyway."

"Go outside and spit." Matt's words came out a little louder than he'd planned, causing the kid to jump a little. Matt lowered his tone. "Go on. I'll bring the sodas."

While Jeremy hurried outside, Matt limped over to the refrigerator and took out two cans. He'd learn the stuff on his own—that would be better, anyway. Then there'd be no chance of Jeremy telling Liz what a dummy Matt was. He took the soda out to the porch where Jeremy was already sitting. After handing the kid his soda, Matt sat down himself. He opened his can, took a sip and leaned back against the post. They sat there and stared at the open fields.

"We're supposed to sit here and do nothing, right?"

Matt shook his head. "We're relaxing. You know? You watch that hawk floating up there for awhile. Then you look at the wildflowers blooming over there. Get tired of that, you close your eyes and smell the air. That's relaxing."

"But that's doing something," Jeremy said.

"So," Matt snapped, "it's still relaxing, right?"

"Yeah. Right. It's relaxing." The kid leaned back and closed his eyes. "See, I'm relaxed."

Matt glared at him, then felt his face slowly slip into a smile. The kid was a real character. Liz had done a good job of raising him. That thought brought Bill back, though, something Matt didn't really want. He looked away from the porch, past Jeremy's bike and out toward the river. He thought of the old trestle bridge.

"Kids still walk to the trestle bridge to prove their love?" he asked.

Jeremy opened his eyes and frowned. "To prove their love? What are you talking about?"

Matt laughed at the look of astonishment on Jeremy's face. "The bridge wasn't in as bad a shape back then as it is now, though it wasn't too great. It was in use until the sixties, when they built that concrete bridge downriver of it. So what's that make it—thirty years of disrepair? Maybe only fifteen back in my day."

"Yeah, but what's this got to do with love? The thing only leads over to Stony Mountain."

"Right. And how else can you get to Stony Mountain?"

"From the bridge over on the other side."

"But you need to cross the river way up at the Bitterroot bridge and drive all around," Matt said.

Jeremy shrugged. "So you need a car. What was the love part?"

Matt sighed, feeling old and outdated. "Crossing the trestle bridge was supposed to be proof that you loved someone. You made a flag with their initials on it and carried it across the bridge, then hung it from a tree for everyone to see."

"Jeez." Jeremy's voice did not reflect admiration. "And a bunch of you guys did this?"

Matt squirmed slightly. "Well, I never did, but some of my friends did."

"Sounds kind of dorky." He looked off at the river, as if trying to see into the past. "Did my father cross it for my mom?"

Matt let his eyes stare out to the past, too, but found it wasn't a place he wanted to visit. "I guess," he said slowly. "He crossed it a bunch of times on dares and to go fishing, so he probably did it to say he loved her."

"Maybe he didn't," Jeremy said carefully. "Love her, I mean."

Matt didn't know what to say. He just stared over at Jeremy, seeing Bill in his eyes and Liz in the way he held his head. What kind of answer did Jeremy want? What was the truth? "I don't know," Matt admitted, and he looked away. But there was no answer floating on the spring air or sprouting among the wildflowers. "I think he did, but I think it got kind of lost later."

Jeremy didn't say anything, and neither did his expression seem to change. So was it the right answer? Matt wished kids came with an instruction manual the way the computer did. There should be a troubleshooting section that you could check when you didn't get the response you wanted.

"People still talking to you about your father?" Matt asked.

"Nah." Jeremy shook his head. "Not really."

Not really? That probably meant not very often.

"I used to dream about him coming home," Jeremy said suddenly.

There was something in the kid's voice that made Matt sit up. Maybe a warning that they were entering dangerous waters.

"And how the whole town would be glad to see him." Jeremy looked at his soda can before looking out over the fields again. "Maybe there'd be a parade and he'd want me to ride up with him."

Another long silence settled between them, but Matt let it be.

"That was a long time ago, though," Jeremy said, as if dismissing his dreams as those of a child. "I guess the part about the town being glad to see him isn't all that crazy. I've got all these newspaper articles that were written about him, and his pictures are all over the school. I mean, a lot of people must have thought he was some kind of a hero."

A hero. Somebody everyone looked up to. Somebody who could do no wrong. "He had his good points," Matt said. "And he had his not-so-good points."

Jeremy shrugged, continuing to look out over the far horizon.

"You just have to remember that any mistakes he made were because of who he was and not who you are."

"Yeah, I guess." The words came out in a whisper, but the kid seemed to relax a bit.

"And I don't care what the town thinks," Matt said. "Heroes only exist in comic books. You go looking for them in real life, and you won't find them. Nobody's going to rush to your rescue. Nobody's going to play the superhero. You look close enough and you see everybody's got cracks in their shoes."

It had taken Matt a long time to figure that out. Maybe he'd save the kid some wear and tear on his heart this way.

Liz was able to convince herself that Matt couldn't read her mind or her heart. The things he'd said when they were shopping for his computer were things anybody could have guessed at. It wasn't as if her life were a closed book. Everyone in town knew all there was to know about her.

All in all, it helped to calm her so that she got through her class in good shape. Matt was there in his seat in the back of the room, but the rest of the students were willing to talk writing this week. She had a little trouble concentrating at first. If she let herself be caught by his eyes, the rest of the world seemed to fade away. Not exactly the best reaction for a teacher to have.

Once class was over, though, she couldn't just let him go with the others, even though her head told her she ought to. People were starting to link them as it was. If she didn't like that, she should just let him go his own way. Except that she wanted to talk to him tonight as a mother.

With a quick wave at Liz, he left the room with the others while she was involved in a conversation with Maggie Alwine. Liz knew he had to be around someplace, though, and spotted him leaning against the front of the school when she was pulling from the parking lot. She stopped the van.

"Get in," she called to him. "I'll give you a ride home."

"I'm waiting for Luke," he replied.

"Luke isn't coming," Liz said. "I called and told him not to bother."

That dark, macho cop look came over his face, sending a chill of awareness down her spine. She felt daring and a tiny bit forward for telling Luke not to come. She bit back the urge to flee. "Get in," she said as she pulled open the sliding side door. "I want to talk to you."

He tried one last glare that said he didn't want to be dependent on her, but she ignored it. She just wanted to talk about Jeremy, she told herself, and that gave her strength. That gave her the armor to fight off the tremors that wanted to shake her being. Once he was inside and seated in the passenger seat next to her, she pulled out onto the road.

"What do you want to talk about?"

His voice teased at her. It tried to push her away, but she had seen into his heart and knew that it was just his manner. "I want to discuss your cheerful attitude," she replied. "Your constant laughing and joking around is getting annoying."

"You're a real humorist," he growled.

"I thought I was," she said, laughing.

He made a face and looked away. She let the silence remain until they hit the outskirts of town.

"I appreciate your talking to Jeremy," she said.

"Had to. He was setting my computer up for me."

"Can't you ever be serious?"

"You just told me I was too serious."

"I said you were a grump. What I'm talking about now is how you get smart-alecky when I try to be serious."

"My humble apologies, madam."

The gate to Matt's farm appeared in the headlights. She slumped slightly. This wasn't how she'd planned this talk. She knew she'd have to ease the tension she felt in her heart whenever he was near, but she hadn't figured on having to get past his wall of gruffness.

"It was nice of you to talk to Jeremy," Liz said. "I wanted to tell you I appreciated it."

"I'm not stopping you."

What was with him tonight? One minute he was grumpy, the next minute he was a joker. Maybe this was how he kept everyone from getting too close. She pulled into the driveway.

"But," he said his voice suddenly light and pervasive, "it would be much better if you showed your appreciation instead of telling me about it."

A shiver danced up and down her spine, sparking a smile on her lips as well as in her heart. But she took her time stopping the van, turning off the ignition and setting the hand brake. Did she want things to stay cool and neighborly? Or did she want to follow that flame beckoning her to go down seldom-explored paths?

The night seemed to close around them, shutting the doors to the past and even the present. There was nothing here but the two of them. There was no reason to hide from her feelings, no reason to run back to safety.

She turned toward him and settled her back against her door. "Is that right?" she murmured.

"I thought that was what we talked about in class tonight," he said. "About showing, not telling."

The moonlight cast mysterious shadows, made him seem larger and more looming. She ought to be worried about protecting her heart—two weeks ago she would have been—but there was such a sweet scent on the night air that caution was a foreign concept.

"I said *good writing* is showing, not telling," she pointed out.

"Yeah," he replied. "But you also said that good writing is life and life is good writing."

"I'm surprised your mother kept you as long as she did."

"She was rather stubborn."

Liz sat there, savoring the spring night. There was no reason to rush. Lingering brought about its own sweet tension, a promise that was as delicious as the night. She was in no hurry.

She couldn't see Matt's rock-hard face or his husky, well-muscled body, but she didn't need any light. She could sense his strength as if waves of it were washing out around her. As if his lips and his caress were imprinted on her soul from years of dreaming.

"You said you wanted to talk," he said. His voice was as slow and soft as a summer's breeze. "But I do wish you'd slow down a tad. I can't get a word in edgewise."

Liz just smiled. "I tried telling you how much I appreciated your talking to Jeremy, but all you did was give me a bunch of smart-mouth comments."

"I already apologized."

"You weren't sincere."

"This environment is not conducive to sincerity."

The kidding tone in his voice fanned the sparks in her soul, teasing them to grow brighter and stronger. "What's wrong with the environment?"

"Well," he replied, "these seats for one. They're separated."

Liz looked down at the space between the seats. A sweet tightness grew in her center, a heat flushed her cheeks. "They certainly are. Plus there's a gearshift between them."

"Right," he said. "And you have a steering wheel filling up the space in front of you."

"Oh, dear. What can I do?" She tried to joke, but her words came out on a breath. "Should I sell the van?"

"Nah, you don't have to do anything that drastic. We can sit in back."

She glanced back at the seat behind them. "You *would* have more space for your injured leg back there."

"That would make me feel so much more comfortable."

"Only a poor driver would let a passenger be uncomfortable."

"And you're a good driver."

They stared at each other through the darkness for several moments, long enough for a few new stars to be born. Then slowly she slipped out of her seat and made her way to the bench seat. Matt moved just as slowly, maneuvering himself to a position next to her.

There was still a space between them. Smaller but still there. It was dark and the night seemed to be closing in on her. Somehow she wanted even more of the night around them.

"You want to open the door?" she asked.

While he did that, she reached up to slide the sunroof back. The van felt open, full of the fresh scents of a heavenly spring night. A planting moon cast warm shadows all around them, and a million stars twinkled and danced for them.

Matt moved closer, putting his arm around her shoulder. She leaned into his body and nestled her head on his chest. She could feel his blood pulse, sending a strength throughout his body.

Here she was, thirty-one years old, with a son, a business, a settled life. Yet she felt a joy rising within her, a secret hunger calling for his touch, his caress, to make her feel home. She ought to go while she had a smidgen of sense.

"I think I hear Jeremy calling me."

"What's with you guys?" Matt growled. "You got some kind of a special communication line between you two?"

"It's a mother-child thing." Her voice sounded about as firm as a melted marshmallow. "When one's in trouble, the other knows."

"You're not in any trouble," he murmured in her ear. "I'm here."

Liz would have laughed if she could. But turning slightly put his mouth so close to hers that she couldn't resist. There was no reason to fight what was so right and necessary and now. His touch was all she wanted and all she needed.

Time had no meaning and neither did place. The only thing that mattered was that the two of them were here together. It was as if their souls had been wandering, searching for each other until now. Until this very moment in time when all things were perfect and ready.

She didn't understand the desperate hunger in her heart or the force of the night. Or that soft breeze that seemed to wind around them, binding their souls and their needs into one. But even as all power to think was fading away in the face of passion, the breeze seemed to shift and a chill settled in the van.

Liz slowly pulled away, sanity coming back with effort. What had come over her? She had more sense than she'd shown in the past few moments.

"Must be spring fever," she said with a shaky laugh.

"Must be." His voice sounded less uncertain, but no less coated with desire.

She sat back, trying to will normality around them. "Guess I ought to get back home. I've got to pick up Jeremy from Mom and Dad's."

"Want to come in for something to drink?"

"No, I really ought to go."

He nodded and shifted his weight to climb out. Suddenly she was afraid to let him leave. Afraid that that chill in the air would never go and that her emptiness would haunt her.

"I'm going grocery shopping Saturday morning," she said. "Want me to pick anything up for you?"

"I don't know."

She felt stupid for asking. As if groceries were all she could think of. "Or I could just bring you along," she suggested.

"Sure," he said. "I guess I'd better refill the cupboards."

He got out of the van and, as she watched, climbed stiffly up the stairs to the porch. A whiff of that gentler air came back, bringing with it a taste of regret, but she refused to let it enter her heart. She wasn't some silly young girl falling under the spell of the night.

"You got the list?" Jeremy asked.

"Yes." Liz slowed as she drove through a wide puddle. "It's not like this is the first time I've gone grocery shopping."

"I know, but you don't want to forget when Matt's around."

Liz just gave him a look, which he was ignoring, and pulled into Matt's drive. "Looks like the storm did some damage out here," she said.

A few branches were down in the yard and the driveway was awash with puddles.

"Betsy really went wild," Jeremy said.

Liz just gave him a quick look before she rounded the house. She tried to tell herself that she wasn't nervous about seeing Matt again. That that strange interlude the other night after her class was no reason to be embarrassed. It had probably been the barometric pressure making her weird before the storm.

By the time Liz parked the van, Matt was out on the porch. Jeremy was climbing out as if he were finally coming home.

"Hi, Matt," he called. "Some storm, huh?"

"Sure was," Matt said. "Had me hiding under my bed."

He was talking to Jeremy, but his eyes found Liz's. The look in them—the pure, raw hunger that was reflected—shook her to the core. Her knees felt shaky, her heart seemed to tremble. When Jeremy gave her an odd look, she realized that she was still sitting in the van and must have looked strange. She got out.

"Had a little damage, I see," she said.

"A little."

She could have sworn he was talking about his heart. Lord, that old barometric pressure must still be low.

"I got some great coupons," Jeremy said. "You need some laundry soap? I got a dollar-off coupon."

Matt tore his eyes from Liz's and smiled down at Jeremy. "Doesn't your mom want it?"

Jeremy made a face. "She buys this weird stuff from Mrs. Alwine."

"It's not weird. And she needs the money."

Matt just shrugged. "Maybe I should get Mrs. Alwine's stuff, too."

Jeremy just groaned and climbed up the porch steps. "Jeez, don't you guys care about saving a buck?"

Matt reached for Liz's hand, his smile surrounding her like a cloak. She felt safe and silly for having worried about seeing him again.

"You ready to go?" she asked.

"Almost. I was trying to board up a window that got broken in the storm." He held the screen door open for her. A sheet of plywood lay on the kitchen table, along with a hammer and some nails.

"Where's the window?" she asked.

"In the attic."

"The attic?"

He had the grace to look slightly sheepish even as his jaw took on a stubborn rigidity. "It's no big deal. I just didn't want the birds to get in. If you just wait a—"

"A month until your leg heals," Liz finished for him. She picked up the plywood and nodded at Jeremy. "Can you get the hammer and nails?"

"Wait a minute," Matt protested even as she started through the house. "I can handle this."

Liz stopped. "Where are the attic stairs?" she asked. "We don't have to climb up a ladder, do we?"

He gave her a black look and led them through the dining room, which was totally bare of furniture, and into the living room with its one chair and television. Jeremy stopped walking, and she turned to see what was keeping him.

"What's that?" he asked, pointing to some sort of black stoppered vase on the mantel.

Liz looked over at Matt. He looked like he'd rather be anyplace else in the world.

"It's nothing really," he said with a shrug. Except that the look in his eyes belied his words.

Jeremy put down the hammer and nails so he could pick the vase up. Matt looked even worse. What in the world could it be?

"Hey, it feels like there's something in it," Jeremy said, shaking it slightly.

Something in it— Liz turned to stare at Matt in horror. His eyes told her she was right. It was Bill's ashes.

"Uh, Jeremy. Maybe you ought to put it down so we can get that window fixed," Matt said. "I don't want to keep you guys here all day."

Jeremy put the urn down, but kept a frown on his face. "But what's in it?"

Liz sighed and led him by the hand over to the chair. "Do you know what cremation is?" she asked.

"Sure." His face darkened with sudden understanding. "Is that my dad's ashes?"

Matt nodded. "Your mom and I were figuring on having a small ceremony around his birthday in August and burying him by your grandparents. But if you've got other ideas, just tell us."

"I don't care what happens to him," Jeremy said, flying to his feet. "Why should I? Do what you want with him."

"I've got papers and stuff that were in his apartment, too," Matt said. "I was saving them for you."

"Well, I don't want them."

"Honey, he was your father," Liz said.

"Hey, it didn't mean anything to him. Why should it to me?" Jeremy picked up the hammer and nails. "So where's this attic?"

Matt just looked at Liz, then led them up the stairs to the second floor. In a closet of a back bedroom, a narrow flight of stairs led up into a shadowy area beneath the eaves.

"Betsy up there?" Jeremy asked, his voice and energy level on high.

"And waiting to jump out and yell *boo!*" Liz said. She scrambled up the steps.

She wished she had known that Bill's ashes were out in the open like that. It had taken her by surprise; she wasn't sure she'd handled it the best way. And Matt looked ready to kick himself. As if it had been his fault, which it wasn't. But it was just like him to blame himself for everything.

She cleared the stairs and looked around at the surprisingly wide expanse as Jeremy climbed up. Sunshine spilled into the far end through the broken window.

"Jeez, this place is neat," Jeremy said, obviously determined to be cheerful and enthusiastic.

"Most of these old farmhouses were built in pieces over the years," Liz said. "This is the oldest section, I think."

She started to move toward the broken window when a noise on the stairs drew her eyes. Matt was climbing up.

"What are you doing?" she demanded.

"Making sure you guys didn't steal anything."

If that wasn't just like him. He felt guilty for one thing and had to make a show of being able to handle another. Shaking her head, Liz made her way over to the window. Jeremy held the board in place while she hammered a nail into the top. By the time she was ready to start on another nail, Matt was there. He took the hammer from her hand with a look that told her not to argue.

Jeremy was looking around the darkened rafters. "Some of the guys say this old place is haunted," he said. "You know, by old Betsy."

Liz looked around, her eyes finding the darkest, shadowiest corners and wondering if Betsy's spirit really did linger here. What was she waiting for?

"They said that when I was a boy, too," Matt agreed.

"But you lived here," Jeremy said.

"Until I left for college," Matt said, finishing pounding in the nail. "But it was no problem. Old Betsy pretty much kept to herself. She had the attic and we had the rest of the house."

"I don't believe in ghosts," Jeremy announced.

Matt shrugged and started to pound a nail into the side. "I don't think they care one way or the other."

Jeremy stared at Matt, his face a mixture of shock, disbelief and just a bit of concern. "Do you believe in ghosts?"

"I haven't seen any," he replied. "But I haven't closed my mind to them, either."

Liz wasn't sure if Jeremy was concerned about ghosts or about Matt's mental state. "Boy, some of this stuff must have been here for years," she said as she wandered over to an old trunk in the corner. "Whose stuff is all this?"

Matt just shrugged as he finished his last nail. "It has to be somebody from ages ago, because my mother rarely came up here. And neither Bill nor I was into old stuff."

Liz fiddled with the catch on the trunk. It didn't seem to be locked, but it was stuck.

"You ought to get a cat," Jeremy said. He had wandered to the other side of the attic. "You got a bad case of mice."

Liz's hands faltered slighty, suddenly imagining a trunk full of mice jumping out at her.

"Hey, look at this." Jeremy brought over a torn cloth bag. It looked like a suitcase. "This is really old."

"Be careful," Liz said, wrinkling her nose at the smell. Though she was glad to see he genuinely didn't seem to be brooding about his father. "There may be something living in there."

But Jeremy was already opening it up. "There's just some old newspapers."

Matt came over to her side as she pulled the faded, yellow newspapers from the bag. They were so old the pages were brittle and cracking.

"Oh, look," she said. "These are over a hundred years old. Here's an article about the Stony Mountain Volunteers." She squinted in the dim light, sensing a change in the air. It was her imagination, she decided. Overactive at the moment. "There's an engraving showing soldiers marching to a train, and it talks about the new train station."

"We heard about the volunteers in history," Jeremy said. "Guys from here went to fight at Gettysburg."

"Old Betsy's sweetheart was one of them," Matt said.

"That's right," Liz said. "He got killed at Gettysburg."

"I thought he got killed in a train wreck," Matt said.

"No, he never came back from the war," Liz said. "That's why the town legend has her crying in the train station. They say the high ceiling caught her cries and lets them run loose during storms."

Matt shook his head. "Are you sure? I could have sworn my mother said something about a train wreck."

"No, the whole town knew she was waiting for Willem Kelleher to come back from the war," Liz said. "Eventually, long after the war was over, she stopped going to the train station and would cross instead over to Stony Mountain. She'd sit on the high hill and watch for the trains to come. Legend has it that she planted a rose garden there and tended them as she waited."

"She was the first to cross the trestle bridge, huh?" Jeremy said with a laugh.

"I guess she was," Liz said as she flipped through the papers gently. There were more articles about the volunteers and the Civil War, some about the area being more widely settled, the opening of the opera house in Michigan City, and one about a train wreck.

Liz peered more closely at the article as Matt leaned over her shoulder. "A Matthias Kelleher was killed in the wreck," she said.

"Who was he?" Jeremy asked. "Was he a relative?"

"I wonder if he was related to Willem," Matt murmured.

"Hey—yo! Anybody home?" The bellow came up from someplace on the first floor.

Matt went to the head of the stairs and yelled. "Up here."

He started to descend the stairs, and Liz put the newspapers back into the bag Jeremy had found. Matt ought to give them to the library, she thought. Maybe they'd have a way of preserving them. Yet it wasn't the yellowed paper that lingered in her mind, but the image of a lonely woman watching the train tracks for the train bringing her love back to her.

Jeremy was going back downstairs, so Liz followed along. Luke Schiller was coming up to the second floor as she closed the attic door.

"Saw your van out there," Luke said. "And since Matt doesn't have a car yet, I was sure someone was home."

Matt nodded at Luke. "What can I do for you?"

"I just dropped by to say that we have our committee all organized," Luke said. "You know, the one to put up a memorial for Billy."

A memorial for Bill? What was he talking about? Liz could feel Jeremy stiffen at her side. She slipped her arm around his shoulder.

"You two are honorary members. Not that you have to do any work." Luke smiled. "We all just thought it was proper. Being as you guys are his only living relatives." He paused a moment. "You, too, Jeremy, if you want."

"Whose idea was this?" Liz asked, her voice quiet as she fought to control the many emotions swirling inside.

"Me and a bunch of the guys," Luke said. "We just thought it was the right thing to do. I mean, old Billy was a hero." Luke started to leave, but stopped at the door. "Anyway, meeting's this coming Wednesday over to my house. Around eight. If you guys can come, fine—if not, no problem."

His exit left a heavy silence. Liz just stood still, trying to sort out the anger from the sadness and resignation.

"Notice how they talk about old Billy the way we talk about old Betsy," Jeremy said. His voice was raw, all his pain and hurt unconcealed. "How come Billy's a hero and Betsy's not?"

"Betsy didn't play football," Matt said, mussing Jeremy's hair playfully. "Too bad. She probably deserves the hero title just as much."

Jeremy moved slightly out of Liz's hold. Just enough to say he was a man and not needing such outward comfort. "Maybe more," he said. "Betsy never left those she cared about. Even when she died, she hung around in case they needed her."

"True enough." Matt put his arm around Jeremy's shoulders and they walked toward the stairs, buddies. "Maybe we should be doing something to remember Betsy."

"Yeah. That would be great. Maybe we could find out something about her love and let her know that he's all right now and she doesn't have to keep looking for him."

Liz just looked away, her eyes stinging. Why wasn't love ever easy? It should have been for her and Bill, but it wasn't. Bill's love for Jeremy should have been easy, but that wasn't, either. Even Betsy was still trying to get it right after all these years and couldn't. She followed Jeremy and Matt to the kitchen.

"Think you could get those fallen branches away from the drive before we go shopping?" Matt asked Jeremy.

"Sure." The boy was out the screen door in a burst of energy, leaving Matt to smile sadly at Liz.

"Sorry about everything. First the ashes, now this memorial thing. Want me to try to talk Luke out of it?"

Liz shrugged. "I don't know. I'm more worried about how Jeremy will take it."

Matt came a step closer and brushed a strand of hair from her forehead. "Crazy how we choose our heroes, isn't it?"

She looked at him. Dark brown eyes filled with so much understanding, so much compassion. She wanted to move into his arms and lie there a long time, lie there forever as the world just moved on without her.

She didn't want to think about Bill and let him back into her life, even for a few weeks' time. She didn't want to worry about Jeremy being hurt or feeling more abandoned. She wanted to find peace.

And why not take a moment of it when it appeared? She moved into Matt's embrace, lightly slipping her arms around his waist so she could lean on his chest. "I suppose Bill deserves something, though I'm not sure I want to be involved."

"I suppose."

"He did lead the team to the state championship."

"Yeah, he did."

"I wonder what he would have thought of this memorial business?"

"Probably would have avoided it like the plague," Matt said. "I don't think he liked to be reminded of his hero days, because he thought he'd fallen so far from them."

"What a shame," Liz murmured. "All he had to do was meet his responsibilities and he'd have been a hero to Jeremy. All he had to do was live up to half his promises and he would have been a hero to me."

"You're pretty free with the hero title," Matt said, his lips brushing the top of her head.

"And what should a hero be, if not somebody who does their very best no matter how tough the fight?"

"Heroes are in comic books," he said. "Yours is just a definition of regular, hardworking folks."

Liz said nothing, only closing her eyes as she listened to Matt's heart beat next to her. Not only was he always on the outside, he didn't see that he could be a hero, too. That he could be more special to everyone than Bill had ever been.

More special to *her* than Bill had ever been.

Chapter Eight

"Give me a call when you're done," Luke Schiller said.

Matt slammed the cab door and turned to Jeremy. "What are we doing out here, anyway?" The kid had dragged him out to the mall on the south edge of town. "We could have found your mom a Mother's Day present at the card-and-gift shop in town."

"They don't have what I want," Jeremy replied as he led them across the parking lot.

"If you know what you want, why did I have to come along?"

"I need advice in getting the right one."

They walked along a line of stores facing an open courtyard. Matt was finding himself moving around faster these days, but the thing he wanted most in the world was to get his damned cast off.

He wanted to be a regular guy so that Liz would start to see him as something other than a charity case. He wanted her to think of leaning on *him*, not the other way around.

"Where is this damn place, kid? We've already walked to hell and back."

"Here it is."

"It's about—" Matt's eyes settled on the filmy night-gowns and lingerie in the window and his mouth fell open. "What is this—a joke?"

"No. No, I need your help. Honest."

"You think I'm an expert on this kind of stuff?" he asked.

"Well, I don't know *anything* about it," Jeremy said. "I'm just a kid. I've never been married."

"Neither have I," Matt snapped.

"But I don't even have a girlfriend."

Matt's mouth opened, but he quickly closed it. Damned if he was going to admit he didn't exactly have a girlfriend, either, unless he counted Liz. And he wasn't sure she wanted to be counted as his girlfriend. He wasn't sure what her feelings were, though he knew damn well that his were growing faster than some of these plants shooting up and filling the May landscape around Stony Mountain. Doubt about her interest in his feelings made him grumpier than the long trek across the parking lot.

"Why do you want to buy your mom this kind of stuff, anyway? Doesn't she need something useful?" Matt desperately rifled through his memory. What kinds of things had he bought his own mother? "Dish towels. Yeah, I bet she needs dish towels."

"Grandpa bought her a whole bunch for Christmas."

"Well, hooray for Grandpa," Matt muttered.

"What?" Jeremy asked.

"Nothing." He cleared his throat. "Anyway, are you sure she wants something like this for a gift?"

"Yeah. All she has is a bunch of old mangy T-shirts that she wears to bed."

"Oh, yeah?" He couldn't see Liz in a mangy anything, but he could easily visualize her shapely little body in a T-shirt. The curve of her soft breasts showing in the front. Those sweet legs falling out of the bottom.

"And they don't even fit her," Jeremy said. "You know, they look like maybe Luke Schiller's old T-shirts."

He doubted that Liz would be wearing Luke Schiller's old shirts, but his mind returned to Liz in her T-shirt, an oversize one. The breasts were now just a gentle swell, but the legs were as shapely as ever. And nothing, but nothing, could disguise that curvy little—

"Come on," Jeremy said. "Let's go in."

Matt gritted his teeth and dragged himself back to reality. A reality of standing outside a lingerie shop with a little kid. "What if your mother doesn't like this kind of stuff?"

"All women like these kinds of sexy clothes," Jeremy replied.

"All women?" Matt's face wrinkled in disbelief. "How did you become such an expert? Let's go look at some other stores first."

"No," Jeremy replied. "I want to buy my mom one of these."

"Have you looked at anything else?"

"Look, Matt. We've been standing out here for five, maybe ten minutes. We don't go in soon and buy something, people will think we're a couple of perverts."

"All right," Matt snapped. "We'll go in and take a quick look-see, but then—"

"Matt?" A pleasant-faced, elderly woman stood in the doorway of the store, staring at him. "Matt Michaelson?" she asked.

Matt started to nod slowly and then suddenly groaned inside of himself. Oh, no.

"I'm Abigail Forycki. George's mother. Don't you remember me?"

He could only keep on nodding as a grin slipped onto his face. He remembered Mrs. Forycki—he remembered her well. He also remembered a sunny afternoon back when he was about twelve when she caught him and George peering out the window at sixteen-year-old Susie Tollson who was washing her car in her bathing suit. Matt could feel the heat filling his cheeks. Now he knew for sure that old Thomas

Wolfe meant a fella shouldn't go home again, ever. Home was filled with people with long memories.

"Are you gentlemen buying or just looking?" Mrs. Forycki asked.

"He—" Matt pointed at Jeremy. "He wants to buy something for his mother."

"Why that's very nice of you, Jeremy. Come on in, then."

Pushing the kid ahead of him, they entered the store. It was filled with more stuff like in the window—all kinds of lacy, abbreviated outfits. Matt could feel a touch of sweat on his forehead.

"So, what size does your mother wear, Jeremy?" Mrs. Forycki asked.

"I don't know." He looked at Matt. "What size does mom wear?"

"How should I know?" Matt snapped.

"You hold her more than I do," Jeremy snapped right back. "You're always holding her around the waist and stuff."

Matt looked up to see Mrs. Forycki's sweet smile, and he knew that she was remembering the time she'd caught him and George.

"I think she's a four," Mrs. Forycki said. "But don't worry about it. She can come in and exchange something if it doesn't fit."

"That's cool," Jeremy said, nodding.

"What color would you like, dear?"

"I don't know." He looked at Matt again. "What color should we get?"

"I don't care." Matt paused a moment to settle his vocal cords. "You buy whatever color you want."

Jeremy turned to Mrs. Forycki. "He's been walking a lot," he said. "His leg is starting to hurt."

"My leg is fine."

"I have some chairs in the back," Mrs. Forycki said. "Would you like to sit down?"

Matt gave Jeremy his best cop stare. "Pick something out—now."

"Sure," Jeremy replied in a disgustingly cheerful tone.

Then he took a quick trip around the store with Matt glaring at him all the while. He didn't want the kid to stretch this shopping thing out into a lifetime project.

Fortunately, Jeremy didn't. He came back with a black nightgown, lots of lace and sheer material. Visions of Liz in it nearly undid Matt.

"That's very lovely, Jeremy," Mrs. Forycki said. "Your mother will look very pretty in that."

Matt knew the woman was watching him, but he avoided her eyes and stared out the window. It was getting warm and stuffy in the store. Come on, kid, he silently urged him. Pay the lady and let's get out of here.

"Uh-oh," Jeremy said.

"What?" The word barely squeezed through Matt's clenched teeth. "Now what?"

"I don't have enough money," Jeremy said. "We'll have to go home, then come back."

Matt sighed.

"Although I don't know if I have enough money at home," Jeremy said. "I'll have to go to the bank and come back tomorrow."

"No." Matt reached for his wallet and took out some bills. "I'll spring for the difference. Just get the package and let's get out of here."

Not too much later, before the rest of his hair turned gray, the transaction was finished and the package was wrapped. They stepped out of the store and Matt began retracing their steps back to where Luke had let them off.

"We can call Luke from the store," Jeremy said. "He can pick us up here."

"What's the matter, kid? Can't you take a little exercise?"

They walked along in silence, Jeremy carrying the package while Matt carried a vision of Liz in the nightgown. Not the kind of image that would help him write that chapter by Thursday.

"Hi, Reverend Bowles."

Matt looked up. First he felt guilty, then he felt foolish. It was that young pastor from one of the churches in town.

"Hello, Jeremy. Hello, Matt."

"Hi," Matt said with a short nod.

"You guys out shopping for a Mother's Day present?" the minister asked.

To his horror, Matt noticed that the bag Jeremy was holding had the name of the store on it. "Yeah, Jeremy bought something for Liz."

"Looks like he bought something nice," Reverend Bowles said with a twinkle in his eye.

"Yeah." Matt cleared his throat. "Come on, Jeremy. We have to get going."

They started to part, when the minister paused. "Jeremy, would you please tell your aunt Jan that the youth center meeting will be at eight o'clock, instead of seven?"

"Okay."

Matt started to edge away.

"We're trying to put together a well-managed set of programs for the kids in town," Reverend Bowles said.

"Yeah," Matt said. "The Stony Mountain Youth Commission. I read about it in the paper. It's something that needs doing."

"Everyone's welcome," the minister said, looking at Matt.

"No, I'm sorry." Matt let his eyes roam and check out the parking lot. "I really can't make it."

"We can get someone to drive you."

"No." Matt shook his head. "I was a cop. I don't know anything about little kids."

"I'm sure that as a former police officer you know a lot about kids of any age," the minister replied. "But we're not just concerned with younger children. We want to serve the junior high and high school age also."

"You won't get them into some church hall," Matt said. "Kids that age want something of their own, away from wherever their parents and siblings go."

"I'm not sure we could afford a building just for them," Reverend Bowles said.

"You don't have to buy anything," Matt replied. "Rent a storefront downtown. There's a few open. You could probably get one for a good price."

"You have a number of good ideas."

"Nah." Matt started to pull away, taking Jeremy with him. "I'm just an old cop shooting off his mouth. You need someone that knows how to handle kids."

He was starting things over in his life, getting out of the taking-care-of-everybody business.

"Oh, Dad," Liz exclaimed, at the same time reaching for a damp towel under the counter. "I'm sorry."

She mopped up the spilled coffee, refusing to let her eyes anywhere near Matt, who had just sat down at the counter. This was all his fault. Sneaking into the sandwich shop like he did gave her heart no chance to steel itself. No chance to pretend he had no effect on her.

"What are you doing here?" she was finally cool enough to ask.

Matt looked bewildered. "I just came in for a sandwich," he replied. "Isn't that the kind of stuff you sell here?"

She took a moment to remind her heart that his voice was nothing special. That it was just the acoustics of the place that made it seem as soft as velvet and as potent as aged whiskey. "What kind of sandwich would you like?"

While Matt reviewed the daily sandwich board behind her, she reminded herself how happy she was with her life the way it was. How much safer it was to rely only on herself. She didn't look at his lips and remember how they'd felt pressed against hers or his hands and think about how closely they'd drawn her to him.

"How about a grilled chicken breast?"

"Lettuce and tomato?" she asked. "Mayonnaise?"

"Mustard."

Liz made a face. "Mustard doesn't go with chicken."

"What do you mean it doesn't go? Is there a law against having mustard on chicken?"

"Just the law of good taste." She turned and gave the order to the kitchen, ignoring the snickering behind her.

"You guys must really be compatible," her father said. "You bicker like an old married couple."

Liz just closed her eyes, horror washing over her as thoroughly as a wave over a swimmer at the dunes. Had they reached that level of ease with each other without her knowing it? Were they so right for each other that they fit together as easily as two pieces of a puzzle?

"I gotta get going," her father said as he stood up from his stool. Then he turned to Matt. "So, young man. You have any plans for Mother's Day?"

Matt looked a bit surprised. "Uh, no, sir."

"Why not join us for dinner, then? I think we're the closest thing to family that you've got here in Stony Mountain."

Matt flashed a look at Liz, but she wasn't sure what those dark eyes were saying to her. Was he asking if she minded or was he asking if he had to? What did she want? A vision of him sitting at her side at her parents' table came into her mind. It felt astonishingly right. She smiled at him before her fears could stop her.

"Yes, thank you," Matt said, turning to her father. "I'd like that."

With a nod at them both, her father left. Matt's gaze returned to Liz. His eyes were trying to read into her heart, to see the secrets in her soul, but she wasn't ready to share them and turned away.

"I think your sandwich is ready." She picked up his plate from the ledge and set it in front of him. "Anything else?"

"Iced tea?"

Liz turned quickly and poured a glass of iced tea. "Here you are."

"Thank you, ma'am." He took a bite of his sandwich. "I got my computer going. Even got a couple of pages written."

"That's good."

He reached into a back pocket and pulled out a folded sheaf of papers. "I don't know if you'd have time to read them before class tomorrow, or if you're even interested..."

There was such an uncharacteristic hesitation about him that it caught her by surprise. He was actually worried about her reaction. She took the pages from him. "Sure. I'd be glad to."

"Thanks." He gave her a flash of a smile before getting back to his lunch.

It had just been a brief glimpse into the Matt that lived behind his defenses, but Liz felt shaken down to her toes. She knew he hated having her help him and that he wanted to be independent, but she'd thought that was just his macho side showing through. This was a vulnerability, a fear of failure.

She glanced down at the pages in her hand. She'd make time to get to them soon so she could reassure him. Right after the lunch crowd left, for sure. Sooner, if she got a moment.

"Hi, folks."

Liz looked up from the papers, folding them so she could slip them into her apron pocket. "Hello, Reverend Bowles. How are you?"

"Fine. Just fine." He settled himself on a stool. "I'd like a ham and cheese on rye, please. And a glass of iced tea."

"Coming right up."

"How are you, Matt?" she heard the minister ask behind her. "All done with your shopping?"

She couldn't quite make out Matt's words; they came out more like a growl. He was so used to being a loner, he was having trouble adjusting to life in a fishbowl. She put the minister's order in and got him his iced tea, then checked the counter for anyone needing a refill.

"I've been thinking about your comments from Monday," the minister was saying to Matt. "You know—what you were saying about Stony Mountain needing a youth center for older teens. One not connected with a specific church."

"Yeah, I guess I said that."

No one was clamoring for attention, so Liz slipped Matt's pages out. It was the first chapter of his book. Her eyes began to scan the words.

"I discussed your concept with our youth commission," the minister was saying. "The response was quite positive."

"That's good," Matt said.

Liz felt a slight sinking in the pit of her stomach as she went on to page two. This would need a lot of work. Matt was so overpowering, so strong, that she expected his writing to be the same. Yet it wasn't. Far from it. Maybe he just didn't have the right beginning.

"We'd like you to work with us on it," the minister was saying to Matt. "We're looking for a full-time director, but we'd be willing to use your expertise on a part-time basis, too."

Liz looked up in time to see the slight twitch in Matt's left cheek. He didn't want to get involved; she could tell that without even looking at him. But that was a shame. He could help a great deal. Based on what he did with Jeremy, he'd be excellent with teens.

"Sorry, Reverend," Matt said. "I'm a little tied up right now."

"Isn't your cast supposed to come off in a couple of weeks?" Liz asked.

He glared at her. "I'm not talking about my cast."

Liz took a deep breath. He was talking about his writing, but was that where his talents lay? From the small sample she'd just read, she'd say no. But it was just a small sample, a beginning sample from someone trying to learn a new computer program. He might have a lot of talent. And even if he didn't, if writing was his dream, she couldn't crush it.

"You're great with kids, Matt," she said. "Maybe you should think about the part-time offer."

"That's not what I want to do."

The words came out hard and definite. He sure didn't look to be in a discussing mood, so she said nothing more, but she couldn't hide that little shadow of worry that fell over her heart.

Was he turning out to be a true Michaelson male? Oblivious to what the world needed from him and only playing by his own rules? She didn't want to think that. She hoped she was wrong, but the stubborn look on his face as he finished his lunch was not the sort to make that cloud of worry disappear.

"Home?" Liz asked gently.

Matt had read his whole first chapter in class. Everyone had been nice and they had been gentle. But they'd also been honest.

Her heart ached for him. She'd tried to warn him that maybe he wanted to do a rewrite on his own before submitting it to the class, but he'd been adamant. He'd set up this schedule for himself and...

"Want to go out for a drink?" she asked.

"No," he muttered. "I just want to go home and slit my wrists."

"Aw, come on. The others were just offering their opinions. You have to evaluate them and decide which are worthwhile and which aren't."

"I stink."

He reminded her of Jeremy when he'd blown a play in a game, especially when he felt that he wasn't measuring up to his father's image. Who was Matt trying to measure up to?

"Relax, Matt. Nobody starts out great. There's a lot to learn."

He made a face and straightened up. "Better get me home," he said. "I have to tuck my field mice in."

He was putting on a good front, but Liz knew he was still hurting. She wasn't about to leave him alone to wallow in his misery.

"They've waited this long," she said. "Another half hour or so won't hurt."

"Nah, you have to get home to Jeremy."

"He always stays at Jan's on class nights. And he has a day off tomorrow. A teacher's institute or something. So he can sleep in late."

"No," he said. "Take me home. I'd have one drink and then another. Before you know it, there'd be a brawl and I'd get thrown out. And everyone in town would know that you were with Matt Michaelson when he got into a fight."

Liz forced a laugh as she turned on the ignition. "I sometimes think I need a little excitement in my life."

"Maybe some other night."

"Yeah, maybe."

She pulled out of the school driveway and turned toward Main Street. Every writer went through this. Maybe it was in school or maybe later, but everyone had to come to terms with the possibility of their mediocrity. And not just writers, either. Actors, singers, athletes.

Her heart seemed to slow for a long moment. Maybe this was what Bill had been going through back when they got married, his attempt to adjust to mediocrity. She hadn't helped him get through it very well. Dared she even try with Matt?

She stopped at the stoplight down the block from the train station and let her eyes wander, trying to keep her mind off similarities with the past. Matt was a totally different person from Bill. He was not going to turn around and propose if his writing career didn't turn out. He—

"That light isn't supposed to be on," she said as they approached the station. "I was sure I turned it off."

She pulled into a parking place in front of the building and turned off the ignition. "Stay here," she said. "I'll check it out and be right back."

"Don't you think you ought to call a patrol officer?" Matt asked.

"Don't be silly," she snapped as she stepped out of the van.

"Oh, excuse me," he said, his sarcastic tone drumming on her ears. "I forgot. Small towns don't have break-ins or any other crimes."

"I'm sure someone just left the light on. So just relax."

Unfortunately, he didn't appear to comprehend *relax*. By the time she'd crossed in front of the van, he was getting out. Liz could feel her stomach tighten up. She really wasn't in the mood for an argument. "What are you doing?"

"Going in with you."

She looked down at his cane. "Ah, I'm not sure how much help you'll be." The words weren't even out of her mouth before she was drowning in guilt. But damn it, why did everybody have to push in on her life? "I'm sorry, but you're a little slow at the moment."

The streetlight shined off his teeth as he flashed her a wolfish grin. "That might be," he said as he pulled back his jacket slightly. "But I've got some fast friends."

Oh, Lord. She'd forgotten that he always carried his gun. Although she didn't like guns, his was so much a part of Matt that she didn't see it anymore. "Let's just relax," she said. "Okay?"

"I'm not nervous."

But she was. "I just know that there'll be nobody inside."

"Good."

"It'll be all quiet and boring."

"I like boring."

"There'll be nobody there," she said again.

"Doesn't old Betsy hang around here at night?" he asked.

"Only during a storm."

He looked up at the clear night sky, filled with stars, and shrugged. "Maybe she came by for a snack. I don't have too much out at the house."

"Matt—"

"Let's go," he said. "Give it a quick check and then we'll head for the barn."

Obviously it was a waste of time to argue with Matt, not with *that* load of mule genes in his system. She opened the door. Better to get this over with.

The outside door opened into the station itself, but it took several steps to get them to the sandwich shop. Now that she was in the building, Liz was glad that Matt had come in with her. The place was spooky at night. A shiver raced through her for a moment as she thought she saw old Betsy in the shadows. If she didn't know better, she'd wonder what the hell the woman was doing, following her around.

"I'll just check the storeroom," Liz said.

"I'm with you."

His words and tone were comforting, like a down cover on a cold winter's night.

He checked the storeroom with her, then insisted that she check out the rest of the shop, following along behind her as she looked through the kitchen, behind the counter and in each of the bathrooms.

"Satisfied?" she asked, feeling bolder now that nothing had been found. She was also happy to see as she turned off some of the lights that old Betsy had gone someplace else.

"Hey, what's that?"

Apprehension returned as she looked toward the corner where Matt was pointing. "You mean the jukebox?" she asked.

But he was already making his way toward it. "Didn't this used to be in that old ice-cream shop down the street?"

"Yeah," Liz replied. "Sam died a few years ago, and the shop was too much for his wife to carry on. She sold most of the fixtures, and Jan bought the jukebox."

Matt didn't say anything.

"I don't know why. Probably sentimental reasons. I imagine she and her husband danced to most of the tunes on it."

He nodded. "This thing was old when I started going to Sam's." Matt ran his hands lovingly over the surface "Does it still work?"

"Yeah."

His hand went in his pocket. "What does it take—a quarter?"

"I can push a button in the back."

He looked at her; she looked at him. The dim light set sparkles dancing in his eyes.

"Make a selection." Her voice came out husky, tight. "It's on the house."

His hand moved carefully, as if in slow motion. Click. He hit the alphabetic button. Then, still moving slowly, his hand glided down to the numbers. Liz was surprised to see how hairy the back of his hands were. Did that mean his whole body was hairy? Click. He hit a number.

The machine whirred, and Matt turned toward her. Still in slow motion, he reached for her and she slipped into his arms. The chords of an old Righteous Brothers song floated out, filling the dark empty corners of the sandwich shop.

"Are you sure you should be dancing?" Liz asked.

But Matt just folded her closer to his chest and led her in a gentle sway to the music. He moved with surprising ease, even with his wounded leg, and she found herself closing her eyes as she dropped her head to his chest.

As they progressed slowly across the floor, a magical mist filled the room, rolling in after the gentle notes coming from the old jukebox. The years rolled away, taking with them the everyday cares of her life. There were no more worries. No more wondering what kind of a man Jeremy would grow up to be. No more concerns of facing her remaining years alone. All that was left was her womanliness and his manliness. And they were as one.

Matt's arms were so strong around her, yet so gentle in their holding. Liz felt free and safe at the same time. Her heart seemed bewitched, mesmerized by the words of the song, by the sweet rhythm wrapping around them, by the feel of Matt's breath against her hair. The music possessed her, sliding under her defenses to bring her soul alive.

They moved in the shadows, their feet just barely brushing the spray of light that came through the kitchen door, as the soulful beat throbbed in the night. An emptiness was trying to capture her, trying to lure her away from the safety of Matt's arms, but she wouldn't go. Here was security, here was peace and happiness and fire and passion.

Then suddenly the song ended, the words fading into the darkest corners, leaving only echoes of dreams in the air. Liz didn't want it to end. She didn't want to lose that magical belief that love was waiting, but Matt's arms were slowly letting her go. She wanted to protest, to somehow will the music to go on while she stayed close to his heart.

And it did. There was a click and then another, and one more mournful ballad filled the air.

"I must have pressed the wrong button," she whispered even as Matt's arms took her once more.

"Or something's stuck."

But she was pressed into his embrace and didn't really care what had happened as long as she was still where she wanted to be. Where she was meant to be. His hands slowly moved across her back, pressing her even closer. She could feel heat wherever they touched, a searing, burning heat of desire that left a trail of longing.

She looked up at him, a stirring deep in her soul as hungers that had lain sleeping for so long were awakened. She felt as if she were coming alive, becoming whole.

His gaze came down to meet hers, and she drank in the hunger burning vividly in his eyes. He bent his head, his lips meeting hers in a sudden splendor. They clung together, his lips whispering sweetness and light and forever to her heart. Need was there, as well as the promise of heaven.

She stirred in his arms; the fire glowing deep in her hidden corners was spreading. She must have been cold, because now she was feeling so warm. She must have been lonely, for now she felt so much like she belonged. Her mouth clung to his, begging him not to leave, not to let her be so alone again.

Then the song changed again to words of lost love. A haunting sadness hung in the air, a fear that what could be might slip away. Their arms tightened with worries unspoken even as a gentle wind cried in the rafters above them.

This dream in their heart was special, and so rare. They had to cling to it and fight to never lose it.

Something was in the air, some magic swirling around them that promised a joy so rare and beautiful that they couldn't dare pass it up. And warning of a sorrow so great as to be unbearable if they should part. They moved in delicate harmony, their hearts intertwining in tender union.

Even in the shadowy corners of the sandwich shop, Liz could feel the charge in the air, the growing needs that remained unspoken. They seemed to light the darkness with sunshine and bring the scent of roses to the stale, closed-in air of the shop. There was a sweet smile somewhere in the recesses of the room, a happiness with which the heavens had blessed them.

And as that happiness grew, as that charge seemed to ignite the melodies that flowed around them, an answering fire began to rage within Liz. It was as if Matt's touch, the nearness of him, was the spark to set the kindling of her heart ablaze. His hands left her skin feverish and needful. His lips left her mouth hungering for more. His embrace left her wanting so much, much more.

"Want to go over to my place?" she asked.

His feet slowed to a stop. He looked into her eyes, looked into her heart, and she let the cravings of her soul rest in her gaze. She needed him as a woman needs a man, not just to hold and caress her body, but to bring her heart to life again. To let her spirit find joy and peace and belonging.

"Are you sure?" he whispered, his voice strained and tense.

"Jeremy's at Jan's," she said as she slipped out of his arms, but only enough so that she could take his hand.

The song on the jukebox had ended and the machine mysteriously turned off. Its lights blinked twice in the darkness, then slowly dimmed.

"How'd you do that?" Matt asked.

"Must be Betsy," Liz said with a laugh. She was more aware of his arm going around her shoulders. Of the strength in his touch and the blinding needs in her heart.

They slipped out the door, the night surrounding them like a velvet cloak that hid them from prying eyes. She leaned against him, not heavily because of his bad leg, but enough to feel his bulk along her side. Enough to feel the tension racing through him that was met with a like urgency in her.

The night air cooled her fevered cheeks and their footsteps sounded softly as they crossed the street. Lights glittered here and there in the distance, but they were like the lights on a Christmas tree—there to make the moment more magical. Liz took a deep breath, but it didn't steady the trembling of her hands or the weakness of her knees. It only fed the fires that were already raging.

They reached the stairs up to her apartment, and Matt turned to her. Pressed up against the outer wall of the hardware store, she looked up into the shadows of his eyes. She could feel his passion in his hands and in the shudder of his breath and knew that his eyes were burning coals awaiting the conflagration of their love.

"Liz?"

His voice was so soft, so much a breathless plea that she barely heard it, but the night carried his dreams to her. It made them hers, winding them into the dreams of all lovers for all time.

She took his hand again and started up the stairs. "Come on," she said to him and to the night. She felt brave and ready. She felt so alive that only wonder and joy could come from this night.

So up the stairs they went. Her heart was ready to sing, ready to shout out her excitement. The apartment was dimly lit, but she didn't wait to turn on lights here and there. She led him through the living room and into her bedroom.

"Oh, Liz," he said, his words more a moan than anything as he pulled her into his arms.

His lips took hers with hunger and need and a desperate sort of urgency while his arms held her against him with such an iron grip that she felt imprisoned. But if it was prison, she never wanted to be freed. She could feel his heart racing and knew that hers was beating as wildly.

His lips moved, burning a trail along her neck as the flames in her soul grew higher and hungrier. She arched against him, her breath coming out as a sigh, a moan, a plea for fulfillment. She was a prairie fire raging out of control, about to consume all in her path.

Suddenly, Matt pulled away slightly. He shrugged out of his jacket and slipped his shoulder holster off, hanging it over a chair back. Then she was back in his arms, his hands pushing her blouse off her shoulders, his mouth running over the bare skin and making the fever spread.

As if their legs could no longer support the weight of such hungers, they slipped to the bed. She lay on her side, resting on her elbow as she smiled down at him. His eyes were ready to devour her; the fire in his soul was raging almost out of control.

She smiled, knowing that *she* awakened that fire and feeling the heady power of being desired. She brushed the hair back from his forehead, then lost that hand to his grasp. He brought it to his lips, and it was as if another fuse had been lit to her heart.

"Are you sure you can handle this?" she asked. "I mean, with your leg and all."

"I'm pretty tough."

"I know that." She planted light, dancing kisses around his lips. "But are we going to rebreak something?"

"Only the previous records for magic," he said as he pulled her down to him.

Their lips met, as did their souls, racing over the universe in a splendid waltz of belonging. There was nothing but the wild sounds of the night, nothing but the hungers and warmth of fire. His hands eased her out of her blouse, then her bra. She unbuttoned her skirt. Then, as his hands ran over her suddenly steaming skin, she did the same for him, touching his hairy chest, running her hands over his steel muscles.

She'd never felt so free, so uninhibited, so consumed by wants. She loved the feel of Matt's hands on her, the ache in every part of her to feel more of him against her. Slipping out of her skirt and panties, she helped him ease his pants over his cast, then couldn't help but kiss the rough skin around it.

"Poor little knee," she cooed, then let her hands slide slowly upward from the knee.

Over skin covered with hair and marked with scars, she inched her caress. It was like finding her way home, she marveled as the wonder and supreme sweetness started overtaking her. It was like being lost and suddenly found.

But then Matt groaned and pulled her close with such urgency that dreaming was over and it was time only to feel and believe. Slipping over him, she let her hands slide along his chest, its every inch a sensuous tale, and took him inside her. They were one at last.

Even as his hands tried to pull her close, to touch and caress and taste and feel all of her desires, she felt herself soaring. Their hearts, their bodies, their souls all moved in unison as the night stood still. Then the stars raced down to join them as the heavens exploded and only magic was alive.

For a glorious time, she and Matt danced through the skies, smiling at the stars and seeing the wild, unpredictable beauty of fire. Then time came back and the night surrounded them once more. She lay at his side, content. Alive, happy and ever so much a woman.

His arms came around her, pulling her close even as her eyes drifted shut. She wanted to stay this way forever. This was where life existed, where the sun rose and set, where her heart resided.

She felt a gentle kiss on her forehead and then let sleep take her.

Liz stretched and slowly drifted out of the soft cocoon of her sleep. She'd left a window open and could smell the new day dawning. She could hear a bird joyfully welcoming the sun. She felt warm and relaxed. She felt wonderful. She sprang up, remembering last night.

She felt awful.

She spun about, but Matt was gone, as was all trace of him. No, that wasn't true. Her treacherous body carried lingering memories of her night. His male essence still clung to her.

The bird kept on singing his praises of the day, and Liz buried her head in her pillow. What was wrong with her? Sure, she had been lonely. But did she have to fall under the spell of Matt Michaelson of all people?

Oh, yeah. Things had worked out just great. She had felt good. She had felt alive. Now she felt like slitting her wrists. How could she face him again? How could she face anybody?

"Oh, no," she groaned in her pillow.

Maybe she should just lie here with her head buried in the pillow and suffocate herself. Even if she wanted to avoid him forever, she couldn't. This Sunday—the day after tomorrow—was Mother's Day. That was the day the whole family, including Matt, would gather at her parents' home.

She rolled over on her back and screamed inside. Tomorrow was Saturday. She always took Matt grocery shopping on Saturday. She screamed again.

"Mom?"

Liz sat bolt upright, clutching at the bedclothes as she came up to see Jeremy standing in the doorway. "What are you doing home? What's wrong?"

"Nothing." Concern crept in around the edges of his eyes. "I just woke up early. And I knew Aunt Jan was going to make eggs for breakfast, so I walked home."

"Why didn't you call me? I could have given you a ride."

Her son was staring at her. Liz drew the sheets even closer around her naked body. "Are you hot?" he asked.

"What?" The word came out in a screech, but she didn't care. "What do you mean? Have you been talking to Matt?"

His eyes darted around the room. "I was just wondering," he mumbled.

"Why?" she said. "You're not old enough to wonder about such things."

"You don't have a nightshirt on."

Her little guy looked very bewildered, and Liz wished that the earth would just open up and swallow her.

"I mean, you always wear a nightshirt."

Liz clutched the sheets to her chest and swallowed hard. She didn't really know where to start. This was a very difficult thing for a woman to discuss with her son.

"Mom?"

"Yes?"

He stared at her with the big, innocent eyes of a child. This wasn't fair. Damn Matt. Where was he when she needed him? He should be here. He should be the one explaining things to Jeremy. It wasn't just her fault. She hadn't held a gun to his head. And Jeremy was his nephew. When were the Michaelson men going to take on their responsibilities?

"I was just wondering," Jeremy said.

"What?" Liz cringed inside. "Now what are you wondering about?"

Her son had backed up toward the door. "I was just wondering if you wanted some French toast for breakfast."

Chapter Nine

Matt leaned forward onto the porch rail and let the morning sun warm him through and through. He felt reborn. Whole. Strong enough to race up Stony Mountain and back. He felt as if the dreams he hadn't known he'd been dreaming had suddenly come true. All because of Liz.

A soft breeze floated past him, carrying the scent of spring and the promise of summer. How long had he been stuck in his own personal winter? How much longer might he have stayed there if he hadn't come back here and been captured by Liz's smile?

He wished he hadn't rushed home last night. The morning seemed suddenly ordinary without her at his side. He wanted to be there when she opened her eyes to the day. He wanted to taste the sweetness of her lips with dreams still lingering in her heart. He wanted to greet the sun while locked in her arms.

He straightened up. He really had to get started rewriting that chapter, though sitting cooped up in his office didn't hold much appeal. Maybe he'd give Liz a call. Just to wish her a good morning.

He hurried inside, but found himself listening to the phone ring and ring and ring at her apartment. Drat. She must have already left for the sandwich shop. He called her there and was rewarded with the sound of her voice.

Suddenly he was tongue-tied. He couldn't think of a single thing to say. "It's me," he finally said, afraid she would hang up if he didn't find his voice. "How are you?"

"Fine," she said.

"Just *fine?*"

She laughed, but it had a touch of distraction in it.

"This a bad time?" he asked.

"Kind of."

He felt under pressure to be clever, to be so witty that she forgot everything but him. It wasn't a pressure he could respond to well.

"I was hoping to see you today," he said. Good thing he wasn't trying to write comedy.

"I don't know." She seemed to be slipping away. "I need to get a gift for my mom for Mother's Day after work."

That was fine. It wasn't as if he owned her or anything. "How about dinner?"

"I promised Dad I'd go shopping with him this evening."

Obviously, Jeremy wasn't the only one who needed help in picking a gift. "Hey, that's cool." He hoped he was sounding better than he felt. "No big deal. Don't work too hard."

Then the day stretched endlessly before him. His computer screen blinked at him annoyingly until he turned it off. It wasn't that he didn't understand she had a life of her own. It was just that he missed her.

He finally took out the box of papers he'd brought from Bill's apartment and spent the day getting to know his brother again. Tomorrow would be a better day. If nothing else, they'd be going grocery shopping.

Except that she called him early Saturday to beg off. "I promised to make the pies for dessert for dinner tomorrow," she said. "And Jeremy's got baseball practice."

"Hey, no problem," he assured her. "It'll give me more time for my rewriting." As if he'd been able to do any.

"If you're low on stuff, I could have Hank run out. Jan could probably spare him for a few hours."

"No, I'm fine. No chance I'll starve." He paused, wondering with sudden darkness if she would care if he did. No sense in asking and finding out the truth. "I'll see you tomorrow. Remember, Mother's Day dinner at your parents."

"Right. We'll pick you up around two."

So he got to spend another day puttering around by himself. He took a carton of yogurt out of the fridge and wandered out to the backyard to eat.

Liz probably had perfectly valid reasons for being too busy to see him yesterday and today, but he couldn't help feeling abandoned. Had he come on too strong the other night? Not strong enough? Had he offended her in some way? Or just not pleased her enough? Now he remembered why he avoided relationships.

He had finished his yogurt and was walking back toward the house when he discovered he had a guest. A large black-and-white cat watched him from under the porch.

"Hi, there." He bent down slightly. "What're you doing here?"

The cat just blinked at him from the shadows.

"You related to Betsy?"

The cat just continued to stare. Matt tore his yogurt carton down the side so it lay almost flat and placed it on the ground just under the porch. Once he had backed away, the cat crept over to investigate. It was a scrawny thing, all legs and belly. Matt frowned, recognizing from his youth on the farm the look of a pregnant cat.

"Looks like you got loved and left, too, huh?"

The cat just gave him quick glances as it licked the remains of the yogurt hungrily.

"'Course, I may not be left permanently," he went on. "I'm supposed to be going to her parents' house for dinner tomorrow. Mother's Day, you know."

The cat finished its licking and looked up at him expectantly.

"Still hungry?" He straightened up. "I get the idea."

He walked stiffly into the house, the cat following him as far as the porch stairs. At least somebody—or something—didn't mind spending some time with him. Inside, Matt scanned his cupboards. Not much in the way of tuna or salmon or other cat-type foods. He put some cottage cheese into a bowl and went back on the porch. The cat was gone.

"Story of my life."

He put the bowl down near the wall and went back inside. Probably what would happen tomorrow, too. He'd be left standing on the porch, waiting for Liz to come by—only she never would.

The cottage cheese was gone the next day, so Matt refilled the bowl. The cat was under the porch again and came out a little less cautiously to greet him. He put the bowl down.

"Happy Mother's Day," he told the cat. "I'll get you something better today. More nutritious. Liz'll take me to the store after dinner."

The cat just stared at him. *Assuming she comes,* it seemed to say.

"She will."

But Matt had no certainty she would as he got ready after lunch. He expected the phone call to come as he shaved. Surely while he was showering. When he was all dressed, then. But he was just putting on his suit coat when he heard the familiar roar of her van.

So maybe she really had been busy the last two days, he told himself. Maybe he hadn't offended her or otherwise been a failure.

She was turning into the drive as he limped out to the porch. She slowed the van to a stop, but didn't turn the motor off. There was only a quick, nervous smile to greet him, then her eyes darted away. It was crazy, but he would swear he could smell the flowery fragrance of her perfume from here. He would swear he could still feel the soft silkiness of her skin beneath his touch.

But she looked different—embarrassed and uncertain— and he just put on his best howdy-do smile. Maybe that's all it was. Just her uncertainty about how to act toward him once they'd been lovers.

"Hi," he said as he got close to the car.

"Hi, Matt," Jeremy shouted.

Liz smiled. "Are you ready? We're running a little late."

He hadn't realized her parents had the stopwatch on them, and some of his uncertainty came back in a rush. Maybe she wasn't embarrassed but repulsed. Maybe she regretted everything and was trying to find a way to avoid him.

He nodded. "Yep. All set."

Jeremy had the sliding side door open for him. "You can sit in front," the kid said with a wink. "I'll stay here with my present." He patted a wrapped package on the seat next to him.

"Thanks," Matt muttered as he swung his leg into place and sat down. He wondered if the kid had shown the nightgown to Jan. Liz was liable to get a lot of razzing from her family.

Liz pulled out of the drive and headed back to town. Matt took a peek at her from the corner of his eye. She was all dressed up and looked gorgeous, but the words telling her so died on his tongue. Did she want to hear that from him? He wasn't sure what the trouble was, but he had the feeling that his stock was pretty low at the moment.

"So how are you?" he asked.

"Fine." She gave him a quick smile, as if it were in her script, not in her heart. "Sorry we've been so busy."

That sounded scripted, too. "No problem. I found a new friend."

"A new friend?" Her voice sounded almost worried.

"There's a stray cat living under my porch."

"Oh. A cat." The worry was gone.

"That's cool," Jeremy said. "What'd you name it?"

"It's a her, not an it," Matt said. "And I haven't named her anything. She's a stray. Probably'll be gone when I get back."

"Not if you feed it," Jeremy said.

"Even if you feed it," Liz said. "There's no guarantees when you're dealing with a stray. Sometimes they like the freedom too much to trade it for regular meals and a warm bed."

Why did Matt think cats were the farthest thing from her mind? He sure wasn't going to press the topic, though, or try to convince her that *he* wasn't a stray. He didn't know what he was, except taken with her smile. They rode the rest of the way to her parents in silence.

"Uh-oh." Jeremy's voice betrayed concern when they slowed to a stop on a residential street. "They're blocking the drive."

Two tall, well-built teenage boys wearing scruffy jeans and cut-off T-shirts were leaning against a customized old car, talking to a girl in a halter top and short shorts.

"Run them over, Mom," Jeremy said.

"There's no need for that, honey," Liz replied. "I'll just park here in the street."

"But why should Matt have to walk all that way?" Jeremy protested.

"Jeremy, there's no need to—"

"Just pull up behind them," Matt said. "I'll ask them to move the vehicle."

"That's the Trager brothers," Jeremy said. "Danny and Donny."

The kid's whole tone indicated that these were a couple of the town's tough boys. All the more need for them to move. Matt'd learned long ago that if you gave the punks an inch, you might as well give them the town.

"Matt, that's okay," Liz said softly. "It's not that far from the street to Mom and Dad's front door."

"Pull up behind them, please." Didn't she think he could handle two punk kids?

She hesitated a moment but let the van glide to a stop behind the kid's coupe. "Be careful," she murmured.

Obviously she didn't. "*Careful* is my middle name," he replied.

He dropped down onto the ground and walked over to the boys. Two studs, ready to perform for their lady. Well, he had his lady, too. And he needed to score a few points himself.

"Hi, guys."

They stared at him, trying for insolence but not quite making it. Finally they nodded in unison. The girl just smirked.

"Nice car," Matt said.

"We like it," the taller one said.

"Dangerous place to leave it." Matt kept his voice soft and gentle. "All the folks going in and out of the drive, especially on a holiday, and before you know you got yourself a bunch of scratches and nicks."

Their eyes shifted from each other back to Matt.

"We wouldn't like that," the taller one said.

"No, not at all," the other added.

"Well, you know it don't matter whether you like it or not." Matt shifted slightly to lean against the car. "Once the damage is done, it's done."

They both stared at him, trying damned hard for the bad street look. And they almost made it.

"So why don't you move the vehicle? That way everyone's happy and—" Matt pushed himself away from the car and winked at them "—your car stays looking all nice and pretty."

Then he turned and slowly made his way up toward the house. He could feel their eyes on his back, but his gut told him the vehicle would be moved. He'd just have to be patient.

He was halfway up the drive when the lads and their ladyfriend slowly eased into the car. There was a screech of tires and they were gone. Liz pulled the van up next to Matt.

"What did you say to them?" Jeremy demanded, looking half disbelieving and half impressed.

"I just asked them to move."

"If I would have done that, they would have laughed," Liz said. "You have a knack for dealing with teens."

That wasn't the area he wanted her admiration for. He took the present from her hand, leaving her with the pies.

"This won't get hurt if I drop it, will it?" he asked.

"No, but I could have managed."

That was obvious, he wanted to say. She was making it very clear that she could manage just fine on her own. There was nothing she needed him for. Not carrying a package, not ridding the street of some young punks. He'd turn around and walk home except that the front door had opened and her parents were calling hello to them.

Once they'd passed the greeting gauntlet, Liz went off into the kitchen and Jeremy slipped into the backyard with some older cousins. Liz's father got Matt a beer before they retired to the sun porch.

"I saw you had a little thing with the Trager boys," her father said once they'd been seated.

"Yeah." Matt took a sip of his beer. "I just had to ask them to move their vehicle."

Liz's father gazed at him and took a sip of his own beer. "They ain't bad boys," he said. "Just need a strong hand now and again. Father's dead and mother ain't got no folks here. Hard for a woman to raise boys alone."

Matt nodded.

"Got a number of boys like that. Kids that need to be brought up short." He looked at Matt. "Hear you had some good ideas on a youth center for them."

Not sure what to say, Matt buried his tongue in beer again. What the hell was this? A campaign to give the big-city cop a job? Well, he had a job. He was a writer. And that needed a hell of a lot of work.

Jan came to the sun-porch door. "We're going to open presents in the living room."

Matt greeted her announcement with relief. He felt like dashing off to the living room, and he would have if it wasn't for his damn leg. He didn't need any more of these "Gee, you're good with kids" conversations. He was starting a new life and he wished people would remember that.

Due to his bum leg, he was one of the last to get to the living room. He would have liked to sit next to Liz, but she was on the floor all the way across the room. To get there he would have had to stumble over a bunch of women and kids, not to mention the fact that, at the moment, he wasn't all that great at getting down to the floor. He took a seat in a straight-backed chair near the door. At least he could watch her undisturbed if not be close to her.

"You're first, Liz," Jan said.

"Why?" Liz asked.

"We decided," her sister replied simply.

"Yeah, open yours," Jeremy said, obvious excitement bubbling in his voice. "We got you a really neat present."

"We?" Liz asked, as she picked up the box.

"Yeah. Matt and I bought it." The kid looked straight at him with a grin as wide as Kansas. "We went in on it together."

Matt wasn't certain he liked the gleam in Jeremy's eye or the look of hesitation in Liz's. His stomach took a definite side shuffle. He didn't buy it; he just lent the kid some money. But now didn't look like the time to discuss such technicalities.

"It's something you really need, Mom."

"Oh?"

Liz carefully removed the wrapping, then stared at the store's name on the box. The air closed in on Matt and he felt a sense of impending doom. He wished he remembered how to pray.

Liz slowly took the cover off, then stared at the contents, her eyes wide as saucers.

"What is it?" Jan asked.

When Liz did not reply, her sister looked over her shoulder and broke into a hoot and a howl. "Oh, my gosh," she screamed. Before Liz could respond, Jan grabbed the item out of the box and held it high. "Isn't this just fantabulous?"

Matt could see the red creeping along Liz's lovely neck and up those beautifully smooth cheeks. She looked at him, her eyes stormy and troubled.

"Jeremy picked it out," Matt said.

"Sure," Jan said.

Everyone joined in her raucous laughter. Well, not quite everyone. Liz's smile came nowhere near her eyes.

"It's really pretty," she said, smiling at Jeremy. "You have excellent taste."

There were times—not often but now was one of them—when Matt wished he'd had a sister. Mom was great and all, but with the three-men-to-one-woman ratio, they didn't always see the female side of things. And there were times when that would certainly have helped.

Like now. He had his suspicions—he wasn't totally sure—but he thought Liz was pulling farther and farther away from him.

"You need more than that," Jeremy said. "That's barely enough food for two days."

Liz frowned at the cans of cat food in Matt's hand. "He doesn't even know if the cat'll be there when he gets back."

They were at the grocery store so Matt could stock up on cat food, anyway. Her parents had forced so many containers of leftovers on him, he wasn't going to have to buy food for a month. But that was a sign to her that they approved of him.

She approved of him, too. She just wasn't sure if she approved of the two of them together, as a couple. There were nice, good people and then there were *couple* people, ones who were made to be paired up with someone, who felt alone and empty and incomplete when alone. Truth be told, she wasn't sure either she or Matt were *couple* people.

"I probably should get some kind of dry food," Matt said. "I think they need a balanced diet."

"And a bed," Jeremy said. "Too bad it's Sunday. Purr-fect Pets is closed. They have really neat beds for cats."

Liz frowned at him. "What are you checking out cat beds at the pet store for?"

He shrugged. "They were next to the dog beds and, you know, I thought I should check them out. Just in case we got a dog someday."

Liz just sighed. Everybody wanted something from her. But what did she want? She didn't know anymore.

They paid for Matt's cat food and drove him back to his house. It was dark out, and with the stars winking down at them, Liz could think of nothing but the evening they'd sat out here and watched the night. She had felt so special, so alive in Matt's arms. Now all she felt was fear.

Fear that she'd be back in them and lose her way, then her heart. Fear that she wouldn't ever be in them again and wouldn't ever feel that rare joy and splendor of belonging.

"Can I look to see if the cat's there?" Jeremy asked.

"Sure," Matt said, handing Jeremy his keys. "There's a flashlight in the closet by the back door."

Jeremy hopped out of the van and raced up the steps to the porch. Liz was all too aware that that left her and Matt alone here in the darkness. That all she had to do was reach over and—

She turned and opened her door. "I'll help you get all these leftovers and stuff into the house."

She climbed out of the van and went around to the side door. Matt was out by then, standing there, waiting for her. Liz's heart said to run, but her head told her not to be so silly. Still, she moved carefully, as if walking in a mine field.

"You weren't upset about that gift, were you?" Matt asked. His voice was so soft it was almost a caress.

Dangerous path for her thoughts to follow. "No, of course not. It's very pretty." Too pretty. Too much a reminder of the side of her that she'd been locking up.

"It really was Jeremy's idea. He said you wore grungy old T-shirts and really needed something better."

"They aren't really grungy," she said. But they were safe. Sexless. No wild imaginings while sleeping in them.

"He also said they were Luke Schiller's old shirts, if I remember rightly."

"Luke Schiller's? They are not." Liz couldn't help but laugh, and when she did, all her walls toppled over.

Suddenly she was in Matt's arms, pulled into his embrace and tasting the hunger on his lips. For a wild, magic moment, she let herself go. She let the flickering embers in her own heart flare up again and try to consume her. She let the passion hiding deep in her secret corners explode into need for his touch, for his caress, for the safe passage his arms offered.

Her mouth tried to draw strength from his, tried to tell him of her fears and her worries even as they turned to ashes like autumn leaves in a bonfire. His lips asked more and more of her, his arms locked around her as if they'd never let her go. She could feel the racing of his heart, the charge in the air around them.

"I found her," Jeremy said.

Liz jumped from Matt's arms and wiped her hand over her face as if the passion were a curtain she could push aside. She took a deep breath, and by the time Jeremy was coming around the side of the van, she was facing him and smiling.

"Did you—" She saw he had a black-and-white cat in his arms. "Jeremy, you shouldn't be carrying her. She could have fleas or be sick or something."

"Mom, she's real friendly."

"But you don't know," Liz said, a franticness taking hold. "You can't just trust everybody and everything. Just because they seem friendly doesn't mean they are. It doesn't mean that they won't hurt you or leave you or—"

Matt put his hand gently on her arm. His touch deflated her panic, leaving her feeling silly and exposed.

"Put her up on the porch," Matt said lightly. "We'll feed her up there."

Conscious that she must have sounded like a fool, Liz grabbed up a stack of leftover containers and carried them up to the house. Matt followed with the grocery bag. And when Liz put her things down on the kitchen table, she discovered the cat had come in with them.

"Jeremy—"

"It's okay," Matt said. "We'll play it by ear."

He opened a can of cat food and they all watched as the cat wolfed the food down. Was that how she had been? Liz wondered. So hungry for Matt's love that she forgot the world existed?

"We ought to be going," she told Jeremy. Ignoring his pout, she pushed him gently toward the door as she glanced over her shoulder at Matt. "We'll be seeing you."

She escaped out the door, certain that sanity lay away from his gaze.

Sanity maybe, but not sleep. She tossed and turned all Sunday night and got up Monday as grumpy as an old bear. It was raining, which delighted her, but didn't help her mood any. Neither did Jeremy's talk about Matt and his cat when the boy came back from a bike ride out to the farm.

Tuesday was bright and sunny, which only increased her annoyance. All around, flowers were blooming, trees were leafing out and the world was celebrating life. She wanted to hide away in a cave and avoid everybody.

Just the thought of Matt was enough to make her knees weaken and her lips tingle. Hearing his name would send her heart into overdrive. Lord knew what would happen if she actually heard his voice or saw him. She needed to remind herself of the hurt that love brought with it, of the pain of being alone after being one with another. After closing the sandwich shop, she dropped Jeremy at his baseball practice and stopped for gas at Schiller's service station.

"Hey there, Lizzie," Luke called over from the service bay. "How ya doing?"

"Just great, Luke. And yourself?" It was all so simple, she realized suddenly. The perfect reminder was right at hand. She walked over to the service-bay door. "Sorry I didn't make your meeting about Bill's memorial last week. When's your next one?''

"I'm going to mail these letters," Jan said. "Then I need to swing by the hardware store for some brackets for that shelf in back, and then I want to—"

Liz had been cleaning off the tables while she listened to her sister. Aware of the sudden silence, she looked up. Jan was staring at her.

"What's wrong?" Liz asked.

"That's what I was wondering," Jan replied.

Liz turned to face her sister. "Why should anything be wrong?"

"Well, for starters," Jan replied, "I was talking to you, and you didn't say one word back."

"What was I supposed to say?"

Jan shrugged. "And now you've got your arms folded across your chest. You always do that when you're bothered by something."

Liz frowned. "You mean, like when people poke at me and ask me dumb questions?"

Her sister looked at her a long, long time. They were at opposite sides of a chasm wider than the Grand Canyon, and no words crossed between them.

They were only a year apart, almost like twins. They'd shared their innermost secrets with each other. They knew each other better than their mother did. Her sister ought to know that Liz didn't want to be bothered.

And she did. Jan gave her a quick nod before turning and hurrying to the door where she stopped. "That little nightie you got on Mother's Day doesn't fit too well, huh?"

The words came out so gently, so filled with understanding, that Liz almost burst into tears. She wished she could talk to someone, to explain her crazy fears and have them tell her that she was right. Or that she was crazy. But she just didn't trust anyone to know how afraid she was or to know how much her heart ached to be loved.

But rather than say any of that, she forced a smile to her lips. "I'm sure it'll fit fine."

"Okay," Jan said, pulling open the door. "See you tomorrow."

Liz just nodded and stood there watching until Jan had left the station and walked around the east corner to the parking lot. Then Liz slowly picked up the washcloth. She had only a few more tables to clean and she could go home. Home—where she could sit and think about how alone she was. How alone she would always be.

As she cleaned, Liz avoided looking at the jukebox. That horrible, insidious machine that was the cause of it all. She almost laughed. It would be nice if she *could* blame her situation on someone or something. But she couldn't. She had wanted to feel alive again and loved. Now she was paying for her moment of weakness.

"Hi."

She looked up to see Matt standing in the doorway, a smile on his lips but uncertainty in his voice. She wanted to send him away. She wanted to fall into his arms.

"Hope you're not here for a late lunch. I'm closing up," Liz said. "About all I can give you is soda or iced tea."

He stepped farther into the room until he came to a table to lean against. "I don't want anything, thanks. I just want to talk."

Liz knew that. He'd called her Monday and then yesterday, leaving messages each time. She'd just been running away from him. She should have locked that damn door as soon as Jan left. Locked the door and ran to the back room where no one would see her. Now she couldn't escape. Her heart beat with the fear of a trapped animal.

"I get the feeling you're avoiding me," he said.

"Avoiding you?" She laughed to show how ridiculous the idea was, but it came out weak and hollow. "Why would I be doing that?"

"Because you regret last Thursday night."

She turned away, too afraid that her eyes would tell him he was right. "Don't be silly," she said as she wiped a table. "I'm a big girl. I knew what I was doing."

"All right. Then you found me lacking in some way."

She let her eyes find his for a moment. But they were filled with dark shadows; it was impossible to read them. Was there anger or doubt lurking in those shadows? She shook her head slowly. "Oh, no. That's not it at all."

"Then what's wrong?" he asked, sinking into a chair.

"Nothing," she said quickly. "I'm just cautious. You have to give me time."

"I thought I was."

She sat, too. "This isn't like some crime you have to solve in forty-eight hours," she said. "I have a lot to do. Things that I've been letting slip over the past few weeks because I've been doing things with you."

"Like driving me around."

Like letting her foolish heart dance out in the open. But she just shrugged and let him think what he wanted.

He got to his feet slowly. "The doctor from Chicago finally called. He looked at the X rays our hospital sent him and he said it looked like my cast can come off in a week or so."

"That's good." She got to her feet also, feeling as if she were seeing off a mere acquaintance.

"Yeah, so I thought we should go out and celebrate."

"Celebrate?" Liz shook her head. "But the cast isn't off yet."

"That's okay." He flashed her a smile, one so full of sweetness and energy that it could set church bells to ringing. "No reason we can't celebrate again once the cast is off."

Liz felt cornered. Felt as if that smile would do her in, that there was no escaping from him or the hungers in her soul.

"So why don't we go out for dinner tonight?" he said.

"I . . . I can't." She found her voice. "I have a meeting tonight. You know, that committee for Bill's memorial."

"I see. I didn't realize you were helping them." He paused a moment. "What about a quick bite first?"

"I really need to get home. Fix something for Jeremy, check how he's doing with his homework." She shrugged. "Things like that."

Matt looked away for a moment, and she was able to catch her breath. She wasn't actually lying. Sure, Jeremy could fix his own dinner and he hadn't needed her help with homework for ages, but a mother should always be available.

"Okay," Matt said. "I'll see you tomorrow, then."

"Tomorrow?"

"We have class, don't we?"

"Oh, right. Class." She laughed. Why had she fallen prey to those eyes? Why had her treacherous senses become addicted to his touch in such a short time?

"This will give me a chance to rewrite my chapter."

Liz nodded. She found a way to smile, but it probably looked about as real as that petrified fish on the wall.

"And we'll just have to have a super celebration once my cast is off."

She nodded. He had to leave soon, before the threads holding her heart together snapped.

He stood where he was a long moment, then finally said, "Good night." And with a wave, he was gone.

Liz watched him walk out the door and up Main Street, and then her vision blurred. She couldn't see him anymore. Ever so slowly, she walked over to lock the door.

This wasn't working. It wasn't working at all. Maybe she could see him and be friends. Maybe she could keep her heart uninvolved.

Sure.

But it was either that or stop seeing him altogether, and she didn't have the strength to do that.

Chapter Ten

Matt hit the delete button and watched the screen go blank. It wasn't nearly as satisfying as ripping up a paper and throwing it across the room. There was no release of frustration. No sense of cleansing.

He leaned back in his chair and frowned. He should have bought one of those really neat computer desks, with power-driven drawers and roll top—all operated with a remote-control gadget. Then he'd be able to write. He was willing to bet that all the top professional writers had one.

Sighing, he spun his chair around and looked out the window. The view outside was nice—folks in Chicago would pay big bucks for it—but it was starting to get boring. Nothing but green, sweet smells, and big-mouth birds singing the whole day long.

Rosie jumped into his lap. "You come to tell me I'm lousy, too?" Matt asked the black-and-white cat.

Rosie just purred and climbed up onto the desk, stepping on the keyboard as she did. An interesting if unintelligible string of letters appeared.

"I see," Matt said. "Not only do you think I'm lousy, you think you can do better."

Trouble was, she probably could. There wasn't anything Matt was doing well these days. Maybe he ought to go back to being a cop. Except his bum leg was proof he hadn't done that very well, either.

"Why'd she go to that meeting last night for that memorial for Bill?"

Rosie had no answer. She probably thought he should figure a few things out for himself. Trouble was, the answers he was coming up with were pretty depressing.

He considered skipping the writing class that night. It wasn't as if Liz would miss him. But when Luke pulled up in the drive after dinner, Matt climbed into the cab. There were some things he just wasn't strong enough to give up.

Liz was as bouncy and bright as usual in class. Her eyes seemed to sparkle, and her lips seemed especially full and tempting. She was wearing a pale blue dress that highlighted her slender waist and soft, rounded breasts. Why had she gone to that stupid meeting last night? She said she didn't love Bill anymore, so why did she go? He didn't hear a word she said all evening.

Suddenly everyone was filing out of the room, laughing and talking as they got ready to go home. Class was over. Matt walked slowly up to where Liz was putting her notes back into a folder.

"So how was your meeting?" he asked.

"Last night's?" she asked with a smile. "Fine. They want to put together a collage about Bill to hang in the school and have a service at the football field."

"Super."

She appeared not to notice his sarcasm. "It should be nice, though they want to do something more lasting, but they haven't decided what. But they figure homecoming's when they should do something, so I guess we have time to decide."

He just grunted and turned to walk out the door.

"Hey, wait up. Aren't I giving you a ride home?"

He turned back around and stared at her. "I assumed you'd be hurrying home."

"Hey, just 'cause I was a little busy this week, it doesn't mean I'm going to make you walk." She grabbed up her folder and purse and followed him to the door. "So how's your rewriting going?"

What a topic to choose. "Okay," he said as she turned off the classroom light and they walked down the hall. "But slow."

"That's normal," she said. "Too many people think writing is something done fast. Most things that are good take time to develop."

Why did he think she was no longer talking about writing? They went out into the evening and got into the van in silence. It felt good to be here with her again, closed in by the darkness, and close enough to touch her. Maybe she was right. Maybe he just wanted everything too quickly.

They'd turned onto Main Street, and as they were nearing the station, Matt held his breath. What would Liz do? Keep on driving toward his home? Or turn into the lot to take him to heaven? She just kept on going.

"Shoot," he muttered under his breath.

"Beg your pardon?"

"Nothing." He coughed. "Just clearing my throat."

"It's probably the night air," she said. "It affects some people that way."

Yeah, right. Getting hauled straight on home also affected some people. Especially old cops with a touch of gray in their hair. "Everything shipshape at the old sandwich shop?" he asked.

"Yep."

"We could have taken a few minutes and checked."

She just kept on driving, her eyes straight ahead. "I've been real careful to turn out the lights when I leave."

"That's good."

"Better to be safe than sorry."

Another mixed message. Matt just stared out at the darkness. He'd have to be deaf, mute and blind not to have gotten the idea. She wanted to move cautiously. She wanted to think things through. She wanted time.

What did he want? That was simple. To be with her.

They rode to his home without speaking. It was amazing how the distance seemed to grow shorter each trip he made with her. She pulled into the drive and around to the back porch. When she turned off the motor, the night seemed to swallow them up. Crickets chirping, the breeze rustling the leaves, the sound of his heart racing.

"I just need some space, Matt," she said softly. "Try to understand."

He turned to look at her. Her features were more shadow than substance, but his mind could see the hesitation in her eyes. "You have a lot of space now," he said, gesturing at the area between the two front seats in the van. "You could probably put another seat in here."

"You know what I mean," she replied. "I don't want to be rushed, pushed or managed in any way."

And apparently he was guilty of all three. He turned his eyes back to the night. He could hear the river in the distance, rushing off to new lands and new sights. He used to share that urge when he'd been growing up here, but no longer. He wanted nothing more than to stay put and grow old. But with the right person at his side.

"I don't want us to quit doing what we've been doing," Liz said, her words breaking into the darkness.

"And what's that?"

"I want us to be friends. Good friends. Like we are now."

"You just don't want to go beyond that." He heard her sigh and slowly turned to face her again. "Right?"

"What's wrong with the way things are?" she asked. "We do things we enjoy. We have a nice time."

What was wrong? Hell, he wanted more. More time with her. More of her. Just more.

"Please understand." She put a light hand on his arm. The spot burned as if she'd put white-hot steel there. "I was devastated when Bill left."

"I can understand that."

"No, you can't. Not unless you've gone through it, too. Bill was the only boyfriend I ever had. I never thought of dating anyone else. I assumed we were made for each other, that we were two halves of one whole. When he left, he took everything. My heart, my sense of who I was, even my memories of growing up, because they were all entwined with him."

He could see all that. But it had happened years ago. People heal and go on. She certainly had. "But you made it."

"Yes, I made it. I learned how to take care of myself."

"And Jeremy," he added.

"And Jeremy," she agreed. "But I'll never be the same. I don't have that history of some relationships working out and some not. I had one and it failed. It's a lot harder for me to take a chance again than the next woman."

"But I'm not just the next guy," he said. "And I'm not Bill."

She swung her legs around so that she was facing him. "I'd like us to stay friends, Matt. Special friends. The way we are now. At least, the way I think we are."

Her hand came over to rub his arm, but he didn't look her way. A distant star winked at him, promising glitter and romance, but if he remembered his science correctly, that star might not even be there anymore. He might just be staring at the light traveling from a dead star. Was he trying to hang on to something that was over already, or had it ever existed in the first place?

"Matt?"

"Yeah." He fought to keep his voice neutral. "That's fine."

"I know that's not what you want, but—"

"That's for damn sure," he said. The hell with this tippy-toeing around. "I want us to be special. Not just special friends, but special everything. Special and only for each other."

"We are."

Gritting his teeth, he paused to take a breath. "I want to take care of you. I want to be there for you. Every day and night."

Now it was her turn to stare out at the night. And she did it long enough to let worry take the upper hand in his corner of the van.

"But I can be patient," he said.

Liz turned to face him, a crooked smile on the shadows of her face. His heart panted and begged like an eager puppy.

"I can be patient," he repeated. "I'll just pretend it's a stakeout."

She leaned forward, sitting just on the edge of her seat so that her lips could reach his. She brushed his mouth with hers lightly, enough to light the fires but not enough to feed them. A gnawing, aching emptiness ate at him, filling his being with thoughts of what might be and yearnings for what wasn't.

"We'll have everything," she was saying. "We can go out. We can do things together. We can love each other."

"But we'll live apart."

"It's a small town," she said. "We're never far from each other."

"I don't care about the distance," he replied. "It just feels apart—far apart."

Liz slid back into her seat. He was losing her already.

"Why don't you come in?"

She shook her head. "Not tonight."

Not tonight, not tomorrow. Probably not ever. He made a face and he could see his irritation reflected in her manner.

"I don't want to force things," she said, her voice getting sharp. "I want to ease into things. I want a natural flow."

"Well, this is my natural flow," he said, snapping his own words short.

"You obviously need more to do," she said.

"Like what? Screw around with that damn youth-center thing?" He was sure he knew what she was leading up to, but he pushed on anyway, "I don't want to be a nanny—I want to be a writer."

It was dark, but he could discern the uncertainty clouding her features. Hell, maybe he was just feeling it. He knew it was there. She didn't think he could write worth a damn and just didn't know how to tell him. He doubted if special friends were supposed to say anything negative about each other. Certainly not things like "Pack it in, fella, you can't even write lyrics on the wall in a men's room."

"Want to do anything tomorrow night?" she asked.

"*I'm* supposed to ask that," he snapped.

"Well, excuse me," Liz said. "But I'm not familiar with all the rules in the macho handbook. I thought we were nineties kind of folk."

"I'm sorry."

"Maybe we each ought to do our own thing tomorrow."

"Sure," he replied. "That'll give you the space you want."

"Good night, Matt."

He opened the door and dropped down to the ground. It didn't sting a bit. That damned cast should have been off weeks ago. His leg was all healed.

"Good night." He slammed the door.

The gears ground in protest as Liz threw the van into reverse. She spun in the gravel for a moment, then roared off down to the road. Damn vehicle was getting noisier and noisier.

"Get a new muffler," he shouted after the rapidly retreating van. "You might as well do something worthwhile with your space."

Liz didn't know why she had bothered bringing Matt grocery shopping. Just because she had done it almost every Saturday since he came back didn't mean that they had to do it every Saturday from now on. Especially if he was going to be such a grump. This was about as much fun as that meeting for Bill's memorial.

"You need any pasta?" Liz asked.

"I don't eat pasta," Matt said. "I eat noodles." And for good measure, he plopped a package of them into his corner of the shopping cart.

"This is going to be a great season," Jeremy was telling Matt. "I hit two homers in practice already. I'm ready to hit one in a game."

"You don't have to hit homers to have fun."

Well, at least with *her* he was in a lousy mood.

"Last year, I stunk. I was always making some stupid mistake. I'm going to be really good this year."

"Just relax and have fun," Matt said.

"Bread?" Liz asked.

He grabbed a loaf, but kept his eyes on Jeremy. "If you put too much pressure on yourself, you rarely do well and don't have any fun. You relax and you usually play better and have a good time doing it."

"I know, but—"

Matt laughed and rumpled Jeremy's hair. "Everybody wants to be the hero, I know."

"You coming to my game today?"

That stopped Matt, forced him to look up at her. "Uh..."

"He can, can't he, Mom?" Jeremy asked. "He could leave his groceries at our place and then pick them up after the game."

"Sure," Liz said. Jeremy wanted him at his game and that was enough for her.

"Great." Jeremy's speed with the shopping cart seemed to pick up. "This'll be super."

There wasn't much that she and Matt could do but be swept along by Jeremy's enthusiasm. They paid for their groceries, stored them at her apartment, then got out to the baseball field in record time, as if it were Jeremy's first game ever. Much to Liz's relief, Matt went off with the boy, allowing her to go over to the bleachers.

"Hi, Liz," the mother of one of Jeremy's teammates called out to her.

"Hello, Mary." Liz climbed the stands to sit next to Mary Quast. "How are you today?"

"Just fine, thank you. And yourself?"

"Okay." Aside from the fact that she was thoroughly sick of Michaelson men.

"Ready for another baseball season?"

"Yeah," Liz replied. "I guess."

"Hey. You get to sit outside in the sun and relax. It beats working."

"Yes, it does."

Though *relax* was not a word that came up in their house with the start of baseball season, or any sports season for that matter. Although Jeremy was a reasonable athlete, he would never be a star like his father. She didn't think it mattered and neither did his coaches, but it sure bothered him. Sports seasons were like one long roller-coaster ride.

"Looks like Jeremy is getting some last-minute advice from his uncle."

Liz looked over toward the far edge of the dugout where Matt was standing with his arm around Jeremy's shoulders. They both looked serious as Matt talked. Then Jeremy burst out laughing and they parted, with Matt giving her son a final slap on the back. A smile hung on his face as he went to warm up with a teammate.

"Whatever he said, it must have been funny," Mary said.

Liz nodded slowly. Obviously Matt had the magic touch that she didn't have. "Yeah."

"Jeremy sure enjoys having Matt around. I know he talks about him all the time."

A lump danced in Liz's throat, making speaking a bit hard. Jeremy didn't lack for male role models, but there seemed to be something special between him and Matt. Maybe it was the blood ties to his father. Maybe it was the similar way in which they looked at the world. Whatever it was, it was definitely there.

"Hey, Matt." Mary had stood up and was waving.

Liz sighed. There would be no space for her today—at least, not here at the game. But then, if she was sitting here and Matt somewhere else, she'd have to answer a million questions. Were they fighting? What was going on? Who was mad at who?

As if they weren't two people with two separate lives.

"Phew," he exclaimed as he dropped down by her side. "That's a rough road for a crippled old cop. Especially climbing up these bleachers."

She moved slightly to give him room, though not enough to keep his thigh from brushing hers. A flash of white heat coursed through her, stealing her breath for a second.

"You could have taken a seat down in the first row," she said.

He just looked at her a long moment, his eyes dark and mysterious. "I'm rather susceptible to loneliness," he said.

His hand was near and she wanted to slip hers into it. She wanted to feel the warmth of him seep all through her, melting the worries and fears that kept her from sleeping. She turned away to stare at the boys warming up on the field.

"Anyway," Matt said, "you were up here. No reason for me to stay down below."

Why in the world had she taken him to the sandwich shop that night? It was old Betsy's fault. That darn woman had messed up her love life, so she wanted to make everyone else in town miserable.

"Why did you come all the way up here, anyway?"

"I like sitting way up here," she said. "It's one of the few times in my life that I'm taller than most people."

"Ah, the true Liz. Power hungry."

She frowned at him, suspicious of his sudden joviality. "What happened to the grumpy old Gus from the grocery store?" she asked. "The 'I don't eat pasta' guy."

Matt just shrugged. "I remembered about catching flies."

"And am I a fly?"

"You are far too beautiful to be a fly."

She gave him a glare that was supposed to tell him she wasn't easily fooled, then turned to watch the kids and coaches milling around down on the field. The game was going to start soon, but with kids it always took a bit to get them in order. She watched Jeremy trot out to center field.

"He's a good kid," Matt said.

Liz forgave him his earlier moodiness. "I think so."

"You've done a hell of a job."

"It's a long way from done."

"I don't think you need to worry. There'll probably be a few bumps in the road, but you've laid a good foundation." He took her hand, squeezing it a moment. "And it really isn't all that long before the job is done."

"He's only eleven," Liz protested.

"Almost twelve."

Liz pulled her hand out of his. She didn't like looking at the future. She liked taking things one day at a time.

"Another ten years and he'll be a man," Matt said.

And she'd be alone. Liz wished the damned game would start so she could jump up and down and holler.

"I bet you have to admit that the past ten, twelve years have just zipped by."

She shrugged, staring hard at the infield. *Come on, guys. Play ball.*

"Time will go even faster now that things are downhill."

That was enough. Maybe she should go sit in the front row. And she should kick him out of her writing class. If he liked long, rambling discussions so much, he should be taking a philosophy class. "You're really a bundle of sunshine."

"Sorry." He took her hand, holding it lightly but firmly enclosed by his. "Cops tend to get that way. Or maybe it's genetic."

"I don't remember Bill being all that dark," Liz said.

His hand tightened around hers. "It's probably the eldest-brother syndrome then."

"Hey, folks. How are you two?" Reverend Bowles was making his way up the bleachers toward them.

What was this *folks* business? Were she and Matt an item now? That's all she needed, more pressure. And pressure from the whole damned town.

"Fine," they chorused. Wonderful, they even sounded like a couple.

Puffing slightly, the minister sat down next to Matt. "I had a chat with Mrs. Trager early this week," he said.

Matt's dark frown was building. Had the woman complained to the minister? Matt had never told Liz what he'd said to make the kids move their car.

"She appreciates your taking time to talk to her boys."

Now Matt looked bewildered. "I told them to move their damn car."

"Maybe it wasn't what you said as much as how you said it," the minister replied.

Matt shrugged.

Liz listened with interest. Since she'd stayed in the van she didn't know how he'd said what, but she did know the kids had moved out of the way, and fast.

"In either case you made an impression on the young lads. A positive impression, I should add."

Matt shrugged again. "They just needed someone to come on firm to them."

"They aren't the only ones who need that," Reverend Bowles said. "We have a number of young men and young ladies who lack direction these days. I guess a lot of parents are afraid to take a stand."

"Tell them they gotta, Reverend. They ain't got no choice."

"That's true," he said. "The parents do have responsibilities, but the community has to support them. You know, in Africa they have a saying that it takes the whole village to raise a child."

"Yeah," Matt grunted. "I heard that."

"So we still need our youth center."

"I imagine you do," Matt said, nodding.

"And we need a good man to run it."

"That's sex discrimination, isn't it?" Matt asked.

The minister smiled.

"I'm sure there are folks around who want to do that kind of thing," Matt said.

The minister stared at him for a long time. Then he stood up and patted Liz's shoulder. "I think right about now we could use your help."

The Reverend was being a tad obtuse, but she was no dummy. They wanted her to convince Matt to get involved. Right now, though, she didn't know what she wanted to do with Matt. She just wanted some space, some distance between them. She didn't want to get involved with anything or anybody.

"Play ball," came a voice from the field.

A great sigh escaped her body. She wanted to shout hallelujah, but settled for wrapping her arms around her knees and staring at the players on the field. She hoped that Jeremy would enjoy himself.

"Okay, there you go."

Jenny Hilliard had shown Liz how to thread the film through the lenses and was now getting up from the microfilm reader. A large class ring, hanging from a gold necklace chain, bounced on the high school girl's chest.

"And when you want a copy, you like press this button here. Then you pay for them at the front desk. The library charges you ten cents a copy."

"Thank you, Jenny." Liz sat down and settled herself in the seat the girl had just vacated.

"How come you want to look at stuff that's so old?"

Liz smiled. The newspaper was from 1948, yet Jenny made it sound as if Liz were trying to decipher hieroglyphics engraved on stone tablets. Apparently, to a high schooler, ancient history was what happened last year.

"I'm helping to put together a collage for Bill Michaelson's memorial service," Liz said. "It'll include things that Bill did, but I thought it would be nice to include other items. For example, Bill's father was also a star athlete back when he attended Stony Mountain High School."

"He's like dead, isn't he?"

"Actually, they both are."

Jenny nodded a few times, holding a solemn look tight to her face. Once she dropped that, her face quickly sprang back to its usual smiling, dimpled form. "So, where's Matt?" Jenny asked. "Like, what's he doing now?"

Liz was about to start paging through the old newspaper file, but her hand paused in midair. "Ah, like I'm not sure."

"I know where Drew is." The teenager fingered the ring hanging from her neck. "He's clerking at Luke Schiller's Gas and Grub."

Her first inclination was to tell Jenny that the girl *thought* she knew where Drew was, but remembering her own fragile emotional state back in high school, Liz decided that wouldn't be charitable. "We both have lives of our own," she said. "We don't keep track of each other."

"Uh-huh," Jenny said, a sly smile lighting up her face as she walked back to her place at the desk.

"Great." Liz could feel the muscles in her back tighten up as she hunched over the microfilm reader, and she knew it was from aggravation. Everyone in the whole damned town had her and Matt linked. "Damn you, Matt Michaelson," she muttered. "Why didn't you stay in Chicago?"

Fortunately, there was no one else in the microfilm room. Anyone hearing her talk to herself would think she was as addle-brained as old Betsy was rumored to be.

The newspaper pages dashed across the screen in front of her and, though she fought the impulse, Liz's mind drifted to Matt. Outside of a few little skirmishes, today had been pleasant. Matt had been a bit impatient at the grocery store, but had mellowed at the baseball game. Maybe he was finally understanding her need to go carefully.

She slowed the film down and saw that she was still in the summer of 1945. Another fast-forward spin and she'd be into the fall of the year. She was sure she'd find some stories or pictures of Bill and Matt's father. While he hadn't done anything as dramatic as Bill, he'd been the big star of his time, she'd been told.

She didn't remember much about Matt's involvement in athletics when he was in high school. Had he been just an average athlete? Maybe the Michaelson mystique had passed him by. That could be in his favor. Liz brought the microfilm to a screeching halt.

She was in September, so she started to page through more slowly, dropping down to a readable speed whenever she hit the sports news.

There were a couple of stories about Mr. Michaelson in 1945. And there were more in the following years, along with pictures of the teams. There were even a couple of action shots of him. She had a lot of good material for the collage.

She scanned the rest of 1948, then 1949. Just as her eyes were glazing over, she hit a Halloween story from 1950. Something about a haunted house. The picture looked familiar.

As she brought the article into focus, she saw that it was about old Betsy and the house where she'd lived. Matt's house. About Betsy's lost love, Willem, and how her ghost was said to live in the house and visit the train station. There was also a small mention of Willem's older brother, Matthias.

"Hey, Mom." Jeremy came rushing up to her side. Mike Quast was with him. "Can I stay overnight at Mike's? His mom said it was okay. She said I could come home with them now."

Liz wasn't sure what she could say with the two boys staring at her hopefully, but her heart softened at the shadows still lurking in Jeremy's eyes. He hadn't been the star of his baseball game as he'd hoped. Maybe a night out was just the thing.

"Sure," she said. "But what about your pajamas and clothes for tomorrow?"

"I got my key. We're gonna stop and pick stuff up." He plopped a book down on the desk next to her. "Here's the book on cats that Matt wanted. Can you drop it off for me?"

She looked at the book as if it were covered with spiders. "I guess."

But she had been through with Matt for the day. She'd withstood his smile and touch and his laughter. All right, not totally, since she found it necessary to do a little work on Bill's memorial to remind herself that men were untrustworthy, but she would be fine as long as she didn't have to see him again.

Once Jeremy and Mike had left, Liz worked some more on the collage, but she couldn't concentrate. The book was there, drawing her eyes and her thoughts. It was as if Matt had put some sort of spell on it.

She finally gave up and went home, but it was no easier to concentrate there. She changed the bed linens and cleaned the bathroom, but relaxation was miles away.

"I've got too much to do," she told the book as it silently called to her. "I can't just drop everything and go running over to his house every time he wants something."

But it was just easier to take the damn book over, then try to find ways to keep busy. She grabbed it up and marched out to the van. She'd drive there, give him the book and leave. Two minutes, tops.

Except that when she got there, Matt was in the middle of weeding his mother's old rose garden. It was so peaceful back there, so inviting, that she couldn't resist staying for a while and helping him. And then it seemed silly to rush home to eat dinner alone.

So they ate canned spaghetti sauce on noodles and then took glasses of wine out onto the porch to watch the sun go down. Liz closed her eyes and leaned against Matt's shoulder, relaxing when his arm came around her.

"Why'd you go to that stupid meeting for Bill's memorial?" Matt asked suddenly.

Liz turned to face him, hearing something in his voice and wanting to see if she could read it in his eyes. She couldn't. "Why shouldn't I go?" she asked.

"I didn't think you were interested."

She turned away, looking out to the river in the distance as it was disappearing into the dusk. It was always changing, moving, rushing ahead. She was always looking back where she'd been, wondering if she should have gone there.

"It seemed like the thing to do," she said. "He was Jeremy's father."

"You said you didn't love him anymore."

"I don't, but for years he was my best friend."

"It still seemed strange."

It had felt strange, too, but she wasn't going to admit that to him. It felt a little like dressing up in her old gym uniform and trying to go back to gym class. Even if the clothes fit, the times didn't anymore. Bill's accomplishments were in the past and didn't seem all that fantastic when matched up against the things all his peers had done since—raise their families, take care of aging parents, meet their responsibilities.

Yet the meeting had been a rousing success in reminding her to be wary of commitment. To avoid being part of someone's plan to rebuild themselves. To remember that some people's heroism only goes skin-deep.

"You going again?" Matt asked.

Liz just turned in his arms. "What is this—the Inquisition?" she asked as she grabbed at his waist to tickle him.

"Hey."

He grabbed for her, retaliation clearly in his fingertips, but the desire for it died suddenly as their gazes caught and held. The fire of the other night wasn't gone, wasn't even just smoldering, for it flared up with the heat and intensity of a raging inferno.

"Oh, Lizzie," Matt moaned, pulling her into his arms.

She didn't fight it. She couldn't have. The burning in her heart was beyond control. She pressed her lips to his and found all the wonders of the universe in his touch. Spring was bursting through her soul, bringing with it all the promises of life unfolding.

Matt's arms tightened around her, her breasts were crushed to his chest in delicious possession. She shared his hunger, shared his needs, shared his wild, tumultuous passion to feel the heights of love again. She ran her hands over his back, feeling the strength that would enfold her and delighting in the mystery of it.

"Want to go inside?" Matt asked. His voice was a mere whisper on the wind.

"Sure." Hers wasn't any stronger.

They got to their feet and walked, arm in arm, through the kitchen. They slowed in the hallway when their lips needed the other's. This wasn't like her, Liz told herself as she gasped for breath under the onslaught of Matt's kisses. She liked to think things through, make rational decisions. Yet she seemed incapable of decision-making when around him.

They made it to the bedroom, where suddenly everything seemed to slow. As if the last time they had made love too fast, this time they seemed ready to spend the rest of eternity making love. Moving as if in slow motion, they made their way over to the bed and lay down.

Matt unbuttoned her blouse slowly, letting his tongue slide over her neck, then her chest and finally the flat surface of her stomach. He loosened her bra and cupped her breasts with gentle hands as if she were something so precious and delicate she might break.

She let her hands roam under his shirt, feeling the mat of hair on his chest and relishing the tingly, tangly touch. With Matt's help, she pulled his shirt over his head and did her own exploring, tasting his chest and the rocklike muscles of his stomach. Her hands wanted more, as did her heart, which beat with longing and delight. She unbuckled his pants and slid them down, over his cast and onto the floor.

"I'll be so glad to get that thing off," he muttered when his pants caught on his cast.

"I see now," she said with a laugh. "You can't wait to be on top."

He grabbed her to him, his eyes intense with his yearnings. "The 'I can't wait' part is right," he murmured.

They tumbled over on the bed. Matt lay on her as his mouth devoured her. The room seemed so still, so waiting, as if a fuse had been set and all that was left was the explosion.

Matt's hands were roaming over her skin, pulling off her jeans and panties, bringing her heat to a ferocity to meet his. They were so right together, so perfect. As if they'd been waiting all their lives for this moment. All eternity.

Then suddenly she took him in her, pulling the heat and fire and passion from his heart to join with hers in a conflagration of love. They held, they moved, they breathed the magic words of wonder and marveled at the oneness of their souls.

When the heavens could take them no higher, soft clouds brought them back to earth, but the embrace was no less sweet. Liz felt Matt's heart slow to near normal, and she smiled in her heart that a few moments in time could hold so much joy. She closed her eyes and cuddled even closer.

Matt's lips brushed her forehead, then her cheek, then found her lips in a kiss of sweet union and promise. The world was still and she was safe in Matt's embrace. When she heard his even breathing beside her, she let her own soul relax even more. It was how it should be, she thought, as she felt drowsiness overcome her.

Chapter Eleven

The phone exploded in sound, filling the silence of Matt's kitchen. He snatched up the receiver before the first ring was anywhere near done. "Yeah?"

"It's me. I'm home."

It had been less than fifteen minutes since Liz's sweet tones last danced on his eardrums, but he reached out for her with every molecule in his body, like a thirsty desert wayfarer plunging into the cool springs of an oasis.

"All safe and sound?"

"And reporting in as ordered, sir."

"Good." He let the smile in his heart climb up on his face. "You're going to work out real well."

There was a dead silence on the line. He couldn't even discern her breathing. Uh-oh. That was a whoops.

"I mean, you follow orders real good."

"I know what you mean, fella. And at the moment, you're skipping around on some very thin ice."

Wow. That ice might be thin, but it felt cold enough to bring on a nuclear winter. "How about we call my words a joke?"

"How about we call them pathetic?" Liz said.

"I can work with that," he replied.

Another block of silence seized the line, but this one was pleasant, like an early summer's morning.

"I need to get to sleep," Liz said. "Otherwise I'll look like a haggard old lady and my kid will beat me to death with his questions."

All things that wouldn't have happened if she'd stayed with him, but he'd probably pushed her enough for now. "Okay," Matt said. "Sleep tight."

"Good night, Matt."

But he couldn't just let her go like that. Not after all they'd shared and not with the swell of emotion freezing up his heart.

"Oh, Liz." For a moment his vocal chords froze up, but only for the briefest of moments. He was a man and ready to take the risk of getting shot down. "I really care about you."

Then he held his ground—and his breath—listening to the silence slowly walk to the edge of eternity.

"You're special to me, too, Matt," she said, then hung up.

Her voice had been light, almost a whisper, but the words had been clear. She cared about him!

He wanted to sing, but that would only wake up the crows. He wanted to dance, but his bum leg wouldn't let him. He wanted to fill Liz's ear with words of sweet love, but he wasn't some damn poet. So all he did was bask in the music of the dial tone and realize he was the luckiest man in the whole world.

He'd proclaimed his love for his lady and she'd returned it. He hung up also, bursting with excitement, wanting to shout the news to all of creation.

Soft fur polishing his ankles and a demanding meow told Matt that his roommate was awake. An audience.

"I told her I loved her and she said she loved me," he told Rosie. "You know what that means, don't you?"

Rosie's reply sounded rather cynical—her instant of bliss would be leaving her with a swarm of little babies to raise by herself. But Matt was too happy to be brought down by Rosie's gloom.

"Want an early breakfast?" he asked.

The cat jumped up on the countertop as Matt took a can of cat food out of the cupboard.

"What did the doctor say about jumping up on countertops?"

Rosie just purred.

"I could put your dish on the floor, you know."

The cat yowled, which Matt deciphered as "Shut up and put out the damn grub." He followed her orders, and she was soon slurping up a generous serving of turkey giblets and bacon. Matt pulled up a stool, sitting down to watch her.

"Liz stayed over for most of the night. It was nice having her here."

Rosie barely paused in her eating to glance at him.

"I would think you'd like having another female around the house."

She chose not to answer.

Maybe Rosie didn't care, but Matt sure would have liked another female around. One female in particular. And he didn't want her just visiting. He wanted her taking up permanent residence.

Matt got up from the stool and walked over to the sink, leaning forward to look out the window that faced to the east. When Liz had left for home, it had still been dark and there were only a few chirps from the early birds. Now they had themselves a full chorus going.

The sun was creeping up over the horizon and it was getting lighter. A slight mist hung down over by the river, but the air smelled so fresh and clean. How could he have stayed buried in the soot and smog of a big city for so long? He was glad he had finally come to his senses and returned to the clean air of home. Now that he'd taken care of his location, there were other things that needed fixing in his life.

Liz spending part of the night here had worked out all right this time, but it wasn't something he wanted to do for the rest of his life. In fact, he didn't really want to play this stealth game too many more times.

Stony Mountain was a small town and, most likely, tongues were already wagging, but most folks were tolerant. For now. But if he and Liz went on like this for too long, it would bother more than a few folks. Mostly because of Jeremy.

And Matt agreed. It wouldn't be fair to Jeremy to play fast and loose with his mother. Heck, the kid had enough of a load to carry with a father who'd never bothered to see him. No, there was only one thing for Matt to do.

A quiver of fear ran through his stomach again, along with that cold chill down his back. The same one that came when he'd told Liz that he loved her. But this one was going to be tougher. He wanted Liz to marry him.

But the caveman days were gone. One didn't just drag a lady out here and pose the question. A guy had to have the proper atmosphere.

Resolve filled Matt's heart. He was going to put the whole package together. Food, wine, himself. He was going to woo and win his lady.

"Hey, Rosie." He went into the living room, looking for the cat. "We got some planning to do."

Liz wasn't certain about any of this. Sure, she and Matt had had a great time Saturday night, and she hadn't woken up yesterday morning in a panic, even though Matt had said he cared about her. After all, what did that mean? That they were friends who had just shared a passionate few hours?

But still, as she drove to his house for dinner on Monday, she had to remind herself that no one was trying to put walls around her, least of all herself. She was free to come and go as she pleased, whenever she pleased, even if Matt had tried to play Mr. Macho by sending Luke over to pick her up.

She pulled into Matt's drive and braked her van as Matt was coming down from his porch. The look on his face was darker than the thunderclouds in a summer's storm.

"What going on?" he demanded. "Where's Luke?"

"I sent him home." Liz stepped down from the van. "There was no reason why I couldn't drive out here myself." This wasn't different from any of their other dates.

"I set it up with Luke to drive you."

Liz sighed. He was determined to play his macho game. "Luke had some deliveries to make."

"That's not my problem," Matt said. "I already paid him."

"Fine," Liz snapped. She should have just stayed home and watched TV with Jeremy. "I'll give you your money back. How much did you pay him?"

"That's not the point."

"I agree," Liz said. "The point is I like taking care of myself."

"I didn't say you can't."

She was ready to match his sour look with one of her own. "It doesn't matter what you say. I like being able to come and go as I please."

The anger seemed to slip away from his face, leaving what looked like hurt. Her irritation left, too, so now guilt nagged at her. He was just trying to play his role in this dating routine; not being able to drive made that even harder.

"Why don't we start over?" Liz said. "I believe you invited me here for dinner?"

He nodded. "Yeah, I did." He gave her his arm. "This way, madam."

She allowed him to lead her up the stairs, then waited as he opened the door for her.

"Thank you," she murmured, stepping in.

"At this point, I'd take your coat."

She stared at him. Something wasn't right. Glancing around the kitchen, she thought it seemed different somehow. Nothing appeared to be out of place. It was just a feeling.

"Was I supposed to wear a coat?" The words stammered and stumbled over her tongue. She looked down at her usual jeans-and-shirt outfit, then back at Matt. He wasn't wearing a coat, but he did have on a dress shirt. "Was this supposed to be formal? I didn't even think to ask."

"Oh, no," he assured her. "You look fine. Better than fine."

Matt seemed nervous. That wasn't at all like him.

Liz looked around the kitchen again. The cat's dish was on the counter and little else. Everything was the same as usual. Well, not quite the same. Things looked a little neater than usual. Maybe a lot neater, she thought as a delicious smell wafted by her nose.

Delicious smell? Matt's cooking consisted of boiling hot dogs and sticking a frozen dinner in the microwave.

"Did you cook tonight?" she asked.

His eyes shifted around as if he were a little boy caught with his hand in the cookie jar. "Not really."

"Then what smells so good?" she asked.

"Come on," he said, taking her arm. "We better eat before the food gets cold."

As he pulled her along, Liz noticed that the kitchen table was bare. Were they going to eat in the living room and watch television? That would be a trick since there was only one chair there as of last Saturday.

"Here we are," Matt said as they entered the dining room.

"You've got dining room furniture," she said, feeling like one of those cartoon characters who'd had an anvil fall on their head. This room had been totally bare Saturday.

"What do you think?"

And it wasn't just a dining table and chairs. A white linen cloth was spread over the table, candles in silver holders graced the center alongside a low vase of red roses, a bottle of wine in an ice bucket was off to one side, and there was china—real china—to eat off of. No, an anvil wasn't enough to cause this hallucination. It had to be a piano—a grand piano.

"We can send it back if you want," he said.

"Huh?"

"If you don't care for the furniture," Matt explained. "You don't like it, the stuff is gone."

Liz could only stare at him. What difference did it make whether she liked the furniture or not?

"I know you women like to pick things out yourself, but I wanted dinner to be special tonight. So this stuff is sort of temporary."

Pick things out herself? An uneasy, gut-wrenching feeling twisted Liz's empty stomach. "Did you get the furniture just for tonight?"

"Sort of."

He was grinning—the same grin Jeremy wore when she'd opened his Mother's Day present. Liz was sure it had been a good idea to drive herself out to Matt's farm. Damn sure. "And you cooked a whole meal?"

"Sort of."

Liz gave him her best "don't mess with Mommy" look.

"I called Delaney's Catering and told Connie I wanted a really nice meal for two."

She sighed, her stomach tightening even more. There was nothing wrong with boiled hot dogs. They were great. They were delicious. They were her favorite date meal.

"Hey, I had to tell them what I wanted." Matt seemed to take her silence as a reprimand. "That's like doing the planning. All Connie had to do was heat the stuff up." Then he spun quickly on his good leg, pulling out a chair. "Come on, sit down."

Liz hesitated for a moment. She considered taking flight, but that would have been cowardly. And the smells reminded her how hungry she was. She took her seat.

Before he joined her at the table, Matt dashed to the side of the room to turn on some music. She hadn't noticed the new stereo until now, but said nothing as he came back to

fill both their wineglasses. They were crystal, not depart-
ment-store glasses. Liz glared at Matt as he sat down and
raised his glass to her.

"To us," he said.

"You're going to a lot of trouble just to get me into bed,"
Liz said. "I mean, at this point in our friendship—" she
stressed the word *friendship* "—all you have to do is ask."

His features tightened for a moment, but after taking a sip
of his wine, he just began serving.

The meal was one of Connie Delaney's usual master-
pieces. Chicken breasts stuffed with deviled ham and
smothered in a champagne sauce. Wild rice and glazed car-
rots. The salad was made with Boston lettuce and accom-
panied by blue-cheese dressing. Liz fought a good fight, but
found her defenses relaxing.

Once they'd finished the chocolate mousse, Matt leaned
back and cleared his throat. "You remember how I told you
that cops don't make good husbands?"

"Mmm." She wasn't interested in cops or husbands, but
she wouldn't mind topping off the evening with a little cud-
dling.

"Well, I'm not a cop anymore," he said.

"Nope, you're not," Liz replied. A bell of some sort was
ringing in the back of her mind, but she ignored it. Should
they do the dishes or the snuggling first?

"I'm a new man," he said. "Solid and dependable. A
stand-up kind of a guy."

Liz smiled at him. "You do good lying down, too."

"Liz," he said, "I'm being serious."

The bell in her head clanged even louder. "I don't want
to be serious," she said, taking his hands in hers. "Not tonight."

Matt pulled his hands free so that he could wrap them
around hers. "Liz, I love you."

The bell turned into a siren. She tried to yank her hands
free, her heart free. "Matt, I—"

"Will you marry me?"

"No!" she cried and jumped to her feet. Her heart was racing as if she'd just run a marathon. Or escaped the clutches of a nightmare.

He looked stunned. "But we love each other. We—"

"What do you mean, we love each other?" she cried. "We're friends. We enjoy each other's company. That's not love."

"It is for me," he said.

"No, it's not." She couldn't believe he was doing this, that he was wrecking the friendship they'd built. "Love is something totally different. You don't love me and I don't love you."

He was on his feet now, too. "You're afraid because of the past. I can understand that, but you have to trust me. I won't leave you."

The scent of the roses wafted over her, so strong that she felt as if she were drowning in them. Her stomach churned. She had to get out of here.

"It has nothing to do with the past," she said. She grabbed hold of the chair back to steady herself. "I'm talking about who we are now."

"But that's just it," he said. "I'm a new person. I'm starting all over and I want you to be a part of my new life."

"No, you're running away from who you are and trying to be something you're not. Just like Bill."

"I'm not Bill."

"And I'm not so stupid and weak anymore," she said. "You don't have the faintest idea what love is. You just want all the trappings that you've missed up to now. You've got the house and the cat and now you need the wife and kid. Only I'm not ready to force-fit myself into someone else's family portrait. Been there. Done that."

"Liz."

But she had already turned and was fleeing out the door. For once, she was thankful for his bad leg. She was able to make it to the van and had the motor running before he was barely out the back door. With a roar from her bad muffler, she turned and sped out the drive, not even noticing she was crying until the tears soaked through her blouse.

"Damn you, Matt Michaelson. Why did you have to ruin everything?"

The scent of the roses was the only answer.

Matt glared around as Luke Schiller put his cab into the parking spot in front of the hardware store. The street was filled with cars, except for this spot right before Liz's front door.

"What the hell are we doing here?"

The big man should have been worried, but he just grinned. "This is where we're meeting tonight," Luke replied. "Guess I forgot to tell you."

Matt felt his insides melt in disgust. It sure didn't take him long to lose it. Good thing he wasn't on the force anymore; he probably wouldn't be able to hand out a ticket to a kid on a tricycle without getting a lot of lip.

"Yeah, I guess you did."

The cab rocked as Luke got out and opened Matt's door for him. "What's the matter?" Luke asked, as he waited for Matt to get out. "You and Liz had yourselves some words?"

"Don't see where that's any of your damn business."

"I agree with you," Luke replied, his smile growing bigger. "I was just curious."

"Didn't you hear that curiosity killed the cat?" Matt said.

"Yeah. But what the heck, all of us gotta go sometime or other. And satisfying your curiosity just makes life more interesting."

It looked as if the best way to bury the conversation was to ignore it. He quietly followed Luke up the stairs to Liz's apartment.

He really hadn't wanted to get involved in this group. And certainly not after the fiasco the day before yesterday with Liz, but Luke had insisted. Said there were things that had to be finalized.

Suddenly a dark cloud descended on Matt's head. He hoped this wasn't some stupid high school trick to get him and Liz to patch things up. He didn't know about anybody else in this damn town, but he wasn't into those kinds of games anymore.

Matt held his breath as Luke battered the door. It was quickly opened and Liz stood there, a radiant smile on her face. His heart fell down into his shoes. He was hoping she would look a little down, as if she missed him, as if she were regretting her words of the other night. But she looked on top of the world.

Maybe she'd lied. Maybe she did still love Bill and that was why she couldn't love Matt.

"Hi, Lizzie," Luke said.

"Hello, Luke." She nodded at Matt. "Matt."

The living room was full of people. Happy people. Friendly people, sitting around and chatting with each other. Matt wondered how long they'd stay happy once he started whacking at them with his cane. He looked around for a place to sit.

"We saved a place for you, Matt," Cindy Schiller called out, grinning like the devil welcoming a sinner to hell. "Right here next to Liz."

The voices in the room quieted for a moment while the smile wattage went up. Matt fought to keep from gagging. And he'd been worried that folks might try to pull some high school nonsense on him. Hell, this was barely junior high.

Unfortunately, there was no other seat available. He didn't really want to stand for long, and his bum leg wouldn't let him get down to the floor gracefully. He sat in his appointed seat.

While Liz flitted about the room playing at being the good hostess, Matt sat and glared at the far wall. He dared anyone to talk to him. Even someone as big as Luke.

Unfortunately, no one took him up on it. And it didn't take long before he was bored almost out of his mind.

"Hi, Matt."

He'd planned on biting off the head of the first person who spoke to him, but found he couldn't. "Hi, Jeremy."

"How are things?" Jeremy asked. "I haven't seen you around."

"Things are a little busy right now," Matt replied. "I have to get to Chicago in a few days."

"And when you get back you won't limp anymore."

Matt smiled. "I'll probably need some physical therapy. But I'm getting there."

"Cool." Jeremy nodded, and his eyes darted around the room for a moment. "Want some cookies? Just about everybody brought some."

"Not now, thanks," Matt said. "Maybe later."

They both saw Liz coming their way. Jeremy gave a quick nod and a "Catch you later" before dashing into the kitchen for his cookie sampling. Matt's own feelings of goodwill quickly disappeared as Liz sat down next to him. There really was no reason for her to be aggravated with him. It was normal for a man to want to marry the woman he loved.

"Okay, folks." Luke Schiller was standing in the middle of the room. "Let's get to business. Abe's got some figures for the new scoreboard to pass around, and Kate's got some ideas for the fund-raising."

Matt took a quick glance at Liz. Her back was as stiff and uncompromising as it was the other night. He could taste the sourness in his stomach. The way she acted, it was as if he'd committed some kind of foul, unspeakable act instead of asking to love and care for her the rest of her natural life.

"What we hope," Luke said, "is to raise the money this summer and get the new scoreboard in place for the homecoming game in early October."

But Matt was barely listening. He was sure Bill would have been pleased with the honor. On the other hand, it was kind of sad that the only thing he'd accomplished had been on a high school playing field almost fifteen years ago.

"Terry has offered to make up a special program for the game that'll include stuff about Bill, and Liz and Cindy are putting together the collage to hang in the school."

Matt just watched as Liz spoke. Maybe she wasn't afraid of the past. Maybe there was no past. Maybe it was all still the present for her.

"Matt."

He started as if awakened from a deep sleep.

"Matt," Luke said, "we were wondering where Bill was buried."

"Buried?" Matt fought to clear the cobwebs from his mind. "You mean his body?"

"Uh, yeah," Luke replied. "His body. We want to have a picture of his grave site in the program."

Matt could feel Liz looking at him and his collar growing a tad tight. "Uh, well, I had him cremated, and Liz and I were thinking about having some kind of ceremony around—"

"I imagine if you asked Bill," Luke said, "he'd say just bury him at the fifty-yard line."

"Yeah," someone else said. "I think he would have been happy to stay on that field forever."

The laughter drifted into chatter, but all Matt could see was the soft smile on Liz's face. No doubt from looking back into the past at perfect Bill. How could she forget his abandonment all of a sudden?

Matt got up to go into the kitchen. Jeremy was doing his homework at the kitchen table. Matt sank down in the chair next to him.

Jeremy looked up at him. "Dumb meeting, huh?" His voice said he still had a ways to go in coming to terms with his father.

"Maybe, maybe not," Matt said as he reached over for a chocolate cookie on a tray on the table. He tried to separate his feelings for Liz from his feelings about Bill. "I think it's nice that they're going to honor him, but it's sad that they have to do it for something he did a long time ago."

Jeremy went back to his math. "Hey, what'd he do since then that was worth talking about?"

"That's just it," Matt said softly. "That's the saddest part. He must have figured that nothing he'd ever do would measure up to that moment when he won the championship. Imagine figuring that you peaked at eighteen and that it'd all be failure after that. What a load to carry."

Jeremy just stared at him.

"I bet he never came back because he didn't have any stories to tell that could top the championship, and he figured that he'd lose the respect of the town."

"That's crazy," Jeremy said.

Matt shrugged. "Maybe. Some people would think he'd failed, but to some people I imagine he'll always be a hero."

Through the kitchen door, he could see Liz, sitting so still and alone. No matter what she said, Matt was sure her heart still belonged to Bill.

Chapter Twelve

"Honey, you're drowning this poor lettuce." Darci pushed the dish of garden salad toward Liz. "Not to mention that I don't even like French dressing."

Liz stared at the plate. It looked like she'd poured the dressing on with a soup ladle. "Sorry, Darci. I'll get you another serving." She hurried away, not giving the woman a chance to talk.

She dumped the salad in the garbage. Then, concentrating very hard and forcing her reluctant muscles to move, Liz prepared another dish of salad. She listed the steps in her mind.

Get a clean plate, pile on the lettuce, add a tomato and cucumber. Put on a few extra cucumbers because Darci likes them. Then top the whole thing off with a small thimble of ranch dressing on the side. Finally with slow, measured steps, and careful not to drop anything, deliver the serving.

"Thanks, honey," Darci said.

"You're welcome." Liz breathed a sigh of relief, glad she didn't flub anything else. "And I'm sorry about the screw-up. I guess I'm just not myself today."

Darci put some lettuce in her mouth and, as she chewed, gave Liz a sardonic look. "Honey," she said, "if you have a good man, you do everything you can to keep him healthy and happy. If he ain't no good, then dump him and forget about him."

Liz just tried to smile. Oh, Lord. Everyone was on her case. Jeremy. Jan. Her father. And that silly little game of making her and Matt sit next to each other that everyone played at the meeting last night. It seemed as if everybody in the whole damned town knew what was good for her. Nobody seemed interested in her opinion, though.

"It really isn't all that simple," Liz said.

"Life is as simple or complex as you make it," Darci replied.

Some people had a sharp retort for everything, a talent Liz envied. She'd always been one of those who had to think things through first, had to analyze the situation and figure out whose feelings were involved.

This thing with Matt had been moving just too damn fast. They needed time with each other. They needed to search out and study each other's motivations. Marriage wasn't something a person just jumped into, like a cool lake on a hot day. She'd done that once and had the scars to prove it.

"Liz, could I have a refill?" Larry Veldeman held up his coffee cup.

"Excuse me," Liz murmured to Darci, then dashed over to give Larry his coffee. "There you go," she said.

"Thank you, ma'am."

Liz lingered by Larry as he sipped his coffee. It was more comfortable by him. Men were different from women. They didn't worry as much about other people's personal affairs, especially no-nonsense guys like Larry.

"Say, Liz," Larry said. "What did you do to Matt?"

"I—" she stammered. "What do you mean? I haven't done anything to him. Why are you asking me?"

"Boy's walking around with his jaw down to his navel," Larry said. "Looks like a hound dog that's forgot where he buried his favorite bone."

It wasn't her fault. Liz wanted to jump up on the counter and scream for everyone's attention. She wanted to tell them it wasn't her fault that Matt was moping around. She wanted to point out that she had never encouraged his marriage proposal. Not in any way.

"I—I don't know what's wrong with Matt."

"Aw, come on, Liz. You and him are as close as two peas in a pod."

"We're two free and independent people, Larry. Neither of us owns the other."

"He's a good man, Liz. Always has been."

It was no use. Folks here had paired the two of them together and, like back in junior high, there was no separating. Their relationship was worse than being married. If they were married and wanted to separate, they could get a divorce. The way things were now, the only option was death.

"Let me know if you need anything else," Liz said before she hurried away to clear some dishes from the other end of the counter.

Liz spent the rest of the lunch hour being very, very busy. She was brisk and efficient. No sooner did a drop of coffee spill and the counter was cleaned. She straightened all the menus. No one lacked for her attention. She was exceptionally efficient, and neighborly and charming. Inquiring about people's children, their pets, how they felt about the weather. Like Bill always used to say when he played football, the best defense was a good offense. She was sorry when the last lunch customer left.

"You're going to rub that counter clean through," Jan said.

"Would you prefer that I left it dirty?"

"I would prefer that you left it in usable shape," Jan replied. "You wear it thin and we'll have to get a new one."

"Ha, ha."

"Not sure we can afford a totally new countertop," Jan said.

"Don't you have anything else to do?" Liz asked.

"Want a bite to eat?"

Liz wasn't really hungry, but if she didn't give Jan something to do, her sister would just hang around being annoying. "How about a grilled cheese?"

"With a tomato?" Jan asked.

"Yeah."

Instead of going back to the kitchen to fix their lunch, Jan stood in the doorway looking at her. "You're going to have to straighten things out sometime," Jan said.

"It's my life," Liz cried, "and I just want everyone to stay out of it."

Jan looked away and stared out the front windows for a long moment. When she turned back to face her, Liz stiffened.

"You want to make some milk shakes?" was all Jan asked.

"Sure." Relief rushed in so quickly that it made Liz feel light-headed. "I'd like that."

Jan stepped into the kitchen and Liz hurried to make the milk shakes. She put two scoops each in the tall metal glasses, then milk and the flavoring. Chocolate for Jan, strawberry for herself. Then she put them on to churn.

Crossing her arms over her chest, Liz listened to the drone and looked at nothing. She didn't want to marry Matt. Right now, she didn't want to marry anybody. And maybe she never would.

She just wanted Matt to be her special friend, her lover. But it didn't look as if he were going to give her that option. Men. Damn their hides. They were so stubborn. The mixer stopped, and Liz removed the containers from the machine and poured the contents into tall glasses.

"Hello, dear."

Liz jumped, almost spilling the shakes. "For heaven's sake, Mother. Don't sneak up on people like that."

"How would you like me to sneak up, dear?"

Liz sighed. "I'm not in the mood for corny jokes." She went back to filling the milk-shake glasses.

"That's rather obvious," her mother said. "You don't look to be in the mood for anything pleasant."

Liz gritted her teeth and concentrated on laying the mixing cups in the sink. She didn't want a lecture from her mother, either.

"I got you a present, dear."

Liz turned slowly, suspicious but not wanting to be rude. There was a plant on the counter. Her eyes took in the small violet flower, and her whole body stiffened. It was an African violet.

"I got you one to start your collection," her mother said, sugar dripping from each word. "I'll get you more as the years go by."

Liz didn't say anything.

"And when Matt's cat has her kittens—" her mother's face just glowed with a nasty smile "—I'll get you several of those."

Matt walked into his office and sat down, but instead of turning on his computer, he just stared at it. It sat there, blank and lifeless, just like his heart.

"Ah, the hell with it." He got up and walked to the window to look out on his country acres. Today, that didn't bring him any more joy or contentment than his blank computer screen.

He tried focusing on the surroundings, fighting hard to prevent any other thoughts from entering his mind, but that quickly led him to his well of depression. Mother Nature made the surrounding fields green and vibrant.

Obviously that was what his computer needed. Somebody who could put words into it that would bring the machine to life. Create stories that would move people. The only place his writing moved people was to sleep.

Rosie came into the room and hopped up onto the windowsill, where she sat and shared his view with him. His hand dropped down to scratch her ears. "How are you, Big Momma?"

The cat was getting bigger. Matt guessed that her family would be here in another week or two. He'd need to set up a box and stuff to handle the babies when they came. Then, as soon as he knew how many kittens there were, he'd have to start looking for homes.

"How about once is enough?" he asked. "Huh, old girl?"

Purring noisily, she leaned back against his stomach. He hoped it wouldn't bother Rosie to be fixed, but he had to admit that he didn't know how or what female cats thought about things. Hell, he didn't know how any kind of female thought about anything.

"I don't know what else I should have done, Rosie."

The cat's purring didn't give him an answer, nor did he expect any.

"I thought I did everything by the book."

He let his hand move down to scratch the cat's back.

"I tried to be understanding, loving, strong, sensitive. I mean, the whole nine yards. No ifs, ands or buts. But what good did it do me?"

Rosie gave him her universal answer, a steady, vibrating purr.

"Nothing," Matt said. "Not a single damn thing."

The rejection was bad enough, but even worse was Liz's whole attitude. She didn't give him one of those "I don't think so's." Oh, no. She had to give him one of her "absolutely, no damned way, even if hell freezes over" kind of answers. Obviously, she didn't want him to carry any misconceptions.

"But," Matt said, "looking at things from her perspective, I guess Liz felt she had to do it that way."

Boy, talk about misconceptions. He had them all.

He thought that they were attracted to each other, that they understood each other, that they shared common values. All in all, that they really liked each other.

But hell, what guy wouldn't? They enjoyed being with each other. They enjoyed talking. They were more than comfortable in bed. And her kid even liked him. Actually, as it turned out, her kid liked him a lot more than she did.

"The only thing I'm successful at is being a flop," Matt said, looking down at the cat. "I can't write anything except my name on a check. And I don't understand women at all."

A rap at the door grabbed his attention, and Matt looked at his watch. That couldn't be Luke. Matt's train for Chicago didn't leave for another three hours.

He'd be back in a few days, minus the cast on his knee. That would make him more able than he now was, but he doubted it would make any difference with Liz. As far as he could gather, the lady thought he was a *mental* misfit.

"Hey, Matt. Where are you?"

"It's our little buddy," he told Rosie as he turned toward the door. "In here, Jeremy," he called out.

The soft padding of sneaker-clad feet announced Jeremy before he stepped into the room.

"How did you get out here?" Matt asked.

"Biked."

"Are you allowed to do that?"

"Yeah," Jeremy replied, "I do it all the time. Ronnie Balmer lives near here." He stopped and frowned. "Your computer's off. Aren't you doing anything with it?"

"It told me it was tired. So I'm giving it the day off."

The kid's face told Matt that better liars than him had tried—without success—to shuck him.

"You're not writing anymore, are you?"

"I'm going to concentrate on grocery lists for awhile."

Jeremy moved over to stand by the computer. He caressed the top of the monitor, almost like Matt caressed his cat. The kid was really comfortable with the electronic marvel. That was good. The way the future looked, he'd *have* to be to make it.

"You always tell me I shouldn't quit, that I shouldn't get down on myself," Jeremy said. "How come *you* can?"

Matt considered telling Jeremy he was an adult. And adults could quit anytime they wanted. But he didn't really believe that.

"I think I said you shouldn't quit *easily*."

The kid shrugged. "It's the same thing."

"Not quite." Rosie jumped off the windowsill and went off on some other business. Matt leaned back and sat on the space she'd vacated. "There's a fine line between stubborn and stupid. You have to give things a chance, but don't hang on when things don't fit you."

"Like baseball doesn't fit me."

From the pain in the boy's eyes, it was obvious that these were demons he'd fought before.

"Sorry I didn't get to the game yesterday," Matt said.

"It don't matter." Jeremy shrugged. "I stunk."

"You might have had a bad day. Sometimes you just have to work it through."

"Did my father ever have bad days?"

Matt hesitated. Like everyone else in town, he saw Bill as a superstar, but Bill must have had some poor days, too. Everybody did. It's just that he had so few nobody remembered. Or what was a bad day for Bill would have been a good day for most other people. "Everybody does, Jeremy."

He remembered Bill's dingy little room back in Chicago. Remembered that Bill had been working as a short-order cook. Bill, who was ranked first in his graduating class. How he never visited Stony Mountain. Most likely because he was ashamed to.

"He had his share of disappointments," Matt said. "It all evens out in the end."

Jeremy rubbed the top of the monitor some more. "Mom didn't come to my game, either." He shrugged again. "She had her class."

Matt suddenly felt very tired, tired and old. It seemed that whenever adults had a disagreement, anything from divorce to war, children suffered. "I screwed up yesterday. But from now on, I'll come to all your games."

"You don't have to . . . if you don't want."

"I want to," Matt said.

"If it works out," Jeremy said casually. "I mean, if your writing is going good, you really shouldn't quit."

Matt laughed. "My writing career is DOA. It's time to bury it."

"You're not going to write anymore?"

"Nope."

"Mom said you weren't at class last night."

Matt turned his head slightly and looked over his shoulder. Thunderclouds were gathering in the west. Looked like it was going to rain.

Making the decision to quit writing was easy. It was a silly little whim, anyway. Not going to class anymore was a little harder. He sure was going to miss his teacher. Miss their little drives when she brought him home.

"The semester is almost over," Matt said.

"Yeah." Jeremy nodded. "But that doesn't mean you have to stop seeing Mom. She's in a lot better mood when you're around."

Confusion churned in Matt's mind. He and Liz had had fun together. Had he pushed this marriage thing too fast or was she still carrying a torch for Bill? He was getting a headache.

"You ought to be heading home, kid. Looks like we got ourselves a storm coming."

"I've gotten wet before," Jeremy said.

"That's nice." He walked over and put an arm on Jeremy's shoulder. "But your mom might be worrying about you."

"I'll look in on Rosie while you're in Chicago."

"The Wilsons are going to do that," Matt said. "But I think she'd like having you around, too."

They walked out of Matt's office and through the living room, where Jeremy paused to look at the urn on the mantel.

"You gonna bury him on the football field?" Jeremy asked.

"No," Matt said with a laugh. "That wouldn't go over real well. Your dad will be buried alongside our mom and dad."

Jeremy nodded as they made their way into the kitchen, where it was Matt's turn to stop. "Hey, I got something for you." He went into the pantry and pulled out an old fishing pole.

"Cool," Jeremy said.

"It was your dad's," Matt said slowly, hoping the light in the boy's eyes wouldn't dim.

It did. But didn't go out completely. "He like to fish?"

Matt nodded. "Yeah, I guess he did. I never thought about it, but I guess he did."

"I do, too," Jeremy said. "It's cool just being outside and waiting, even if you don't catch anything."

Matt eyed him strangely. "That's just what your dad thought, I was told."

"Oh, yeah?" The boy's voice was uncertain.

"You want to leave it here for now?" Matt asked.

Jeremy nodded and put the rod back in the pantry, but with a hesitation about him that belied his earlier anger with Bill. Maybe some progress was being made, Matt thought. They went out on the porch.

"What are you going to do now that you ain't writing?" Jeremy asked.

Matt looked around and sniffed the air. That old storm was coming in fast. He shook his head. "I'm probably going to run the Stony Mountain Youth Center."

"You think you'll like that?"

"I think so."

"I heard some people say it'll be a hard job."

Matt shrugged. "Life ain't no fun unless you got yourself a mountain or two to climb."

Matt followed Jeremy out onto the porch where he stopped to lean against a post and watch Jeremy dash over to his bike. He was a good kid. A special kid to Matt. But there were a lot of good kids in Stony Mountain. He was going to have fun shaping them up. Watching them grow into men. It would be a lot more fun if he had a partner, but—

"Matt?"

"Yeah, kid?"

"When you gonna visit my mom? She misses you, you know."

Matt's eyes wavered and he looked out over the fields. Sometimes kids wanted something so bad they believed it was right even if it wasn't. You probably needed a bunch of gray hairs before you accepted that.

"When I get back from Chicago."

The wind tore in from the west, moaning up in the eaves of the old train station. One of those warm weather squalls was coming in. Liz looked up toward the roof for a moment, then up and down Main Street. Little bugs of worry fluttered around in her stomach.

"Boy, will you listen to old Betsy howl?" Jan stepped into the street by her side, smiling fondly. "Sounds like she's telling us to head for high ground."

Liz nodded. Most of the time the lake squalls were just heavy showers that didn't last all that long, but the darkness in the sky said that today's storm was going to be more.

"Where did you say Jeremy went?" Liz asked.

"I told you. He went to visit Matt."

"You shouldn't have let him go."

"Matt's his uncle," Jan replied. "Besides, they're good friends."

Liz looked away. Jan didn't have to finish anything for her. What she meant was Jeremy and Matt were good friends before Liz and Matt got into their little snit, so there was no reason they shouldn't stay good friends.

"I'm worried about the weather."

"They weren't forecasting this when he left."

That wasn't unusual. Sometimes these storms came up quicker than the weather service could react.

"I'm not blaming you," Liz explained. "I'm just afraid that this is going to be a bad one."

"Aw, don't worry now," Jan said. "That kid of yours has lived here all his life. Plus, he's a sharp little guy. If he's caught out in bad weather, he'll know what to do."

That was true. Jeremy was in Boy Scouts and the environmental club in school. He knew the outdoors and the area. If the storm turned bad before he got home, he'd most likely stop at somebody's house. There was really no reason for her to be irritated with Jan.

An especially loud moan dropped down from the roof and swirled around them. Both she and Jan looked up.

Face it, Liz told herself. This little problem between her and Matt wasn't all that little. Everybody and their brother had paired them off, and in a small town like Stony Mountain, that kind of a notion wasn't going to die easy.

But the biggest problem was that Jeremy and Matt had gotten close to each other. That wasn't going to change. And it shouldn't. But it was going to make for some touchy times.

"Here he comes."

Liz turned to look up Main Street with Jan. They could see Jeremy, head down into the wind, racing toward them. She breathed a sigh of relief.

Jeremy skidded his bike to a stop and put it into the rack beside the door. "Hi," he said, a broad smile covering his face.

"Where were you?" Liz asked.

The tone of her voice quickly wiped off his smile. "I was with Matt." He glared at her. "I told Aunt Jan."

He hadn't done anything wrong, but Liz had a hard time holding back feelings of resentment. A Michaelson man had walked out of her life and she wished the other one had stayed out. "You mean your Uncle Matt, don't you?"

"I mean Matt," Jeremy snapped. "He says his name isn't Uncle."

They were on the verge of trading glares, but Liz forced her pride back. There was no reason to get into an argument over nothing. Liz pushed her lips up into a smile. "So, how is Matt?"

"Okay."

Jeremy's tone of voice indicated that his guard was still up. Well, like her mother always said, it takes longer to fix something than it does to wreck it. "So, what's he doing? Is he keeping busy?"

"Yeah." The tone was still guarded. "I guess."

"Is he writing?"

"No, he's going mountain climbing."

Her smile dropped quickly, like snow off a tile roof. Apparently her son was making an early start on his smart-mouth teenage years. "Don't be a smart aleck, young man. There aren't any mountains around here."

"Sure there is." His smile had a very annoying know-it-all tinge to it. "There's Stony Mountain, the one our town was named after."

Stony Mountain? That was out in the middle of the river. And the only way a person could get to it was by crossing the rotting old trestle bridge.

The wind roared and howled, seeming about to rip the train station's roof off. The storm was upon them. Jan and Jeremy ran inside, but Liz stayed out. The rain beat down on her face.

She'd told the man he had no idea what love was. Dear, God. Was he going to cross the bridge to prove her wrong?

Chapter Thirteen

Liz couldn't believe it. Crossing the trestle bridge in the middle of a storm was just the kind of idiotic, stupid thing Matt Michaelson was bound to do. What did he think it would do—convince her he really did love her?

Nobody crossed the trestle bridge anymore. Nobody. It was some old stunt from their high school days, but how would he know that? He'd been gone for the last fifteen years.

She was drenched already by the minute or so of standing in the rain, but hardly noticed as she spun and stalked back into the train station. This was just unbelievable. The man could barely walk, and he was going to cross a wet, rotting old bridge.

"What's the matter?" Jan asked, looking up from the coffee she was brewing.

"Men are fools," Liz snapped. She grabbed her purse and dug in it for the keys to her van. As her fingers closed around them, her feet began hurrying back to the door. She had to get there in time to stop him. She had to.

"What's that have to do with anything?" Jan asked, her eyes looked worried. "Where are you going?"

"To stop a fool from crossing the trestle bridge."

"What?"

But Liz didn't wait to discuss it anymore. She was outside, racing across the street and squinting into the downpour as she unlocked the van. If she really hurried, she might beat him to the bridge, depending on how he was getting there. Surely Luke wouldn't drive him.

Or maybe he would. He was living in the past just enough to think it was a grand, romantic thing to do.

Liz pulled into the street and headed west. The windshield wipers were on high, but they barely allowed her a flash of the road ahead. The rain was coming down in buckets. She saw a blurry image of the pizza parlor ahead and turned right, onto the river road.

The gravel road was filled with potholes and ruts, so she had to slow down, but every bounce jarred deep in her fearstruck soul. Surely he would have known better once he'd gotten this far. Surely he could have seen that the weather was just too bad to try any kind of stunt.

The wind was picking up, and between the ruts in the road and the buffeting by the gusts, she was having trouble staying on the road. A branch came out of nowhere to slap at the windshield, stopping her breath momentarily. She leaned forward as if it would help her see better.

"Don't let him try crossing," she whispered into the silence.

Not that it was really very quiet. Everything seemed to be roaring around her. The wind. The rain. Her racing heart.

She rounded the curve and, between swipes of the windshield wipers, caught a brief glimpse of the river up ahead. No cars were in sight. Her eyes flooded with sudden fears. Did that mean he'd already crossed? It was only a mile or two from his house. Could he have walked here?

"Damn you, Matt Michaelson." Why did men have to be so stupidly stubborn? Why did they think they were tougher than life itself?

She pulled off to the side of the road and flew out of the van. The bridge loomed ahead, the yellow Warning—Do Not Enter sign on the barricade mocking her fears, but not hiding the bridge from sight, either. It was empty.

The river below was a seething cauldron. What if he'd fallen in?

Stony Mountain rose up in the shadowy distance. What if he'd crossed over and fell?

Without wasting another moment, Liz ducked around the barricade and started across the bridge. The center walkway had long since rotted away, so she had to step from tie to tie, all the while seeing the raging river through the spaces. There was nothing to hold on to, just the occasional angled timber on the open sides, but her hands balanced against them whenever they could.

Why couldn't men be sensible like women? Why did they always have to be some sort of hero?

Her vision blurred. She wasn't sure if it was from the rain or tears, but didn't try to find clarity. If she saw too well, she wouldn't go, and Matt could be lost.

The wood was wet, slimy. Her feet wanted to slip; she felt she had no traction. She tried a few more steps, getting only about ten feet from the shore before stopping, as if hearing a voice in the wind.

"The trick is bare feet," Bill had once said when she'd given him hell for crossing the bridge on a dare. "You stay to the right and go in your bare feet."

"I sure as hell hope you knew what you were talking about," she murmured. "Be right, and I'll forgive you everything."

Liz crouched down and untied her running shoes, slipping her feet out of her socks as she slipped them out of her shoes. Her bare feet did feel surer on the wooden ties, but colder, too. She turned cautiously and tossed her shoes back to the shore, then went forward again.

The rain seemed determined to blind her, the wind determined to knock her down, yet she kept on.

A quarter of the way across. Then halfway across.

The wind seemed to change. It was almost like a moaning, a crying, and, for a split second, she thought she could smell roses.

"I must be hallucinating," she muttered. Wasn't that a sign that something dire was supposed to happen?

The next timber sagged and swayed even as she touched it with her foot. She pulled back and took a deep breath. Might Matt have fallen here? No, surely there'd be a sign, some broken edges of the wood at least. Without taking time to think, she leapt over the tie and onto the next one. Thankfully, it held and she continued her passage across.

Three-quarters across, then all the way. When her feet touched the muddy earth on the other side, she sank to the ground in blessed relief. Her hands were shaking; so were her knees. She took deep breaths that should have steadied her, but it seemed that the wind was stealing all the oxygen from the air.

Finally she felt strong enough to stand and look around her. There was no sign that anyone had been there for ages. She took a few steps up the hill, following what must have been the path the railroad used to take. Matted grass and decaying leaves made a spongy path for her to walk on, and she followed it across the hill until she could see the bridge on the other side.

No one had been here recently. Certainly not today. If Matt had been planning to come, he had changed his mind. She felt a curious mixture of relief, embarrassment and annoyance. Turning, she retraced her steps back to the trestle bridge.

It was raining no less hard on Stony Mountain, but somehow it didn't seem as noticeable. And though there was no trace of anyone else around, Liz didn't feel alone.

"Now what, Betsy?" she said into the storm.

She found a rock alongside the old railroad path and sat down. The underbrush beside her was all atangle, and looking closely, she found it was rosebushes. Dead leaves were caught on dead thorny branches, but strong, sturdy shoots were growing from the roots. Life overcoming death. Betsy's rose garden.

Liz looked up and saw that the town's rooftops were visible from here. "Did it bring you peace to sit here?" she asked Betsy. "Did you miss Willem less?"

Liz almost thought she felt anger and impatience in the air. Surprised, she frowned and looked down at the roses.

"Why would you plant your rose garden here on the west side of the town when Willem died in Gettysburg, way to the east?"

Liz got up and walked over to the water's edge. The churning, raging river raced below. There had been a terrible train wreck here in Betsy's day. Liz remembered reading about it in those newspapers from Matt's attic. Willem's brother had been killed. Matthias.

"But everyone said you loved Willem," Liz muttered. "Why would you plant a garden here where Matthias died?"

Because Matthias had been the one she loved. Liz knew it as surely as if Betsy were here talking to her. After Willem had died, Betsy had fallen in love with Matthias, only she'd been afraid to do anything about it until it was too late.

Liz sank onto the muddy ground, staring across at the bridge, but seeing a hodgepodge of the past and the present. Willem, Matthias and Betsy. Bill, Matt and Liz. It was almost as if they were reliving the past. But could she learn from Betsy's sorrow?

"There you are." Luke Schiller stopped his cab in front of the train station and turned toward Matt. "Got you here plenty early. Give you time to grab a cup of coffee and chat with Lizzie."

Matt glared out the window by his side. Damn people in this town were always trying to fix up someone. He considered asking Luke what the hell he was doing trying to share his misery, but his years of police work taught him not to irritate someone who outweighed him by a hundred pounds.

"Come in and have a cup of coffee with me," Matt said. "It's the least I can do, considering how you've been hauling me around for free all these weeks."

"Sure, why not?"

Luke ran through the rain while Matt hobbled along behind him. It was going to be great to walk and run like a normal guy. His cast was coming off tomorrow, then the doctor figured a month or two of physical therapy before Matt was as good as new. At least, physically.

They hurried into the coffee shop. Jan and Jeremy were the only ones there. Liz must be in the back someplace. Matt was glad Luke was with him. The more people around, the less reason for him and Liz to talk.

"What are you doing here?" Jan asked, picking up two cups and the coffeepot.

He frowned at her. "I'm taking the train to Chicago," he said.

Jan put the cups down and filled each with coffee. "You happen to pass Liz on your way?"

"Pass Liz?" Matt repeated. His frown deepened. "Why would I pass Liz?"

"Because you're the only fool around here."

"What?"

Jan put the coffeepot down. "She ran out of here about an hour ago, saying she had to stop some fool from crossing the trestle bridge. I figured it had to be you."

"From crossing the bridge?" Matt didn't know what the hell was going on, but he couldn't deny that a sliver of worry was working its way into his heart. "Why would she think I was crossing the bridge?"

"Maybe she was making some kind of joke," Luke suggested.

"She wasn't laughing," Jan said.

"Maybe it's my fault," Jeremy said, sounding close to tears. "I told her that you were going to climb a mountain."

"What?" Matt could feel his heart rate going up.

"Well, that's what you said," Jeremy said on a wail. "I didn't say anything about the trestle bridge."

Matt stared at them. Outside, the wind gusted, rattling the windows in the old train station. Rain struck the panes like shotgun pellets as old Betsy screamed and yowled up in the eaves.

"She's in trouble," Matt said. "I can feel it in my bones."

Jeremy's tears started flowing in earnest, making Matt sorry that he'd spoken.

"We'd better get out there," Matt said.

"Cab's waiting," Luke said, and they all tumbled after him, packing into the back seat. They weren't even settled when Luke slapped a flashing blue light on the roof of his cab. Then, driving with one hand, he sent the cab squealing into the street while he held his two-way radio in the other hand.

"Cab one to base. Cab one to base. Damn it, base. Come in."

"Luke Schiller, what are you fussing about now?" came a woman's voice from the radio.

"Honey." Luke calmed somewhat as he spoke to his wife. "Sound the civil-defense siren. Code three. Dispatch all units, including the boats, to the old trestle bridge."

"A code three? You want to send thirty or forty folks out dashing around in this kind of weather? Someone'll get hurt."

"Damn it, Cindy," Matt called, leaning forward over the seat back to shout into the radio. "Lizzie's stuck up on the old trestle bridge."

"Oh, Lord."

Within seconds the town's civil-defense siren began wailing, rising above the wind and the rain, filling the country-side with its call for help. Luke roared out of town and onto the river road, swaying and fishtailing all the way.

Cold fear fought irritation for possession of Matt's heart. Boy, he was going to give that woman one good dressing-down. Once they got her down off the bridge.

Suddenly Luke hit a chuckhole and almost went spinning. *And if he lived.*

The sound of a siren wailing across town awoke Liz from her thoughts. Lordy, it was the civil-defense siren. Someone was in trouble.

She thought of Jeremy and Jan back in that drafty old station. Anything could happen there in a storm. Or to an old house like Matt's. She got to her feet and hurried over to the bridge.

The rain was falling just as hard, but the wind seemed to be letting up some. She wasn't crazy about the notion of walking back over, but she couldn't hang around, waiting for good weather. She stepped out onto the slimy, wet wood with extra care.

She wasn't sure if she was going to kill Jeremy or Matt for sending her on this wild-goose chase, but she definitely was going to give someone a piece of her mind. Not that the trip over hadn't been interesting and just a little unsettling.

She was a quarter of the way back over, just past the rotting tie, when she noticed the flashing blue light heading her way through the downpour. The trouble was out this way?

She eased farther along. Her feet were getting cold and the water splashing on the bridge from the river below wasn't helping any. She looked up and saw two motorboats speeding through the tumultuous water.

"Where's everybody heading, Betsy?"

A car was swerving to a squealing stop behind the van. No, it was a cab. Luke's cab. And Matt and Luke and Jan and Jeremy all spilled out of it. Luke was peering into the van while Jeremy found one of her shoes. Matt was standing at the edge of the bridge, staring at her as the rain drenched them all. Nice time for him to show up. Why hadn't he been here a little bit ago and saved her the trip over?

She waved, and even from this distance she could see the horror on his face. She could also see the hook-and-ladder truck racing up behind them. What was going on?

"Jump, Lizzie. We'll get you."

She stared down between two ties as she crossed from one to another and saw Leo Tuttle manning one of the boats. He was talking to *her*. He was telling her to *jump*. Good gracious! They thought she was in trouble!

This was just too much. What brainless idiot had called out the rescue team for her?

Who else? Matt. Mr. Macho.

Liz was fit to be tied. She was surprised that the rain hitting her didn't sizzle and turn to steam. What did he think she was—some helpless, simpering female?

And to think she crossed the bridge for him!

Liz's feet froze in place. Good Lord, she had. She had crossed the bridge for Matt. Not as part of some high school stunt, but because she had been scared half out of her mind with worry. Because she loved him. This was history repeating itself.

"Just wait there," Matt was calling. "I'll come get you."

It was her turn to watch in drenched horror as he—bad leg, cane and all—started to climb around the barricade. Luke was trying to pull him back, but Matt was too stubborn to listen to reason.

She felt Betsy's anguish wash over her. The wind was a mournful wail, telling her to stop him. To not let Matt try to cross the bridge. To not let history totally repeat itself.

Well, she wasn't. She wasn't going to lose her Matt.

A cold terror shut down her feelings. She reached down to the rotting bridge floor and yanked a loose spike from the tie she was standing on. Bracing herself as best she could against the side, she flung the spike toward the shore. It landed just short of Matt, causing him to pull back slightly.

"Hey," he cried.

"Hey, yourself," she shouted back. "Don't you dare come out on this bridge."

"Are you okay, Mom?" Jeremy called out.

"I am just fine. I don't need help." As if to prove her point, she crossed to the next tie, then the one after that.

Why couldn't this be happening in August when the rain would have been warm?

Matt must not have been listening to her words. "Look, Liz—"

"Damn it, stay there." She crossed to another tie, then stopped to brace herself as she shouted. "I am not going to spend my eternity haunting the train station, Matt Michaelson. If you take one more step forward, I'll have Luke break your legs. I'd rather have you on crutches than floating in the river."

Matt looked stunned, but Luke just saluted her with one hand as he put the other on Matt's shoulder. "Just say the word, Lizzie," he called out.

"Mom, are you crossing the bridge for Matt?" Jeremy shouted to her.

"Damn it, yes!" she shouted back. "And I intend to clobber both of you once I get over there."

She couldn't see Matt that well for the rain, but she could feel his added urgency. She could sense him wanting to throw off Luke's restraint and rush out to her.

"Liz," he called out, "I love you."

"You're still in major trouble."

"Does this mean you love me?" he yelled.

"Yes, damn it, it does."

She was almost halfway across now, and keeping a steady pace. Then past the halfway mark. Betsy's rose fragrance swirled around her, urging her on. Liz could even feel Bill with her, checking out each step.

"Liz?" Matt called out.

"What now?"

"Please be careful."

As if she wasn't going to be now that she had even more to live for. "It's going to be all right now," she whispered to Betsy. "I won't make the same mistakes as you."

Step after step, she was drawing ever closer to the shore. "Find peace," she whispered into the rain to Bill. "I forgive you."

Then she was at the barricade, and eager hands pulled her to the shore. Jeremy was hugging her, crying warm tears into her soaking blouse, and Jan was grinning, smashing Jeremy as she held Liz close for a moment. Luke was clapping her on the back while Leo was calling up his good wishes from the boat.

Finally it was just her and Matt, his eyes boring into hers, his face alive with every emotion for all to read—fear, love, relief, joy, anger.

"What the hell did you think you were doing?" he snapped as he pulled her into his embrace.

She'd never felt so much like she was home. "Rescuing you," she snapped right back. "I was told you were going mountain climbing."

"Well, not that mountain."

"It better not be that mountain, ever. You hear? That bridge is off-limits for you."

"Well, it's off-limits for you, too."

She broke into a grin. "That's okay. I don't need to cross it anymore."

"Evil woman," he murmured as he buried his face against her neck. "Do you know how terrified I was?"

"Yep. Because that was how I felt when I thought you were over there." She let herself relax in his arms, loving the feel of them around her. "You really didn't have to call out the cavalry, though."

"I couldn't risk losing you," he said, pulling back to look into her eyes. "Do you believe now just how much I love you?"

"He must, Mom," Jeremy said. "He was real worried."

"He's been a bear since you dumped him," Luke pointed out. "Must be love."

"How can I refute such expert witnesses?" Liz said with a laugh that died as she looked back into his eyes. "Yes, I believe you now."

"And you'll marry me?"

"She better," Jan said. "I'm tired of her moods."

"I'm tired of standing out here in the rain," Jeremy said.

"I'll marry you on one condition."

Matt sighed. "I'm giving up writing," he said. "And I'm going to talk to Reverend Bowles about the job at the youth center."

"Really?" Liz just shook her head. "And all I was going to ask for was a rose garden in the backyard."

Epilogue

Jeremy coasted his bike to a stop, then dismounted. He wiped the sweat from his brow and looked out over the old trestle bridge. The moon was so bright that you could read the mushy messages kids had carved in the timbers over the years.

He pulled his T-shirt away from his body and waited for a cooling breeze, but none came. It was one of those hot, muggy summer nights common around the middle of August in these parts. Sort of a last punch from summer before the cool nights of fall came back again.

Giving up on the breeze, Jeremy took a medium-size cookie can and a small bundle of rose cuttings from the basket on the back of his bike. Then he walked out onto the trestle bridge, stepping carefully on the ties until he got to the middle.

He put the can and cuttings by his side, and sat there looking out on the river, not moving except to swat a mosquito or two.

"Hi ... Dad." He stumbled on the word, never having used it in regular conversation. "Matt said you used to do this when you were a kid. That you used to climb out of your bedroom window onto the porch roof, then down the center post and jump. He said you told him it was easy."

Jeremy paused for a moment to watch the river lazily slipping along on its way to Lake Michigan.

"And you know what? It is easy." He laughed—a nervous little sound, but still a laugh. "I got your old room now."

Jeremy slapped at another mosquito, noting with satisfaction that he'd squashed the sucker. A dog yipped somewhere over to the east, and Jeremy took a look over his shoulder. It was just a normal night sound in the country, so there was no reason to worry.

"Matt's a real cool guy. We talk about all kinds of things. You know, guy stuff."

There was no reason to describe that any further. Jeremy was sure his father knew what he meant. Guy stuff was stuff all guys were interested in. Sports. Girls. School. What things were going to be like when you grew up. Stuff that a guy couldn't talk to his mom about.

"Matt said you were sorry about the way things turned out." Jeremy took a deep breath and held it for a moment. "I'm sorry, too."

Now that he was done with his apology, Jeremy felt much better. Like a weight had been lifted from his shoulders.

"I don't know if you know, but Mom's gonna have another baby. Matt and her are always bickering and stuff. You know, like Matt says, 'Are you supposed to pick that up?' And then Mom says, 'I know more about having a baby than you.' And then they get all sloppy, hugging and smooching."

A stone lay next to him, and Jeremy dropped it into the river. The water wasn't that far down, but he'd heard it was fairly deep at this point.

"Football practice starts next week. Wade Rembow is gonna be quarterback. Everyone says he's good, but not as good as you were." Jeremy almost felt sorry for Wade. "I'm not going out for football. I'm going to play soccer. Maybe I'll play in high school. I don't know yet."

He and Matt had had many late-night talks about this, too, out on the back porch as they watched fireflies.

"Matt says that I shouldn't play nothin' unless it's fun." He nodded a few times. "Soccer's real fun. I mean, like most of the men in town don't know nothin' about it."

That meant they couldn't really yell and scream at you from the sidelines. They couldn't take you aside and tell you what you were doing wrong. They couldn't tell you how other people used to be better. It was great.

"I gotta be going soon, Dad."

He picked up the cookie can and took off the cover. This was one thing he was going to be glad to get rid of. He'd kept the can in the back corner of his closet for most of the summer now. Man, if Mom had ever found it, she'd have had a pony.

Back in May, after Matt and Mom had gotten off the trestle bridge and did all kinds of kissing and making up, they'd gone to Chicago for Matt's leg. Jeremy had spent a lot of time at the house taking care of Rosie. And every time he'd been there, he'd look at the vase holding his father's ashes. And every time he'd gotten really, really mad.

Finally, one day, right before they were going to bury the vase next to Grandma and Grandpa Michaelson, he'd put the ashes in this cookie can and some sand in the vase.

"I hated you and I was gonna do something really mean with your ashes." His lower lip quivered a bit, and tears rolled down Jeremy's cheeks. "But like I said, Matt and I talked a lot. So now I'm not really, really mad at you. Kind of. But only sometimes."

He wiped the tears with the back of each hand.

"So, anyways, I gotta do something with you." He took a deep breath and let it out slowly. "I was first thinking of putting you on the football field by the school. You know, almost everybody says that's where you were the happiest. But lately I've been thinking about you and fishing. And how I like fishing, too, and it was something that we could do almost, sort of, together.''

He looked down at the pile of ashes in the can, trying to imagine a tall, broad-shouldered man with a big smile on his face, like in the newspaper clippings back in his room. But the ashes just stayed ashes. He quickly sprinkled them out into the river.

For a while he thought he could see the dust floating on the surface of the river and glittering in the moonlight, but it quickly disappeared in the current. "Good luck, Dad."

He slowly pulled himself up, the roses in his hand. ''I don't know how things work where you're at, but if you see old Betsy, will you give her these?'' He threw the roses into the river. ''They're from her rosebush by the station. It finally bloomed.''

He watched the roses float downstream. ''Nobody's sure where she's at, 'cause she don't howl around the old train station anymore. Luke says some dirt musta blown into the cracks in the roof during that big storm when Mom crossed the bridge for Matt, but Mom says Betsy's just at peace now.''

Jeremy waited as a cloud passed in front of the moon, then there seemed to be no reason to hang around anymore. ''Well, see ya, Dad. Maybe next time, I'll bring my fishing pole.''

*   *   *   *   *

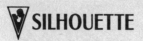

SILHOUETTE *Desire*

Opposites Attract

A new mini-series from Nancy Martin

Who says opposites don't attract? Watch the sparks fly as these handsome hunks fall for the women they swore they didn't want!

In August look for:

THE PAUPER AND THE PREGNANT PRINCESS

Princess Cordelia had a scheme for avoiding inheriting the throne of her tiny country; she was going to have a baby with someone penniless, unrefined and downright common. Someone who would horrify her parents and her subjects. Someone like Crash Craddock.

The second novel in the series will be published in October.
So make sure you don't miss

THE COP AND THE CHORUS GIRL

Only from Silhouette Desire.

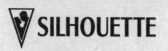 **SILHOUETTE**

SPECIAL EDITION

COMING NEXT MONTH

WHERE DREAMS HAVE BEEN...
Penny Richards

That Special Woman!

Someone had taken her child! And Julee Sutherland's
enigmatic neighbour, Cain Collier, might be able to help her
find her baby. They'd stepped back from their attraction
because of the past, but now it was pushing them together.

A SELF-MADE MAN
Carole Halston

Twenty years after being rejected by Rachel, Lee Zachary still
wanted her. Worse still, his teenage son was interested in her
pretty young daughter. With history about to repeat itself,
Rachel hungered for the love she'd denied...

ROCKY MOUNTAIN RANCHER
Pamela Toth

Luther Ward had plenty of pent-up passion as Maddy Landers
found out when she hired him to ranch her land. But, too late,
she wondered if Luther truly wanted her...or her land.

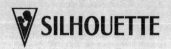
▼ SILHOUETTE

› SPECIAL EDITION ‹

COMING NEXT MONTH

WHAT PRICE GLORY
Marianne Shock

Paige Meredith had big dreams that left little time for grand
passions. But rugged Ross Tanner was an irresistible
distraction from her lifetime goal. He made her wonder what
she really wanted…

INSTANT FAMILY
Patt Bucheister

Cord Thomas was determined that Michele should meet her
long-lost parent, but Michele didn't believe in parental love or
any other kind of love for that matter. So why was she
tempted to do anything Cord asked?

THE SECRET BABY
Amy Frazier

Meg Roberts suspected that her son had a twin, a child she'd
been told had never existed. Only one man could help her, a
man who'd loved her for years. But would Meg be tempted to
shoot the messenger who brought her bad news?

GET 4 BOOKS
AND A MYSTERY GIFT

Return this coupon and we'll send you 4 Silhouette Special Editions and a mystery gift absolutely FREE! We'll even pay the postage and packing for you.

We're making you this offer to introduce you to the benefits of Reader Service: FREE home delivery of brand-new Silhouette romances, at least a month before they are available in the shops, FREE gifts and a monthly Newsletter packed with information.

Accepting these FREE books and gift places you under no obligation to buy, you may cancel at any time, even after receiving just your free shipment. Simply complete the coupon below and send it to:

HARLEQUIN MILLS & BOON, FREEPOST, PO BOX 70, CROYDON, CR9 9EL.

No stamp needed

Yes, please send me 4 free Silhouette Special Editions and a mystery gift. I understand that unless you hear from me, I will receive 6 superb new titles every month for just £2.20* each postage and packing free. I am under no obligation to purchase any books and I may cancel or suspend my subscription at any time, but the free books and gifts will be mine to keep in any case. (I am over 18 years of age)

2EP5SE

Ms/Mrs/Miss/Mr _____

Address _____

_____

_____ Postcode _____

Offer closes 31st January 1996. We reserve the right to refuse an application. *Prices and terms subject to change without notice. Offer only valid in UK and Ireland and is not available to current subscribers to this series. **Readers in Ireland please write to:** P.O. Box 4546, Dublin 24. Overseas readers please write for details.

MAILING PREFERENCE SERVICE

You may be mailed with offers from other reputable companies as a result of this application. Please tick box if you would prefer not to receive such offers. ☐

COMING NEXT MONTH FROM

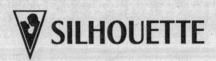 SILHOUETTE

Intrigue

Danger, deception and desire—
new from Silhouette...

TRIAL BY FIRE Rebecca York
THE SHELTER OF HER ARMS Jean Barrett
HER OTHER HALF Saranne Dawson
VEIL OF FEAR Judi Lind

Desire

Provocative, sensual love stories for the
woman of today

MR EASY Cait London
THE PERFECT FATHER Elizabeth Bevarly
MISS LIZZY'S LEGACY Peggy Moreland
THE MADDENING MODEL Suzanne Simms
BEACH BABY Karen Leabo
ERRANT ANGEL Justine Davis

Sensation

A thrilling mix of passion, adventure
and drama

MIND READER Victoria Cole
BANISHED Lee Magner
MICHAEL'S FATHER Dallas Schulze
FADE TO BLACK Amanda Stevens